What the critics are saying...

"Taber and Roni's story is absolutely wonderful, and it has a strong sense of tenderness. If you have enjoyed the first *Feline Breeds* series, without a doubt know that this one is one you'll not want to miss." - *Robin Taylor, In The Library Reviews*

"SUBMISSION was a very enjoyable read. Again with each book Lora Leigh creates a bigger picture I love this ability in Lora Leigh's writing it keeps you guessing and with each novel you learn more about each of her characters and introducing new ones with just enough information to tease you until the next book. I am very much looking forward to reading SEDUCTION the next book in the Bound Hearts series." *-Gail Northman, Romance Junkies*

"What an extraordinary ending to this wonderful series...This story will entrance you from the first chapter and the sex is so hot you will need to take a shower when you are done. The ending is wonderful with a conclusion that will make you cry. My only disappointment is that the series is now ended. I will definitely miss those wonderful August men. How could you do this to us Ms. Leigh, how could you?" *-.Raven Jackman, Just Erotic Romance Reviews*

THE MAN WITHIN
FELINE BREEDS 2

Lora Leigh

THE MAN WITHIN Feline Breeds 2
An Ellora's Cave Publication, February 2005

Ellora's Cave Publishing, Inc.
1337 Commerce Drive Suite 13
Stow OH 44224

ISBN #1-4199-5107-6

THE MAN WITHIN © 2003 LORA LEIGH
ISBN MS Reader (LIT) ISBN # 1-84360-688-7
Other available formats (no ISBNs are assigned):
Adobe (PDF), Rocketbook (RB), Mobipocket (PRC) & HTML

Cover art by Syneca

THE MAN WITHIN
FELINE BREEDS 2

Lora Leigh

Prologue
June
Sandy Hook, KY

"Roni, dammit, what kind of trouble did you manage to get yourself into this time?"

Roni Andrews tried to suppress her grin as she heard Taber's voice echoing through the corridor of the cells housed in the county jail. She sat back on the uncomfortable bunk, trying for nonchalance. No way in hell would she give him the chance to see just how much he could intimidate her. And boy could he intimidate.

Well over six feet tall, his body corded with powerful muscles, his expression often savage, remote, he could set her heart to pounding in both fear and arousal. The fear she could handle. It was the arousal she often had problems with. It had first hit her right after she turned sixteen. It had intensified several months ago after her twenty-second birthday. There were nights she burned for him, and it terrified her.

She welcomed the sensation of cool stone at her back, easing a bit of the summer heat that surrounded her. The heat that built inside her as well. The air conditioner had broken down that night and the cells had been stifling. Thankfully, old Mort, the jailer, had opened the windows rather than let her suffer.

The hard smack of Taber's boots on the stone floor caused her to wince. He only walked like that when he was pissed. She carefully pasted an expression of bored amusement on her face. Wouldn't do for him to know she was really scared to damned death of him when he got pissed.

Not that Taber would hurt her. Instinctively she knew he would never lay a hand on her. But there was something about him when he got mad. Something primal, predatory. He wasn't a man she wanted to risk pissing off too often. Unfortunately, trouble just seemed to find her and more often than not it was Taber who bailed her out of it, one way or the other. She was terrified that one day he would get tired of being her knight in shining armor and write her off entirely.

What would she do then, she wondered. There were times she wondered if she could survive without him. He had been there for her for, when she needed him, for so long, that she didn't know if she could make it without him.

Within seconds, he was standing at the cell door, his hands braced on his lean hips, a frown etched on his proud, sun-darkened face. Overly long black hair framed his savage features, intensified his eyes, and gave him a predatory, savage appeal. He exuded strength, protectiveness and sheer sexual heat.

He made her want to start rubbing against him, like a cat. He was tall and muscular, his shoulders broad, his chest powerful and tapering to a flat, corded abdomen that tempted her to touch.

Long powerful legs were encased in snug denim and there was no way in hell she was going to let her gaze drift to…oh hell. That bulge between his thighs just looked too good to be true. Hastily she jerked her gaze back to his face.

His eyes were narrowed on her now, the jade-green color brilliant and snapping with fury. She swallowed tightly. He was none too pleased with her this morning. Not that she could blame him. In the past few months, she had been in trouble more often than she had stayed out of it.

"I didn't do a damned thing," she snapped back, allowing all the awakening senses he managed to flip into overdrive to fuel her own anger. "I was just standing there, Taber. Honest. That sheriff has lost his mind."

She fought to hide her amusement. Of course, he knew she was lying. He always knew when she was lying.

"I should let you rot here." She loved that growling thing he did when he was pissed. His voice would lower and just vibrate…like a cat. She had a fondness for cats.

She rolled her eyes in mocking amusement. They both knew he wouldn't do it. He liked her too much. The muscles in her lower stomach quivered in reaction to that tone of voice though, striking sparks that flamed in her womb. She could literally feel her breasts swelling, her nipples peaking at the sound, and she knew he hadn't missed the reaction.

Instantly his expression shut down. No anger, no ire. Like a damned robot. Everything in his face seemed to tighten, to chill, causing her to shiver in reaction. She hated it when he did that, hated when he hid from her any response he might have to her. As though his effect on her was her fault and something she should be able to control. She wished it was, it would certainly make her life a hell of a lot easier.

"Are you rescuing me here or what?" she snapped seconds later, hurt by his cool retreat. "It's damned hot in here, Taber, and getting hotter." In more ways than one.

He sighed then, shaking his head as though being in trouble was no more than he had expected of her that early in the morning. At least it wasn't that bland, I-don't-know-you look that she so despised.

"I ought to paddle your ass." He stepped aside as the jailer, well into his fifties and grinning at her knowingly, unlocked the cell door.

Roni didn't fight the shiver that worked over her body at the dark sound of his voice. He could spank her any day, she thought. As long as he touched her. Maybe he would kiss it and make the hurt all better later? Her own thoughts had her suppressing her smile as well as the tight clenching of her buttocks at the thought. Okay, so she was a perv. But Taber was a man that just inspired a more lusty way of thinking of things than most men did.

"Spank me, daddy," she drawled softly as she rose from the cot and strolled over to the opening door.

He snorted in disgust. "Your father obviously neglected discipline while he was here or else you wouldn't tempt me this far."

Roni scooted past him and walked over to where the sheriff had thrown her pack by old Mort's desk the night before. She kept her back to Taber, bending at the waist to pick it up, feeling his gaze on her backside like a caress. It was a game. He had never touched her, and she feared he never would, but she wanted him to look. Wanted him to see her as a woman rather than the child he insisted on believing her to be.

As she rose, she slung the strap over her arm and turned back to him with a bright smile. "I'm ready whenever you are. Think Sherra would let me stay with her for a while? That old house is getting boring this summer."

To be honest, it was getting terrifying. She didn't know who was playing the little pranks on her lately, but she was going to find out. She might be wrong a time or two about who the culprits were, like she was last night, but she would figure it out eventually.

The hard look he shot her assured her that even that small lie hadn't escaped his notice. He knew damned well she wouldn't be asking to stay with his sister unless she was scared to death. She considered asking him to let her stay at his place. But she knew her weakness for him and she was terrified of begging him to touch her. The quiet isolation and intimacy of his home would only shatter the control she fought so hard for. She didn't want to beg for his touch. Didn't want to risk the heartbreak when he rejected her. She didn't want to destroy the friendship she valued so highly with him. If she couldn't have his love, then she didn't want to risk losing him entirely. A little was better than nothing at all.

This reaction to him was getting out of hand, she admitted. She blamed it on her lack of social skills, her fear of dating over the years. You never knew when a guy really wanted to go out with you or when he was trying to find a way to get back at your father. Unfortunately, she paid often anyway for the myriad crimes, both petty and felonious, that her father, Reginald, committed.

"Sherra's out of town this week." He gripped her arm firmly as she made to pass by him again. "How long has it been since you've eaten, anyway?"

She knew she had lost weight over the past month. Fear and worry had a way of affecting the appetite on the best of days.

"Yesterday." She tried to pull this lie off, though by the tightening of his fingers on her upper arm she had a feeling she had failed. "Come on, Taber. You bailed me out like a good boy, now I'll just go home and twiddle my fingers a few days until you get over your mad. Do I still have a job?" She glanced back at him as that thought hit her.

She needed that job. Pesky little things like food, electric, and water cost money.

"You should be back in school, not working in a greasy garage," he snapped as he led her outside to his pickup. "When is your father due back?"

"Hell if I know," she sighed, biting back her regret at the thought of college. It wasn't that she hadn't wanted to go, dammit. But she needed to eat, too. The two weren't coming together very well. "He took off last week. Left a note that he'd call. I haven't seen him since."

Not that she really cared if she didn't see him anytime soon. Even when he was home she was alone. Unless he needed money and she didn't have any to give. It was then that the rages would build until she gladly handed over whatever she had, wherever she could get it, just to get him off her back. If he would just stay gone for longer than a month or two, maybe she could save enough to actually afford her own place.

He jerked the truck door open without releasing her arm. She looked up at him, swallowing tightly at the look in his eyes. They were darker than normal, glittering with some emotion that made heat sweep through her body, made her thighs tingle, her vagina clench. For once, he was watching her like something more than a pesky little child.

"What happened last night?" Uh oh. He was using that tone that brooked no refusal. The one that made her heart speed up in her chest, the blood to pump hard and heavy through her veins.

She shrugged carelessly. "Some boys playing pranks, most likely. You know how they are."

There were several men in town who believed the debts her father owed them should be taken out and paid off in her bed. She tended to disagree.

He was silent for long moments. "What. Happened." There was that freaking rumble again. She shivered beneath it.

"Someone tried to break into the house, okay?" She tried to jerk away but there was no getting free of him. "I chased them as far as the main road before I could shoot. Then I shot. Unfortunately, either old Reverend Gregory is into breaking or entering, or I was shooting at the wrong car. I still haven't figured out how they got away from me."

She hadn't been shooting to kill. Just to kind of maim a little. Fortunately the Reverend seemed to have a sense of humor and only demanded a night in jail to teach her a lesson. It wasn't her first night there. She doubted it would be her last.

"Shoot?"

Damn. He was really mad now. His voice was almost a pure, raw growl "Why didn't you just call me, Roni? What the hell are you doing with a gun?" His voice had steadily lowered rather than risen. That was never a good sign.

"I know how to use it." She twisted out of his hold, but was more than aware of the fact that he had let her go only because he made the decision, not her. "Dammit, Taber, I'm tired of those bastards trying to torment me. Every time Reginald leaves they pull the same crap on me."

They were terrifying her. The phone calls Taber didn't know about. She could never reveal the brief, horrifyingly descriptive notes, either. She paled to think about them. They were graphic, explicit, terrifying.

"In the truck." She had never heard that tone before. Danger resonated around her and the shiver that washed over her had nothing to do with arousal and everything to do with flat dread.

She did as he ordered, though she watched him carefully. The door slammed behind her and Taber proceeded to stalk— yeah stalk, there was no other word for it—around the front of the vehicle and to the driver's side.

"What did he do this time?" She assumed he meant her father.

She shrugged carefully. "I don't know. He came in late last week, threw some clothes in a bag, told me to stay with friends and left."

She should have known, hell she had known, that whatever he was running from was going to affect her.

"And you're still at the house why?" he snarled. Man, he was an animal when he was pissed, she thought worriedly. That deep voice was driving her insane, though.

"Where am I going to stay?" Her laughter was self-mocking. It wasn't as though she had a lot of choices. "I called Sherra, but she wasn't answering. I called you a time or two, but you weren't around either. That left the gun and me. The gun is always there."

She wasn't used to Taber ignoring the messages she left him, or refusing to help her. But she hadn't heard back from him. For a week she had waited, worried and finally realized he wasn't coming. She was surprised he had bailed her out of jail.

She didn't like the look he was giving her. Furious and…hungry. He looked like he was looking for a meal and considered her fair game all of a sudden. He shook his head, amazement flashing in his eyes.

"You have got to be insane," he finally sighed. "Certifiably insane. Goddamn, Roni, why didn't you leave a message?"

Incredulity washed over her at his irate tone.

"How many do you want me to leave?" she yelled back at him. She hadn't slept in a week, she was hungry and sick of being frightened. "I called three days straight, Taber, and left messages. Why don't you check the damned machine? Better yet, go do that growling thing at the damned people who haven't fixed cell phone reception in this county yet. Even your cell wasn't picking up and by then I was tired of begging you to help me." Cell phone reception, or the lack thereof, wasn't unusual in the small, mountainous area they lived in. But she knew the voice messages would have been held for him.

He stilled, his hands clenching on the steering wheel. "There were no messages." Dangerous, rumbling, he was only growing more furious by the moment. "Besides, Dayan had the phone this week. He lost his."

"Then one of your brothers erased them," she told him, just as angry. "I left the messages, Taber. I'm surprised you came this morning. When the sheriff said he had to leave a message…"

"There was no message." His voice lowered further. "The sheriff met me at the garage when I came in this morning."

She snorted. "Well there you go. Did he tell you he left a message last night?"

"No. But I'll be asking him about it." From the tone of his voice, he'd be getting answers, too.

Her gaze flickered away from him as he stared at her intently. His eyes were so dark, intense. The look reminded her that she was female, and made her ache for things that often left her blushing when she thought about them. He had rarely looked at her like that. Having him do so now threw her completely off balance.

"You can stay at my place, over the garage." He started the motor and backed from the jail as he spoke. "There's a good bed and a small kitchen up there. No one will bother you."

But she didn't want to be alone. She was sick of it. "Look, just take me back to my house. I'm sure Reginald will be back soon."

Actually, she hoped he stayed gone for a long time. She almost had enough saved for that apartment of her own she dreamed of. If she could just keep him from stealing it.

He snorted at that. "I don't have time to bail you out of jail every morning, Roni. We'll go get your things and move you in over the garage. You'll be going back to school this fall..."

"I don't have the money yet..."

"I'll fucking pay for it," he snarled, his gaze slicing over her, his fury almost tangible now. "Shut the hell up and listen to me for a change before that crazy father of yours gets you killed."

His voice rose with each word. Roni looked over at him warily. She had never heard him raise his voice.

"I don't need your charity." She crossed her arms over her breasts, staring back out the windshield, her chest heavy with anger and pain. "I'm a grown woman, Taber. All I needed was the damned job."

"You're about to get something you're going to regret and sure as hell don't need right now."

Her head snapped around as the truck jerked to a stop behind the garage.

He was losing his temper. She could feel it. Like electricity, the tension between them began to crackle, stroking over her, almost taking her breath.

It was still early morning, hours before the garage was due to open. The back lot was deserted, enclosed by a high fence, leaving them sheltered, hidden from view. The intimacy of it hit her like a ton of bricks. She was suddenly breathless, achy, and much too aware of the man beside her.

He was watching her with that look that never failed to arouse her. And it *was* arousal. Roni was a virgin, but she wasn't stupid.

"Would I regret it?" The words passed her lips before she could halt them.

A blush burned her face as she turned quickly away from him, shaking her head, feeling just as immature and stupid as she knew she was being right now.

"Forget it." She shook her head as she stared into the deserted lot. "I'm sure I didn't mean that."

But she did. She was honest enough with herself to know it.

"Roni." His voice was softer now, resonating with a power, a heated emotion that had her heart tripling in speed.

"Look, I don't need any sweet little speeches," she said as she fought to hide her humiliation. Damn, when would she learn to keep her mouth shut? "Why don't you just take me home and we'll forget I ever said a word…"

"Do you think I wouldn't love anything more than to take you to my bed? To give you what I know we both want?"

She stilled. She whimpered. Oh God, that pathetic little sound did not come from her throat. She turned back to look at him, feeling the desperation that she fought inside her welling to the surface. Hope surged inside her like a tidal wave of emotion as she stared back at him, her breathing becoming rough, heavy. Need ripping through her with erotic talons.

It was there on his face. Heavy lines of regret, the hunger she only glimpsed occasionally in his eyes. The heat that seared her every time she was around him glowed in his brilliant gaze. But he wouldn't do anything. She saw that as well. Saw the taut control that held his body rigid.

"But you won't," she whispered, her heart breaking. "Will you?"

A bitter smile twisted his lips.

"Look at you," he said gently, though his voice was rough. "So innocent and sweet and you have no idea the animal you're trying to set loose here."

"You wouldn't hurt me." She knew that. Knew that if she gave herself to him he might break her heart, but he would never hurt her physically.

"You can't be sure of that, Roni." He lifted his hand from the steering wheel, reaching out to touch her cheek.

The warmth of his calloused fingertips, the touch of his thumb at her lips had a sobbing breath of need escaping her throat. She had to touch him, to taste him. Her tongue peeked out, swiping over his flesh as they both groaned. The sounds were hot, hungry, filling the interior of the truck with a tension that tightened every cell in her body.

"You make me ache." She couldn't hold back the words or the need. "Sometimes I can't stand it, Taber, I need you so bad. I love you."

They had been friends for years. His cabin wasn't far from hers and he had been a presence in her life for so long that she wondered if she could survive without him.

He swallowed tightly. "You don't know what you're saying."

"I've loved you since I was eleven, Taber. Ever since you carried me out of the damned mountain and took me back to your mother's house. Don't you know you own me?" She hated that thought. Hated how much she needed him, how much she ached for him. "Am I so terrible, Taber, that even you don't want me?" Were the upright, uptight prudes who judged her for Reginald's actions right? Was she somehow tainted? Unworthy of love? The thought of that pierced her soul.

Taber's eyes flared with hunger, as though her words had set loose something inside him he could no longer contain. Hope surged within her. Arousal heated further, searing the already moist depths of her cunt.

"Not want you?" he almost snarled then. "Dammit, Roni, it would terrify you if you had any idea what I do want from you."

There was nothing he could ask of her that she wouldn't give him.

"Then it's yours," she whispered as his thumb stroked across her jaw, drawing slowly to her lips. "Anything, Taber. I would die for you."

The tension in the truck cab was thick enough to cut, hot, heavy with an eroticism that prickled over her skin and stroked her sensitive nerve endings.

"You're still a baby," he groaned, his thumb pressing against her lips until she enveloped it in the heat of her mouth. "God, Roni..." She bit down on it, holding him there as her tongue raked over the rough pad.

Roni had always hated her lack of control, the hungry needs that often pushed her to hurt herself, to reveal her emotions in ways that allowed others to hurt her. She was hungry, starving for Taber in a way she never had for anyone else. She needed him now worse than she needed the air that sustained her.

"Let go," he whispered as his other hand pulled her closer. "Let's see if I can't fill your mouth with something a hell of a lot more enjoyable."

Before she knew what was happening he had her back pinned to the seat, rising over her as he jerked the handle under it to slide it farther back and allow him more room. Roni whimpered, staring up at him in dazed disbelief as he moved between her legs, the hard, hot heat of his denim-covered cock notching between her thighs perfectly.

She jerked against him, inhaling in shock and a pleasure so harsh it was nearly painful.

"Taber..." Her womb convulsed then. Like a punch to her lower stomach it stole her breath, leaving her gasping.

"Feel me, Roni," he ordered her hoarsely, grinding against her, his eyes darkening further as she felt the moisture spill between her thighs. Feel him? How could she do anything but feel him?

It was too intense. A broken cry escaped her throat as she arched to him, feeling her breasts throb, her clit swell. Her hands gripped his arms as he braced himself above her, his expression pulling into a painful grimace as he stared down at her.

She glimpsed the longer than normal canines, had a second to wonder at them, before the thought dissolved beneath the incredible sensations, the knowledge that he was touching her. Finally, Taber wanted her.

"I bet you're so fucking tight I won't last minutes inside you." His voice was grating, exciting her senses in ways she could have never imagined.

"Find out." She could barely breathe, let alone speak, but she forced the words from her lips, needing him now with a ravaging hunger she couldn't dispel.

One touch. That was all it had taken. Just one touch from him to destroy any self-control she might have had.

Her hands went to his waist, clawing at his shirt as she jerked it from his jeans, desperate to touch him, to taste him. She wanted to run her fingers down his chest, test the hard packed muscles of his abdomen, loosen his jeans and see if his cock was as thick and hard as it felt.

"Inside." He lowered his head to her neck, his lips trailing down the side of it, his breath hot and heavy against her flesh. "I refuse to fuck you in the damned pickup like a kid."

"I need to touch you." Her hands flattened against his skin, her fingers curling against the heat of it, her senses overloading with the silken feel, the impression of small, downy hairs covering what she'd thought was a hairless chest.

He jerked against her, a pure primal growl issuing from his throat as her hands trailed down to his abdomen, then to the waistband of his jeans. Her fingers moved to the wide belt buckle, her gaze locking with his as she slid the leather of his belt through the metal loop.

"No. Not like this." His hand covered hers, though his hips thrust fiercely against the mound of her pussy. "Not like this, Roni. Get your ass in that garage and think about this. Think about it hard and deep, baby, because I promise you, once I get inside you, that's how I'll fuck you. Hard and deep and without mercy. And I'll be damned if I'll let you ever walk away from me once I do it. So you better be real fucking sure it's what you want."

He jerked away from her, groaning at the effort she could tell it cost him. He wanted her. The thought rushed through her brain as pleasure heated her body. Roni stared up at him, amazed, a little frightened, but more than willing to give him whatever he needed from her.

"I have to get the hell out of here before I rape you." He settled back into his seat, watching her carefully as she sat back up. "Open the garage up for me. I'll be back later. And do as I said, Roni. Be sure. Because once I take you, there will be no escape. Remember that. This is your last chance, baby. I won't have the control to give you another."

"I don't want to escape." She promised herself she wouldn't beg, but God knew she was within seconds of it.

He was breathing hard, heavy. His face flushed, his eyes glittered with stark, unabashed lust. "I'll be back this evening. If this happens, I want it to happen right, baby. I want you to be sure."

She turned to open the door, to stumble her way from the cab of the truck. Before she could do more than turn to leave he caught her around the waist, his mouth pressing against her neck.

"Taber." Her entire body weakened, her eyes closing at the feel of him against her back, his arms going around her, his tongue stroking over her skin.

"I need to taste you." She could hear the war being waged within him in his voice.

His tongue was rough, rasping, almost like a cat's, causing her to shudder with the sensual pleasure streaking through her body. It licked over her lower neck at the point where it met her shoulder. Then his teeth raked, tearing a strangled moan from her throat as he bit her a little roughly, the pleasure-pain overwhelming her, destroying her.

His hands flattened beneath her breasts, pulling her tighter against his chest as he suckled gently at her skin, then licked over it with a rough growl of pleasure.

"God, how good you taste," he whispered at her ear. "Will you be this good, Roni, when I lick your soft pussy? Will your sweetness drive me insane for you?"

"Oh God." Her head fell back against his shoulder as his lips and tongue continued to torment the sensitized skin.

"You'd better rest today," he whispered as he slowly released her. "Rest well, Roni, because if you're still here when I come back, it may be days before you sleep again."

Roni fought for breath. Fought to find the strength to leave the truck. She didn't want to let him go, didn't want to take the chance that he would change his mind and leave her aching like this forever.

"I don't have to think about it." She didn't look at him, terrified if she did, she would beg him to take her. "I want you now, Taber."

"Then it won't change in a few hours." His voice was strangled, rough. His expression tight and heavy with sensuality. "Go. Before I lose all control."

She moved slowly from the truck before turning back to look at him.

"You'll be back? For sure?"

"Oh, I'll be back," he said softly, a wry smile twisting his lips. "We may both regret it later, Roni, but I'll be back."

She closed the door, stepping back so he could leave, so she could think about and anticipate the coming night.

The night came, but Taber didn't. The next morning, his brother Dayan was there, and in his hands he held the destruction of all her dreams. The letter Taber had sent her had shattered everything inside her.

You're still just a child, Roni. I'm a man. Mature and needing more of a woman to fulfill the needs I have. Someone old enough to understand those needs, not a ripe little virgin. Go home. You're just a little girl playing with something you and I both know you can't handle. Upon reflection, I've decided it's best that our friendship terminate. I'm sick of rescuing you. Sick of the burden you've placed on me to protect you. Learn to protect yourself, and how to grow up. I have no idea how to raise a child, and I don't want to start with you. Taber.

She returned to her home, the silence, the fears, and a hunger for Taber that had grown to nearly painful proportions. And fury. Sweet, hot fury coursed through her, both at Taber and at herself. *Little girl.* The words haunted her. He may not have fucked her, but he had made certain she had grown up quickly. One day, she swore, he would pay for that alone.

Chapter One
Three Years Later

"If you'll notice the small mark on her shoulder, you'll see it appears to be a love bite." The reporter pointed to a bruise-like shadow on the picture of Merinus Lyon's shoulder, at the point where it met her neck. "We have no confirmations, but rumors are suggesting it's a 'mating' mark. That there is an instinctive mating recognition between the Feline Breed, Callan Lyons, and his wife. It includes the mark, as well as a semen and saliva-based hormone that essentially acts as an aphrodisiac on the female. The Feline Breeds are denying this, but the reports that were slipped from the labs where the tests are being conducted are proving the supposition…"

Roni was in shock. She stood beneath her father's regard, watching the report, feeling the blood drain from her face as her eyes centered on the mark revealed by the photo. It would be easy to claim it was no more than a love bite, but several photos in the course of three months showed it never changed, never healed. The reports smuggled to them said it never would.

Roni's hand rose to her shoulder, covering the mark she knew marred her own flesh, just as it did Callan's wife.

"What the hell possessed you to fuck that freak?" her father sneered as he paced the room, his breathing harsh, fury outlining every inch of his body.

Reginald Andrews was a big man, not as muscular and tall as Taber, but strong enough that his anger caused Roni to flinch at the thought of remembered whippings. She was an adult now. She wouldn't tolerate a whipping from him anymore, but she had never gotten over her fear of him. Her fear, or her hatred.

"Go back to wherever you came from," she told him harshly as she continued to stare at the television screen. "They're wrong."

She had survived just fine without Taber, even after the way he marked her skin, destroyed her dreams. She had survived the endless threats and attempted attacks her father's creditors had staged, and she had survived it alone. She could and she would get through this.

"You think you can lie to me?" he spat out as he came up beside her. He jerked her around until he could stare down at her, his washed-out brown eyes darkening in fury. "Do you look in the mirror often enough to see that disgusting place on your neck, Roni? Or does it sicken you too much to remember you spread your thighs for an animal?"

Roni watched him suspiciously. He didn't care about her one way or the other and she had enough sense to know it. She highly doubted that he cared who she fucked, which meant there was more behind his anger than any parental concern or personal insult.

"Take your hands off me before I call your last employer and let him know exactly where the hell you are." She kept her voice low, but there was no disguising the hatred that welled up inside her for her parent.

She hadn't seen him more than half a dozen times in the past three years. None of those sightings had been pleasant. This one least of all. Stubbornness had kept her in the home her mother had loved so dearly, but she had learned how to hide her money, how to provide for herself and ignore him during his few visits.

"Roni, you've gone and ruined everything," he yelled back at her furiously, but he did release her. "I nearly had you married, girl. Mr. Tearns would have paid for the use of you, while you let that cat have it for nothing."

Ah, so now we get to the real story, she thought mockingly. How very typical of Reginald. Marriage to his boss, though, was a little bit extreme.

"My marriage? To your boss?" She laughed at him. "Is that why you showed up, Reggie? Do you think I'd so much as talk to the snakes you run with? I don't think so. Fend for yourself. It's what I do."

What she had always done. She turned back to the television, nearly losing her breath at the recorded interview with the five Feline Breeds. Taber's voice sent a surge of heat flowing through her body that she didn't even attempt to fight. She had learned over the years not to fight it. It only hurt worse when she did.

"Beats fucking an animal," he sneered again. "You'll be lucky to live if anyone sees that mark on your neck, Roni. I bet those Council bastards would love to get hold of you."

Fear shot through her as she turned back to her father. How desperate was he, she wondered? She wasn't stupid enough to think that any parental bond would keep him from selling his information to the highest bidder. He would turn her over in a heartbeat, if he hadn't already.

"Don't look at me like that, girlie." His mouth twisted in disgust. "I'm not about to tell anyone. Hell, like I want it known my kid is a dirty cat fucker."

She almost flinched at the term. Almost. She hadn't fucked him. Hell, he hadn't even kissed her. All he had done was mark her, ruining her forever for any other man, then left her in a way that made her father's desertions pale in comparison.

"Leave, Reggie." She turned off the television. "I don't need you here now any more than I've needed you over the past years. I don't have any money, and I don't want to put up with your crap. Just go away."

She had learned that it wouldn't do her any good if she did need him. The minute he thought she might, he ran.

"You can use this, Roni," he finally said, his nasal voice wheedling. "We could give 'em a story that could make us millions. We wouldn't have to worry anymore."

Horror rushed over her in a wave of sickening realization. She hadn't seen him in months, and now he was here. Another scheme, another get-rich-quick idea and once again he didn't care how he used her to attain it.

It was time to leave. She silently admitted that there was no way in hell her father would ever keep this to himself. She might have a few days at the most to get her things together and run.

She stared around the small house she had lived in all her life. It wasn't much, but it was all she had. The home her mother had dreamed of, but hadn't lived long enough to enjoy. She would lose it now.

The small cabin was no longer the shack it had been. The job she had found in Morehead as an accountant had allowed her to fix it up—new curtains and appliances, a comfortable sofa in a dark forest-green color with matching chairs, a small cherry coffee table and matching end tables, a delicate glass lamp. And she had a new bed rather than the mattress on the floor she had used for years. And now she was going to have to walk away from all of it.

"Go away," she told him again. "And keep your mouth shut unless you want to die. Does it sound like the Council is something you really want to tangle with, Reggie? They would kill you before they paid you a penny." There wasn't a chance he would listen to her.

Fury flowed through her veins like acid, eating away the peace she had managed to find in her life in the past three years. Just what she needed. To be drawn into something so dangerous that it made her father's escapades look like tea parties.

"I'll leave. But I'll be back. You think about this, Roni. The bastard fucked you and left. What do you owe him? Make him pay, like he should have to begin with."

He stomped to the door, casting her an angry, narrow-eyed look before he slammed from the house, leaving her alone once again. Roni shook her head wearily as she collapsed in the new chair. Leather, sinfully soft and supportive beneath her body. Usually its warm comfort was soothing, peaceful. It wasn't now.

"God, now what?" She raised her eyes to the ceiling as she fought back her tears and the reality of this new blow.

She didn't want to leave her home. She had fought most of her life to stay, to hold together the fragile remnants of happier days and comfort herself with them. Now that was being taken as well.

She would have to fix the truck. It was more dependable than the car, and would get her further. Unfortunately, like the car, it wasn't in the best of shape. But it could be fixed. And she'd better fix it damned soon, because sure as hell her father wouldn't wait long before trying to sell her to the highest bidder.

She shuddered in fear.

"Why did you do this, Taber?" she whispered with bleak sorrow into the empty living room, her empty heart.

She had been alone since the day Dayan had handed her the letter Taber had sent her. At first she had dated, determined to get over the one man she had always dreamed of loving. But she had learned quickly that her body would never accept the touch of another man, and her heart ached for what she knew she couldn't have. But at times like this, when she desperately needed a shoulder to cry on, being alone really sucked.

* * * * *

Roni stared into the guts and glory of the pickup truck she was working on, hours later, and sighed wearily as she finally admitted failure. It just wasn't going to get fixed today, no matter how badly she wanted it done. And time was running out.

The ever-present trembling in her hands, the ache in the pit of her stomach, were too severe, and the fear washing through her mind did little to allow her the concentration she needed to fix the stubborn vehicle. Her father wouldn't wait long before he made his move. When he did, her life wouldn't be worth spit. But if she didn't control the effects of what Taber had done to her, then she was in more trouble than she needed anyway.

It was the arousal, a burgeoning, advancing heat that struck without warning and held her in its grip for days.

It was getting worse, the weakness that assailed her, accompanied by an arousal that came just short of painful. This was one of the more severe spells that she had suffered over the past years, and the knowledge of where it stemmed from terrified her.

She lowered her head wearily as she braced her arms on the front of the vehicle and shook her head. She wanted to run, to hide. She wanted to return to a time when she could dream and find comfort in those dreams, but reality refused to allow her the vacation she needed.

There was no escaping the news stories, no escaping the truth that had exploded across the world. Roni had tried to bury herself in work rather than become glued to the television screen, as many others were. Or worse yet, being interviewed by many of the television crews that had invaded the small town of Sandy Hook, Kentucky. She had ignored it, until her father had forced the truth on her.

Thankfully, so far she had managed to avoid the intrepid reporters and suspicious journalists. There were plenty of others more than willing to talk, though, and those interviews aired several times a day. As though the world couldn't get enough of this newest sensation.

Project Alpha. The creation of a special army designed to fight, to kill. Part animal, instinctive in their fighting responses and in their savagery. Rumor and innuendo hinted that the animal genetics they possessed went much deeper than just surface awareness or their incredible fighting skills. It had been hinted that the sexuality of the creatures was in question as well.

Leaks among the scientists that had tested the five Breeds and Callan Lyons' wife, Merinus Tyler, hinted at a hormonal infection, a biological "marking" that had bound Merinus to the fierce Callan.

Roni trembled as she remembered the news story, her hand moving instinctively to her own neck, her own "bruise". It didn't matter that the Breeds were firmly denying this, that many in the scientific field were scoffing at it. She knew it was the truth. She knew because she carried Taber's mark. Suffered, often painfully with an arousal that couldn't be dimmed no matter what she tried. And yet couldn't be assuaged by another, either.

In the three years since the stolen moments she had shared with him outside the garage, she had been unable to allow any other man to touch her. The very thought of being with anyone besides Taber made her ill.

She dropped the wrench she was using in the lip of the truck's frame and jumped off the plastic crate she used for the extra height to reach the motor.

Anger spread through her system, helpless, searing anger in the face of the truths she was learning. He had touched her knowing what he would do to her. Knowing he was marking her, binding her to him in a way she would never escape and then he had just walked away from her as though it had never happened.

Had she taken him seriously? Of course not, she grunted. Hell, no. Why would she do something like that? She slammed the hood closed before turning and stalking furiously back into the house.

This had to stop. She had been shaking with anger, with emotions she didn't want to deal with ever since the first news report hit the air. This was worse than the constant arousal she couldn't seem to rid herself of, the irritation if anyone touched her, the mood swings that often plagued her. There was a deep, overwhelming feeling of betrayal.

She washed quickly, changing into clean jeans and a light blouse before grabbing up her car keys and purse and heading back outside to her car. She needed to buy groceries and maybe a set of spark plugs for that stupid truck, she thought. And she needed to forget about Taber, whether it was what her body wanted or not.

The drive into Sandy Hook took less than twenty minutes. Getting through town took longer. Tourism had boomed, but it wasn't the beauty of the Laurel Gorge they had come to see, it was the town and the gossip they were after.

"Home of the Breeds", a sign proclaimed outside the county limits in every direction. Several new motels were being built and signs outside larger homes advertised rooms for rent. They were even organizing freaking tours into the gorge and cliffs where it was known Callan and his family often hunted and hid. New lies were being created daily for the hundreds of visitors that were flocking to the small town, rumors of missing hunters and animalistic roars disturbing the night.

By the time she pulled into the auto parts store, Roni was irritated and running low on patience, which wasn't high to begin with. She felt like snarling as she managed to work her way to the counter and purchase the parts she needed for the truck.

"Here you go, Roni." Harried and appearing nearly as frustrated as she was, John O'Brien handed her the small plastic bag and her change as he glanced behind her and snapped out angrily, "Damned news vans are blocking my parking lot again. Stupid asses."

Roni glanced over her shoulder to the large windows that looked out on the parking lot. Sure enough, two vans were blocking the driveway as several journalists milled about talking to customers who had left the store. She felt her heart jump in her chest, her palms moistening with fear.

She checked the collar of her shirt to be certain it hid the mark on her shoulder. She sure as hell didn't need anyone to see it now.

"Yeah, they're a nuisance, all right." She shot John a commiserating smile. "Let's hope they let me out of here soon. I wanted to fix that truck by nightfall."

She wanted to get the hell out of here and hide. Being in such close proximity to the vultures ready and eager for the latest news sensation was nearly too much for her nerves. Especially knowing her father.

She lowered her head as she pushed through the exit, heading to the car she had parked on the lower end of the lot. She didn't want her face caught in a roving camera's eyes, or have one of those stupid microphones pushed under her nose...

"There she is!" The shout rang out as she headed along the side of the building.

Roni had a second to feel a surge of sympathy for whoever they were targeting before she was grabbed from behind and jerked around, the collar to her shirt pulled aside with such force it ripped.

Terror surged through her like a tidal wave as hard hands held her, faces flashing before her eyes, and the microphone was shoved in her face.

"Who's your mate, Veronica?" The fanatical eyes of a hungry journalist met hers as she fought to tear herself free. "Who marked you? Are you in heat? Have you been tested?"

She screamed out in fury as her flesh protested the grip on her arms, the sweaty male bodies surrounding her. She dropped the bag and her purse as she began to claw, to fight.

"Tell us, Veronica, who is he? And what's it like to be mated to an animal?"

Fractured voices, raised in both protest and demand, echoed around her as she kicked out at the journalists, clawed at the hands holding her, fighting desperately to be free, to escape.

She was unaware she was crying, unaware of the camera catching every whimper, each hoarse scream that echoed around her. Her vision was dazed, blurred by fear and fury and the overwhelming instinct to fight.

Roni heard the material of her shirt ripping as she finally tore free of the rough hands holding her. She didn't hesitate, didn't look back, she just ran. She didn't know in which direction she was moving, didn't know where to go, who to run to. Her only thought was escape.

"Roni." John O'Brien's voice ripped through the panic as she passed the side of the store. "The truck. Back here." He waved her over frantically, his face pale, his light blue eyes glittering with fury. "Son of a bitch leeching reporters. Come on."

The crowd was surging behind them as he threw open the door to the parts truck and she jumped inside. She pulled the panel shut, locking it as several cameras and microphones were thrust against the windows.

The heavy truck jerked as John slammed it in gear, lurched and began moving forward as reporters and hungry curiosity seekers attempted to block it.

"I'll run over your damned asses," John yelled out, his usually pale face flushed with anger, his red hair standing on end as he swiped his fingers through it and pressed his foot to the gas.

They bumped over a curb, tore through several yards and a pristine fence that enclosed the insurance offices.

"Son of a bitch, there goes my policy," John cursed, though excitement sizzled in his voice as he took a narrow alley, the truck increasing in speed, tires screaming as he turned on to one of the back roads that led out of town. "You okay?"

She stared back at him, confused, shaking, her stomach rioting with fear as she shook her head and blinked over at him. What the hell had happened? Her skin was still burning from the unfamiliar touches of the men who had held her, protesting the contact, screaming out for Taber.

She shook her head, fighting for a semblance of control. Dear God. They knew. Reginald had wasted no time at all in selling her out, she thought. Betrayal, thick and bitter, clogged her throat, despite the knowledge that she could have expected nothing less from a father who had never been a father to begin with.

"Take me home." She winced at the hoarse sound of her voice, the pain that was reflected in it. "I need to go home."

"They'll be waiting there, Roni," he told her softly as the truck's motor surged, pushing the vehicle up a steep road that wound around the cliffs outside town. "You need to hide for a while, figure out what you're gonna do."

"Going to do?" she whispered brokenly as she rubbed at her arms, trying to free her flesh of the remembered feel of another's touch. Dear God, what was she going to do? Her father had moved faster than she expected. He had to have already sold her out before showing up at the house.

She couldn't go home. John was right. They would find her there. They would invade the house. There was no way she could hide from them. But what else was left?

"I know a place," John finally sighed. "You'll be safe there for a while, if they don't catch up with us before we get there. Everything's going to be okay, Roni, at least until we can contact Callan. And you know you have to contact him."

He flashed her a hard, demanding look. His eyes still gleamed with the rush of the chase, adrenaline glittering in his gaze, as well as conviction.

No, it wasn't Callan she had to call, Roni thought. It wasn't his fault. It was Taber's and by God, Taber would pay. Her hands clenched as fury surged through her, nearly as hot as the arousal that often left her weak and helpless. If she managed to get her hands on him she would kill him. And her senseless, mercenary father would be the next one to go.

Chapter Two

Taber rolled his shoulders as the late spring rays of the sun speared through the window behind him, soaking through the cloth of his shirt and heating the flesh beneath. It was the next best thing to being outside, and all he could allow himself for the moment.

Being trapped within the confines of the mansion the Feline Pride now lived in shouldn't have been considered a hardship. Spacious though it was, the walls seemed to close in on him, the confinement pricking at his mind, reminding him of things best left forgotten. And as always, when he sought to escape the memories of his creation and his time spent confined in labs, tested, poked and prodded, his thoughts went to her. Deep blue eyes, skin as soft and silky as a dream, the heat of her arousal burning through his mind.

Roni. In the past few weeks, thoughts of her had been stronger than ever before. His need for her was only growing rather than diminishing, as he thought it would. And that worried him. He knew many of the details of Callan's mating with Merinus. Knew the signs. He had carried those symptoms for over a year, just not as extreme, not as strong. But then, he hadn't kissed his mate. He hadn't allowed the potent hormone to release into her body in the same way.

If she was his mate, then she carried his mark. Not once in the years that had passed before his move from Sandy Hook, had he been close enough to her again to remember if the slight, never-healing wound marred the flesh of her shoulder. Not that he would have been looking for it. But getting close to her had been impossible.

She didn't talk to him. If she saw him coming, she went the other way. If he caught her gaze then fury lit hers, sparkling with female ire as he tried to sort out the cause of her anger. Hadn't he honored her wish that he leave her be? He hadn't called her, hadn't visited her. He didn't speak if he happened to pass her. What right did she have to be angry? What right did he have to care? Surely if he had marked her, some signs would be apparent. Hell, Merinus had been in such pain during the early phase of it that if Doc Martin hadn't suspected its cause, they would have likely had to hospitalize her.

Taber had always kept up with news on Roni. She had shown no unusual illnesses, nor had the records he had checked months before shown any hospitalizations. Yet his body ached for her. Ached in ways that left him frustrated and irritable, barely able to keep his mind on the job he should be doing, rather than worrying about the woman he wanted to do.

As he turned his gaze back to the readout in front of him, the office door burst open.

"Turn on the news." Sherra rushed into the large office Callan and Taber shared within the mansion the Genetics Council had once owned. The one-hundred-and-fifty acre estate in the mountains of Virginia had been deeded to the Feline Breeds, with Callan and Taber named as overseers for the time being until a Pride governorship could be formed. Which would be years down the road, they figured.

Taber looked up from the computer printout he had been reading as Sherra snagged the television remote and turned on the large plasma screen television that hung from the opposite wall. Irritation flashed across his senses at the disturbance.

They had three reports of yet more Feline Breeds coming in, but even more disturbing were the reports of other various Breeds that had been created. Tracking down the rumors and basing them in fact was a tedious process. Reading through the odd codes the Council soldiers used and the myriad transmissions they were catching was even harder. He didn't have time for another news report.

The picture that flashed across the screen froze everything inside him, though. The eager eyes and excited voice of the journalist chilled the blood in his veins. But the face of the woman had a growl rumbling in his chest.

"Veronica Andrews, part time mechanic and accountant in Sandy Hook, who also carries the mark of a Feline mate..." Roni's shirt was ripped, her voice hoarse as she cried out in pain and the camera locked onto the small, bruise-like mark that marred her shoulder.

Taber came slowly to his feet, shock resounding through his body as the events of that stolen day surged through his mind — his mouth on her flesh, his canines raking across the area as he suckled at the skin, his tongue laving it. The taste of her had gone to his head faster than liquor. Even now, she haunted his senses.

"Miss Andrews, how does it feel to be mated to an animal?" Another reporter drowned out her cries as she clawed and kicked to be free. The eager, almost fanatical expressions of the reporters and onlookers sickened him.

The fear in her expression tightened into a coil of rage in his stomach. How dare they touch her! Hold her still for their barbaric displays in such a way. He snarled silently, a promise of retribution searing through his brain.

It was one of the most horrific scenes Taber had ever witnessed in his life. Veronica's eyes were nearly black in shock and pain as rough hands tried to hold her still, pushing at her head to show the mark in stark relief as the journalist droned on about the supposed mating habits of the Breeds.

He drew slowly closer, his eyes centered on that mark...his mark, his woman. He felt his heart beating sluggishly, the blood boiling in his veins at the sight of hands — male hands — holding her still as she fought, bruising the delicate skin they gripped.

He was barely aware of the growls rumbling from his chest, stark and animalistic, as he watched.

"Let her go, you bastards!" A familiar male voice joined the melee as one of the employees of the auto parts store literally jerked several of those holding her back, slamming them into the wall behind him.

It gave Veronica her chance to jerk free. She didn't hesitate as she began to run. The camera followed her, showing the burly storeowner yelling at her, waving her to the parts truck parked to the side. She dived into it, only seconds ahead of the enraged journalists.

The camera zoomed in through the closed window as she glanced back. Her expression was stark with terror, her eyes glassy, tear-filled, her shirt nearly ripped from her body, bruises showing on her arms and the upper curves of her breasts.

Every mating instinct in Taber's body went into overdrive. He had known years before that Roni was different, special. That something about her drew him as nothing else ever had. Staying away from her as she asked him to do had been the hardest thing in his life. Staying away from her now would be impossible.

"I need Tanner and Cabal." The rough Bengal Breeds were as charming and yet as savage as Taber himself could be. "Sherra…"

"I'm on it." She already had the phone to her ear, barking out orders. Weapons, supplies, and a heli-flight into the county would take little more than an hour as opposed to a day's drive. "I'll have you ready to go in twenty minutes," she called out to him.

He watched the truck tip as it turned a sharp corner, took out a fence and disappeared up an alley. The transmission was a live feed and broadcasted internationally. He cursed softly. Every fucking scientist and Genetics Council soldier was most likely watching the same display. And he knew damned good and well several of those soldiers were placed in Sandy Hook.

John O'Brien was a good man. His friendship with Callan had stood through the news reports and the rumors that had gone crazy over the months. But he was still just one man, and despite his army training, he was no match for the men the Council would have in place.

"Callan. Get someone on her," he called back to his Pride leader almost absently, feeling as though the world was centered on the replay of the attack.

"Got it, Taber." Callan's voice was hard, dangerously cold. "O'Brien's with her. He's good. I have a pretty good idea where he'll head, and I'll contact him when you get airborne."

"Helicopter's warming up, Taber," Sherra reported. "It's being loaded. Tanner and Cabal are heading out to it now. Everything's a go."

Taber's eyes narrowed as he memorized the faces of the men holding her. A few were citizens of the small county where she had grown up. The other two were strangers. They would all pay.

Roni's scream echoed around him again, her eyes large, terrorized, her face pale. His fists clenched in fury and only then did he become aware of the low, ominous growls issuing from his throat.

He didn't speak before leaving the room. He turned on his heel and headed quickly out of the office to the front door of the three-story mansion. Outside, a Jeep awaited him. The young Feline Breed driving it put the gas to the floor as he sped to the landing pad where the helicopter awaited.

"Good luck," the younger Breed called out as Taber jumped from the Jeep and headed to the waiting aircraft.

He ducked as he ran to the open door of the small, sleek little copter and jumped inside. Three years he had waited, never certain, unwilling to force his life on any woman, but especially one he had tried for so long to protect.

"Ready," he yelled out as Tanner glanced back from the cockpit.

He pulled the headphones over his head, strapped in and braced himself as they lifted off. Every second it took to get to her now was too long. A smile edged his lips. He had respected her wishes over the months because he was unaware of the instinctive mating process. Now the beast inside was free to claim what was his. She could rage, she could bitch, she could hate him until hell froze over and cracked wide open. But she was his. And soon—very soon—she would find there was no longer a choice...for either of them.

* * * * *

This wasn't happening to her. Roni tried to convince herself that the mad dash from town into the mountains rising above it was all a nightmare. She would wake up soon. Of course she would. It was just the stress. It wasn't every day you learned you had mated with a new species of human that you hadn't even known existed.

"You doin' okay?" John glanced at her worriedly from the driver's seat of the parts truck, his red brows lowered over the light blue of his eyes.

Roni gripped the overhead strap tighter as he swung around another curve. Sure as hell he was going to end up going over one of the treacherous cliffs and kill them both. He drove like a madman. Her life may have deteriorated rapidly, but that didn't mean she wanted to die any time soon.

"Aren't you going a little fast?" she asked, striving for calm despite the frantic pace of her heart.

"We're almost there. I want to make sure we aren't followed." He turned quickly up yet another side road, bouncing over a rough gravel path that led through a densely wooded area. "I'm heading for my hunting cabin. Thankfully, it's up high enough that the cell phones will work and Taber won't have a problem landing there."

She blinked in confusion. "What are you talking about?"

Taber wouldn't come for her, he wasn't going to rescue her. Didn't they know? Weren't they aware that he had washed his hands of her months ago?

He sighed roughly. "That was a live feed, Roni. The world knows now, and I'm sure Taber's on his way. When he gets close enough he'll call me. Taber knows and the bad guys know. You aren't safe here anymore."

She swallowed past the thickness in her throat, fighting the roiling of her stomach. She had seen reports of the "bad guys". Monsters was more like it. Holding on to her control wasn't an easy thing to do. God help her, she had seen more than one report on the news regarding the fate of the poor souls the Council had targeted. It was the worst nightmare she could have imagined.

"God," she whispered bleakly. "I'm sure I'll wake up soon. But Taber won't be here, John. He didn't care when he made that mark and he sure as hell won't care now."

He had spent a decade pulling her out of one scrape after another. He had reached his limit and now she knew she couldn't depend on his help to pull her out of this one.

John grunted as he cast her an incredulous look. "You keep dreamin' that, Roni, and when you see Taber be sure to let him in on that little secret."

She shook her head and started to pray. She was running seriously low on any other options to pull herself out of this particular problem.

Roni closed her eyes and drew in a deep hard breath as the shrill sound of the cell phone began to ring.

"Yeah?" John barked into the small phone. He was silent for long moments.

"On my way there. What's your ETA?"

Roni wished she could pinch herself awake. She listened only distantly to the one-sided conversation, trying to avoid the fact that the past was about to bite her in the ass. Just what she needed, something else to disrupt the nice little routine she had established for herself. She might not be happy, but she was content. Content was a good thing.

"Told you so," he announced softly, his voice triumphant. "Taber will be here in thirty minutes. We should be secure that long."

Incredulity spread through her. He would be here? After fifteen long torturous months of letting her scrape by on her own, he would be here? That was right friendly of him, she thought, considering it was his fucking fault she was in this mess to begin with.

Roni glanced over as he clipped the cell phone back to his belt. She frowned, watching him intently. She hadn't known John long, she admitted, but he was suddenly different, harder-edged than she had been used to. It reminded her uncomfortably of Taber. That narrow-eyed, dangerous look that assured anyone daring to oppose him they could be in for a world of hurt.

She clenched her teeth, refraining from saying anything in reply. What could she say that wouldn't be less than complimentary toward Taber? He created this mess, then left her to suffer the consequences. Fixing it would be a damned good thing for him to do.

"Here we are." He nodded forward as Roni turned back to look at the cabin that appeared as they rounded a turn in the road.

Situated beneath a thick growth of trees, the small cabin and attached garage would be damned near invisible from the air, and just as hard to find on the ground. He pulled into the rough garage, shut off the engine and jumped from the vehicle.

Roni moved much slower. There had to be a way out of this, she thought with an edge of desperation. Things like this didn't happen to people like her. Her life was supposed to be uneventful. She was dull. Boring. Hell, Taber hadn't wanted her when he had the chance, what made anyone in his right mind think he would want her now?

He had fired her from the job she loved, the only escape she had known at the time from her demanding father. He had disappeared for months. Didn't even speak to her the few times they had run into each other over the past years. A mark on her neck was not going to change that, was it? Not as far as she was concerned it wasn't.

The interior of the cabin was decorated with a miser's hand. There was a lone couch in front of an unused fireplace, a dusty kitchen table and four chairs. No rugs, no curtains and dust damned near thick enough to plant petunias in.

"Bathroom's in the back." He pointed to the closed door at the far end. "Make yourself at home."

He was too casual, too accepting of his sudden role as rescuer and guardian until Taber showed up.

"Why are you doing this?" She turned back to him, watching him carefully.

He looked at her, his eyes glimmering in surprise. "Doing what?"

"Helping me, so certain Taber will show up. What's in it for you?"

He arched a flame-colored brow, amusement replacing the confusion. "I was just helping, Roni."

"Bullshit," she muttered, shaking her head in denial. "I'm not stupid. There's more to it. What?"

She needed to make sense of something, even if it was the only helping hand that had been offered to her.

He sighed heavily. "More or less, that's all there is to it," he told her firmly. "I help Taber and the others when I can. That's all. Besides, you're a friend. I would have helped you anyway."

Which still didn't completely answer her question.

"Why is he coming here?" She pushed her fingers through her tangled hair, ignoring the trembling in her hand. "That mark didn't mean anything when he made it. Why should it now?" This was the question that plagued her more than most.

"You can ask him when he gets here. I'm going out to make sure we weren't followed. Stay in the cabin." He unclipped the cell phone at his side. "Taber's number is the first one keyed in. If something happens, you call him. You hear?"

She glanced down as he laid the phone on the table, feeling her mouth dry out with fear. "What could happen?"

She met his gaze as she raised her head, her heart racing in warning. He watched her, his expression somber.

"Like I said, others would have seen that broadcast. And some of them are a hell of a lot closer than Taber was. I just want to be cautious."

She swallowed tightly. "Mercenaries?" She had heard the reports of the constant battles Taber and his family had fought through the years with the men sent to either recapture or kill them.

A glimmer of sympathy lit his eyes. "Yeah," he finally muttered. "But we should be secure. Only a few people know about this place, and by the time anyone figures out where we are, Taber should have you safe and sound wherever he thinks is best. You'll be fine."

He turned before she could comment and left the shelter. Only then did she notice the gun he carried in his other hand. It was black, lethal, and he sure as hell carried it like he knew what he was doing with it.

Great. She collapsed into one of the dusty kitchen chairs and stared around the one-room cabin with a sense of despair. Mercenaries were after her. Just what she needed on top of everything else.

She lifted her hand, rubbing the mark on her neck that had caused so many problems. It ached more than normal. Not a painful ache, rather one with the remnants of pleasure, reminding her of the incredibly sensuous feel of Taber's mouth there. His teeth scraping her skin, his tongue laving it heatedly. She shivered uncontrollably at the memory.

Jerking her hand back down, Roni stared at the cell phone for a long second before she rose to her feet and paced to the small, dusty window beside the door. She could call him. She should let him know just how much she appreciated the mess she was in right now. Dammit, he wanted her out of his life, had made that plain. How was she was supposed to feel good about any help he would give her now?

She stared out the window, knowing that for now, there was nothing she could do. That sense of helplessness ate at her. She hated being dependent on anyone, especially for her life.

As she stared into the forest, she could see John canvassing the thickly forested area. His body weaved in and out of the trees, relaxed, yet on guard. He reminded her of some of those military types she had seen profiles on during the few times she found time to watch television.

Time was passing too damned quickly. There was no chance to think, to become accustomed to the sudden changes sweeping around her. No time to prepare herself to face Taber again. It seemed mere minutes before John re-entered the cabin and picked up the cell phone. He glanced at her as he coded in the call.

"I hear a 'copter. That you?" he asked quietly, his pale blue eyes cold and confident. "Good. We're safe and sound so far. I'll have her waiting in the clearing." He disconnected then looked over at her. "Ready to go?"

"No." She pushed her hands into the pockets of her jeans. Wake up now, she thought desperately. Come on, Roni, time to wake up.

"Too bad." He grinned as though he was more than aware of the fact that she was desperate to deny any of this was taking place. "Time to move."

* * * * *

It was surreal. Roni stood at the edge of the small clearing, watching as the helicopter swooped in and executed a perfect landing. Motioning her to stay back, John ducked and ran to the small aircraft while Roni tried to still the racing of her heart.

She wanted to turn and run, to escape back to the life she had led before the fateful trip in to town no more than an hour ago. But instinctively, she knew there was no escape. She wondered a bit distantly if she even wanted to escape. Hadn't she dreamed of him nightly, ached for him every minute of the day since he had walked out of her life?

When Taber jumped from the helicopter, every cell in her body sprang to life. Between her thighs, an urgent pulse of desire began to beat, moisture pooling, gathering, preparing her for him. Her breath caught in her chest and not for the first time, she was caught completely off guard by the rough sexuality that seemed to shimmer around him.

He wore jeans. They rode low on his lean hips, lovingly conformed to his muscular thighs and long legs. The wide, dark belt accentuated the white shirt and the flat contours of his abdomen. His shoulders were wide. His devil's black hair tied back at his nape, giving him a savage, earthy appearance that speared straight to her pussy. She felt her juices spill from her hot vagina, her body beginning to ache, to throb for him.

She backed up as his gaze stayed locked on hers, his long legs covering the distance between her and the helicopter. She could see the fierce purpose on his darkly tanned face, his intention to claim her. She shuddered in sudden fear. This wasn't the man she had known before. The man who had been gentle, considerate, the kiss he had bestowed on her neck a whisper of passion, his touch restrained.

She felt the sobbing breath that escaped her throat as she continued to back up, her legs weak, her mind consumed with the vision stalking toward her. He was acting on instinct. He was no longer controlled as she had always known him to be. He was harder, savage. And he terrified her.

"Taber." She stopped suddenly as her back met the rough bark of the tree behind her.

He stopped inches from her, his eyes a brilliant jade-green, intense, overpowering. In that moment, three years of pain and anger overwhelmed her. Here he stood, staring at her as though he could devour her in a single bite, after destroying every dream she ever held in her heart.

Her fist clenched, and before she knew what she was thinking she struck with all her strength into the hard, tight muscles of his stomach. She had a feeling she hurt her fist more than she hurt him.

"Dammit," she yelled as he barely flinched, his body tightening, his eyes narrowing in anger. "Look what you've done to my life. Thanks for nothing, Taber."

The air around them seemed to still, to flame as she struck him. Danger, dark and thick tightened his expression.

"Mine," he snarled. The sound echoed through her body, her soul, as she felt her breath falter, her eyes widening at the sheer animalistic sound.

Before she could react, he caught her hands in his, pushing them back against the tree, ignoring her frantic struggles, her strangled curses.

He leaned closer, his expression stark, primal. His gaze held hers captive as his large body pinned her smaller one to the rough bark. Roni fought to breathe, to draw precious air into her body, to clear away the dazed arousal spreading through her mind.

She could smell him—dark hunger, intense male and heated lust. The scent of him wrapped around her senses, drowning her in the bleak knowledge that he had come to her only because his animal instincts demanded it, not because the man within desired her.

"Let me go!" she screamed, trying to kick out at him, to break the hold that was both fierce and yet gentle. She was trembling, shuddering with her own anxiety and surging emotions, and her need to hurt him as much as she was hurting now.

He leaned closer, his hard chest pressing against her breasts, sensitizing her nipples even through her bra and torn shirt. Her head was pressed back against the tree, her lips parting as she fought to breathe, to ignore the call of lightning-hot desire ripping through her body that mixed with the blistering rage.

He was touching her. Pressed against her. Nerve endings were flaring to flaming life as her knees weakened with an overwhelming sensation of dazed vulnerability.

And then he growled. His lip lifted at one side, revealing the longer, dangerous canines at the side of his mouth. The sound—a rumbled warning of danger and excitement—came a second before his head lowered and his heated, demanding lips covered her own.

She would have fallen if he hadn't kept her pressed so tight against the tree, his hands holding hers, his head angled, slanting his lips across hers, his tongue pressing forcibly into her mouth.

Drugging, exhilarating, the touch was lightning and heat, a morass of conflicting sensations that swept through her body like a tidal wave of impressions, swamping her beneath their force. She couldn't breathe. She didn't want to breathe. She couldn't think, couldn't make sense of anything but his kiss.

Her fingers curled, her hands straining against his grip on them. Her nails bit into her palms as she whimpered against the demanding thrust of his tongue. God, the taste of him. Dark honey, sweet and tempting, lured her with the promise of passion even as it pulled her into a lust that threatened to destroy her.

Her tongue swept over his. Feeling the small, swollen glands just under the sides, she moaned in pleasure at the taste that was released from her caress of them. She needed more. She needed to fill herself with it, to discover the full, heady promise of the intriguing flavor.

His tongue pressed more demandingly against hers then. A growl lingered in the air around them, completely feline, male, a demand that speared through her womb.

Roni allowed her own tongue to caress, to taste, and yet still he wanted more. She could feel it, sense it as his tongue tangled with hers. When her lips closed on him, her mouth drawing at the sweet elixir of his taste, his groan rocked her. This was what he wanted of her. His lips ground against hers, his tongue thrusting into the tight grip of her mouth as her senses were overwhelmed with the flavor releasing into her mouth.

She was on her tiptoes reaching for him. He released her hands then, though she had no fight left in her. They gripped his biceps, her nails biting into the cloth of his shirt, feeling the muscles underneath clench and bunch as he lifted her closer. Taber pressed her against the tree, his thigh insinuating itself between hers, rocking against her woman's core. Sweet heaven. Her head swam with the pleasure, the exquisite heat suddenly building deep within her womb.

She pressed closer to his thigh, moaning at the pressure against her swelling clit, needing more, so much more than what he was giving her now. The helicopter's motor was a distant sound, the wind sweeping over them, caused by the rotation of the blades, was just another caress to her rapidly sensitizing body.

"Taber, goddammit, now!" John's voice was an intrusion she fought to deny. Not now—nothing could separate them now. Not until she could fill herself with the taste of him, had enough to ease the painful hunger beginning to claw in the depths of her vagina.

"No," she whispered desperately as his head raised, his gaze narrow, staring down at her, blistering with the heat of lust and a glimmer of fury.

"Mine," he growled again as though intent on forcing her to admit this.

Roni shook her head, shuddering, needing more of his kiss, more of the drugging sensations that weighed her body with heavy sensuality.

"No time," John yelled again, his body a hazy blur at the edge of her vision. "Dammit, get her to the 'copter before you get caught on the ground. You want to lose her forever?"

Taber didn't speak. He spared a second to shoot the other man a furious look before his arm tightened around Roni's waist, forcing her forward, moving quickly for the helicopter awaiting them in the clearing.

Roni fought to move her feet, to keep up with him, to voice her protest, her anger, but nothing seemed to work. Her senses were cloudy, so dazed that she feared she was beginning to lose her own grip on reality.

"'Bout damned time," a strange male voice called out as Taber practically forced Roni into the helicopter.

No sooner had he jumped in beside her and slammed the door closed than the craft was lifting into the air. The surging power echoed through Roni's body, the vibration of the motors nearly painful to her sensitive nerves.

Confused, frightened, she glanced over at Taber. He watched her, his eyes narrowed, lust gleaming in the rich green depths, determination marking his proud features. This wasn't the gentle man who had protected her for years. It wasn't the tender lover who had left her at the garage three years ago, promising to return. This was a side of Taber she had never seen. It was both arousing and terrifying, leaving her lost amid the conflicting feelings sweeping over her.

She could sense the change in her own body now. The painful longing building in her pussy, burning her clit. Her breasts were tight and swollen, her nipples so hard and sensitive that each breath she took was torture as it forced them to rasp against her bra. She felt drugged, unsteady, so aroused now that it would take very little to push her over the edge of reason into an orgasm that would shatter her.

"What have you done to me?" She whispered the words as her body began to ache, to plead for his touch, his kiss. *Just once more*, something inside her screamed out in agony. *A touch, a taste...*

"I made you mine." He mouthed the words back to her. Slowly, clearly. "Mine, Roni. Forever."

Her eyes widened. Panic and lust churned in her body, throbbing through her veins, setting fires in her breasts, her womb, her vagina. She was burning, aching for his touch.

Roni shook her head, fighting her confusion and the sudden fear of exactly what he had done to her. She swallowed a moan as her womb rippled, her cunt spasming as a shudder worked up her spine, along her scalp as the heat began to build.

She fought to breathe as she watched Taber's nostrils flare, his eyes darkening further as though some stimulus had caught his senses. His cheekbones appeared flushed beneath the dark tan, his lips fuller, more sensual. His eyes glittered with sexual intent.

Roni licked her dry lips nervously, wanting, *needing* to touch him, but terrified of the intense arousal beginning to build inside her body just under her skin, like an internal fire burning through her nerve endings. Her fists clenched as she fought the spiraling sensations, determined to control them, just as she had years before.

But it hadn't been this bad then, a part of her whispered. The hungry need that had eaten at her had been irritating, uncomfortable, but nothing like this. This was intense, slowly building, overtaking her as it flowed through her system.

She forced her gaze from his, turning her head and staring desperately out the bubbled window of the helicopter. Taber was pressed close against her, his side molded to hers, one arm stretched behind her, his fingers playing almost absently with the strands of hair that fell down the back of her shirt.

She closed her eyes as she breathed in raggedly. She could resist the temptation eating her alive. Surely she could. She had before.

She bit her lip as she felt his fingers move her hair, pushing it back from her shoulder, revealing the small mark just below her neck. She would have turned her head, would have blocked his gaze if he hadn't moved to hold her in place.

Roni whimpered. She couldn't help it. When his tongue stroked over the small wound, and then his mouth closed over it, suckling the flesh softly, tenderly, her womb spasmed. Her pussy throbbed, pulsed, sending her into a near-orgasmic delight as she felt his teeth scratch along the surface of the mark he had made.

Her hands clenched at his forearm as it stretched across her chest, his hand holding her other shoulder, keeping her still as he tortured her, tormented her.

"Please." She knew he couldn't hear her, and she didn't have the breath to scream as pleasure seared her body, washing from the point where his mouth held her captive to her tight, sensitive nipples, down to her throbbing clit and soaked cunt. It was destroying her.

He lifted his mouth slowly as he eased back into his seat. But there was no relief for Roni. She gritted her teeth, cursing him, cursing herself, and vowing to die in agony before she begged him to take her, begged him to ease the need that seemed to only grow rather than lessen as he moved away from her.

This wasn't good. Not good at all.

Chapter Three

Life couldn't be much sweeter as far as Taber was concerned. The ride from the hills of Eastern Kentucky back to the mansion in Virginia was made quickly, efficiently, in the powerful little 'copter the military had graciously granted them. A few perks came from outraging society against a government whose leaders had been up to their ears in the corrupt little experiments that had created them.

His body was humming with desire, perfectly attuned to the arousal climbing in Roni's. He could smell her heat and it was about to drive him insane. It was sweet and wild, and sent his senses humming with the pleasure to come. His cock ached like a raw wound, pulsing and throbbing beneath the restriction of his jeans as he forced himself to wait, to keep his hands to himself. For now.

He watched the terrain outside the helicopter's windows, tracking each landmark, counting the minutes until he could get her to a bed, spread her thighs and surge into the heated depths of her wet little cunt. For three years he had suffered a lust that made no sense, and refused all explanations. Control had been chancy at the best of times. There had been days when he had been certain he wouldn't survive if he didn't possess her, brand her as his.

He had waited three years. Three long, miserable years. A black aching void had taken root inside his soul during that time. There had been a desire, torturous and unending, for one woman and one woman alone. He had been unable to touch another, unable to tolerate the scent of any other female's lust when Roni's remained so deeply a part of him.

It was one of the reasons he had never understood why she had left the short, curt note on his desk so long ago. No other woman had affected him as she did. And he had known for a fact that she had wanted him as well. So why had she pulled back? He still had the note. He still felt the fury and clenching betrayal those words had brought him.

He had denied himself for nearly all those years where Roni was concerned. Fought his desire and his hunger because he hadn't wanted to subject her to who and what he was against her wishes. He knew at the time that her decision had been the best one. He didn't blame her, had no desire to make her pay for the hell his body had put him through. But he would be damned if he would let her go now.

His kiss was insurance that Roni would never walk away from him in the same manner ever again. The hormone released into her body would prepare her and heighten her arousal to a point that she would be unable to deny his touch. She would be lucky if she could even walk when he finished slaking his hunger for her. He had a lot of time to make up for.

"We're heading in," Cabal yelled back to him as the mansion came in sight.

It was three stories of gracious, stately elegance. Balconies wrapped around each story, tall pillars rising up to support them and lending the white monstrosity an air of genteel comfort. The centuries-old plantation house had been kept in excellent condition. Previous owners had done all they could to keep the historical air of the house intact, while inside, renovations had assured the owners' every comfort.

His arm tightened around Roni's back as he felt her stiffen. The dark scent of fear mixed with her earthy, sweet desire. But rather than easing her need, the fear seemed to only intensify the addicting smell. The adrenaline racing through her body carried the hormone that much faster through her system.

The helicopter landed with smooth efficiency, settling onto the landing pad and slowly powering down as Taber unclipped his and Roni's safety belts. He glanced into her eyes, his body tightening as he saw the dilation of her pupils, the flush on her cheeks. Her blue eyes glittered with hunger. Her body trembled from it.

"What did you do to me, Taber?" Her voice was husky, confused, as Tanner and Cabal exited the helicopter.

"Come on, we'll get up to the house and I'll explain everything." He jumped from the helicopter before reaching in, his hands gripping her waist as he helped her from her seat.

She gasped as he drew her against his chest before allowing her feet to settle to the ground. The sensual drag of her body against his had him growling with arousal. Thank God they didn't have much farther to go.

Taber gripped her hand and pulled her to the Jeep Tanner had running at the side of the landing pad. Her fingers trembled beneath his, but no more than her body. He could feel the fine shudders that worked through her as he helped her into the Jeep, glimpsed the desperate edge of control in her gaze.

His kiss had done exactly as Callan had outlined to all of them months before. The sexual hormone contained in the glands of his tongue had almost immediately swept through her system as he kissed her. Her level of heat had raised, the need for his touch, his taste, sweeping over her. But it was no greater than his need for her.

He had been helpless this time, caught in the grip of a hunger he could not contain and had no desire to hide. The animal within had been denied once before. It wouldn't be again.

"The house we now live in once belonged to the Genetics Council," he told her, fighting for calm as Tanner raced along the paved road that led to the mansion. "It's now our home base. We're safe here, protected by the growing numbers of our kind, which rise daily. You'll be safe here as well, Roni."

"Will I?" Her tone assured him that she wasn't so certain. Too bad. He wasn't about to let her go.

She held herself as far from him as he would allow, which wasn't much. She was heated and warm, her scent sweet and potent. He had been separated from her for too long, fighting to be noble, to protect her from the truth and the price of being in his arms. But nature had deemed otherwise, and the animal inside had no intention of ignoring that lust-filled call.

He ran his fingers down her arm, feeling the tremors of response that shook her as his gaze met hers.

Taber held back a wince as she shot him a hateful look. Evidently, most of the confusion caused by the events of the day was wearing off. She was getting mad. He ignored the fierce surge of excitement that rocked through his veins at the thought. Her eyes glittered with fury and lust. The scent of her was hot and wild, making his chest ache with the need to roar in triumph.

"I would have been safe where I was," she snapped, "if it hadn't been for you."

Her voice was thick with the emotions, the sensations, washing through her body. She was fighting it, unaware that in doing so, she would only make the symptoms worse. Taber suppressed his smile. Her fury would only cause her blood to beat faster, the hormone to surge through her body, to build and grow in its extremity.

"It takes two, Roni," he told her darkly as the Jeep shuddered to a stop at the front entrance.

Large oaks, ages old, towered above the circular driveway, growing so close to the house that they had once considered cutting several of them down. But the majesty and grace of the hardwoods had been impossible to deny. They had been there for far too long, had protected the home for too many years, to destroy.

As he helped her from the Jeep the large, double front doors opened as Callan and Merinus stepped out onto the cemented landing. The other man's gaze was hard, fierce, as he inhaled slowly, making Taber more than aware that any Breed who came near would know Roni's state of arousal.

Taber led her up the wide, circular steps to meet the couple, feeling the shudders that swept over her body. She was tense, holding herself rigidly erect as they approached Callan and Merinus.

He met Callan's gaze, seeing the concern in the depths of his leader's amber eyes.

"Roni, it's good to see you again," Callan said gently as they reached the other couple. He didn't touch her, didn't offer to shake her hand, as Roni stood stiffly before him. "Allow me to introduce my wife, Merinus. Merinus, Roni Andrews was a good friend to us all during our time in Sandy Hook."

"Hello, Roni." Merinus' smile was gentle as her gaze flickered between them. "I'm sorry we had to meet under such circumstances."

"It's nice to meet you." Roni's voice was soft, husky with tension as she smoothed her hands over her arms. "I'm sorry, too…"

"Please, don't be." Merinus shook her head, a small smile tilting her lips. "These men tend to shake up a woman's life more than should be allowable. But in the end…" She glanced at her husband's faux-mocking expression. "They can be worth it."

"I think I'll wait to comment on that one." Roni breathed in harshly. "If you don't mind."

Merinus' concerned gaze was filled with knowledge as she glanced at Taber. She, more than anyone else, was well aware of the need pulsing through Roni and the stress she was under.

"I understand completely, Roni. If you need anything, be sure to let any of us know. We want you to feel at home here."

Roni nodded, murmuring her thanks, but Taber could see the fine film of sweat on her brow, the flush in her cheeks.

"Please, come in. Taber can show you up to your room and you can rest before dinner. We can talk later." Merinus frowned at Taber, a dark, disapproving look that he met head on.

They entered the marbled foyer as Taber gripped Roni's upper arm and led her to the wide, circular staircase at the right of the large entrance. His suite of rooms was on the second floor, but all that concerned him was getting Roni to the large, well-built bed that occupied them. There he would do more than mark her. There he would claim all that had been his, all she had sought to deny them both over the last lonely, hunger-filled months. There she would pay.

What was wrong with her? Roni felt feverish, uncertain, almost dazed with the sexual needs that threatened to bring her to her knees with their intensity. As Taber led her up the stairs she fought the nearly debilitating weakness that made her grateful for the steadying hand that gripped her arm. His body was large, so hard and warm beside her that she could feel the heat radiating from him.

His hand steadied her, but all she could think of was having it run over her body, stroking her, soothing the fires burning in the very depths of her womb. She had never been so crazed with arousal. No, this wasn't arousal. It went even beyond lust. It was a compulsion, a hunger that tore through her, making its demands nearly irresistible.

"What did you do to me?" She tried to jerk away from him, to get away from the insidious pleasure that heated her body at his touch, but he wasn't letting go of her. "This isn't funny anymore, Taber. I'm sick of the silent, he-man treatment."

They entered a large sitting room. A cherry desk, complete with computer, printer and fax, were at one end of the room. He drew her past a relaxed sitting area with an entertainment complex that would have impressed her if she had time to care about anything other than the fire raging in her pussy.

He led her through another opened door into the bedroom. The room was dimly lit, with dark, cherry furniture and thick curtains shading it from the lowering sun, giving it an intimate, sexy feeling.

At the far end of the room was a large sleigh bed, the mattress and box springs so thick she would have to jump onto it to sit on it. A dark burgundy comforter was turned back, thick pillows plumped and placed against the headboard.

She shivered as she imagined herself on it with Taber, his body covering hers, his hands stroking her. She bit her lip, fighting the whimper that threatened to escape her throat.

"Answer me, damn you." Roni turned on him angrily as he moved away from her, closing the door behind them.

She stared into his eyes…those deep, brilliant eyes. A predator's eyes. She could see the evidence of his unique DNA now. In the high cheekbones, the narrowed gaze. The long canines he no longer bothered to hide.

"You're coming into heat," he answered her, his fingers going to the buttons of his white shirt as she watched him loosen it slowly.

Her knees weakened, her mouth watering as each fastening came loose, exposing more of his tanned, sleek skin. She shook her head, wanting to close her eyes, to escape the power he suddenly held over her. She wanted his shirt off. She wanted to run her fingers over the bulging muscles of his body, feel his hard heat, touch him, taste him as she had dreamed of years before.

Then his words hit her. *Coming into heat.* She felt her heart begin to race in fear. She blinked over at him. Each breath shuddering through her chest felt labored, painful.

"What do you mean?" She swallowed tightly, fighting her shock.

Taber shrugged the shirt from his shoulders, the hard, well-defined muscles of his chest and arms flexing with power and strength.

"Exactly what I said." His voice was hard, but his gaze had hot, liquid lust glittering in the jade depths. "You're in heat, Roni. Your body's preparing itself, assuring that neither of us can refuse what nature demands."

He dropped the shirt carelessly to his feet as he moved to the padded chest at the bottom of the bed and sat down. His eyes never left her. They raked over her, darkening, heating, as he watched her breasts heave with her fight for oxygen.

God, she wanted to taste him. His stomach was flat, hard, the well-developed abs flexing as he removed his boots.

"How?" She couldn't make sense of anything except the hunger flaying her body. "It's never been like this. Even after you bit me. Why now?"

He came to his feet, towering over her, walking to her slowly, his gaze never leaving hers.

"I hadn't kissed you, Roni," he said softly, as he came within touching distance.

The scent of his body infused her senses. It was male, hot and dark, captivating, as she trembled before him.

"What..." She shook her head, fighting the compulsion to touch him, to taste him. "What did the kiss have to do with anything? Dammit, Taber at least answer me before you undress." Her fists clenched as she forced herself to back away from him, to fight the driving hunger thundering through her body.

"The kiss allowed a special hormone to release from my body to yours." He followed her, stalking her as she continued to retreat. "A hormone that is only present when I touch my mate. When I touch you. It allowed me to mark you, physical proof to any other that you belong to me. But it wasn't enough to heighten your senses or your arousal to this state. Only my kiss can do that, Roni. My kiss marked you in a way nature will not let you deny."

His voice was rough, deep, almost rumbling as Roni backed into the wall, staring back at him in horror, in fury.

"My God. You knew." She almost winced at the grating sound of her voice. She sounded as shocked, as frightened, as she knew she was. "When you kissed me, you knew you would do this to me. You knew what would happen."

His hands slapped the wall beside her, his expression turning savage, almost feral, as he bared his teeth in a warning growl. She flinched, her eyes widening, her pussy clenching at the sound.

"You will not deny me this time, Roni." His voice rumbled with power, with determination. "This time, you will not escape me."

She would have fought him, she assured herself. She would have moved from him, would have shoved his balls to his throat with her knee if he hadn't swooped in, his tongue piercing her mouth as his lips covered hers. The moment he did, every cell in her body sang out in relief, and the fury coursing through her whipped into lightning-hot desire.

Sweet, dark honey filled her senses once again. She whimpered beneath the onslaught, her hands rising to grip his waist, her nails biting into his flesh as the feel of his skin seemed to sink into her cells. She moaned, her tongue tangling with his as an inner voice screamed out in warning. Danger. Temptation. Run!

He didn't touch her other than with his lips, with his tongue, and they were voracious in their demand. His strong teeth nipped at the curves. His tongue soothed the slight sting then thrust back demandingly until she closed her lips on it, desperate to hold it still as she fought to make sense of his taste, his power over her.

He tasted like sin itself, wild, hot and addictive. She couldn't get enough. She didn't want to get enough. She wanted to immerse herself in it, drown in the sensations surging through her, burning her with need.

He growled. A feline rumble of hunger as she tightened on his tongue, drawing on it, moaning at the faint taste of honey, suddenly needing more. His hands gripped her head as his lips slanted over hers, driving her insane with the hot, sensual provocation of the ever deepening caress.

Second by second, she could feel her body burning brighter, hotter. Her breasts ached, the nipples hard little points begging for his attention as his chest settled closer.

"God, you taste good." His roughened voice caused her to shiver with pleasure as he pulled back, staring down at her, his eyes narrowed, intense. "I wonder how much better the rest of you tastes."

His knee slid between her legs, pressing against the sensitive mound between her thighs.

"Don't do this to me, Taber," she whispered desperately, her hands tightening on his waist as she shuddered with an exquisite pain that rode much too close to heated pleasure.

His hard thigh rocked against her cunt and she wondered desperately if he could feel the moisture seeping from her body. She wanted to tear herself away from him. She wanted to jerk him closer. The conflicting needs warred within her, fighting an insane battle for supremacy.

"Do what? Make you mine?" he growled. "It's already been done, Roni. I can't take that back. And I sure as hell won't regret it."

His lips moved to her ear, his tongue swirling around it sensually as she fought for breath.

"I can't do this," she cried out, yet her body writhed against his, needing to touch him, to feel the heat and hardness he offered her.

Her head fell back against the wall as his lips trailed down her neck. His fingers pulled at the buttons of her blouse, releasing the torn fabric as the air around them heated with blistering need.

"Shush, baby," Taber whispered as his lips stroked over her collarbone. "It's going to be okay. I promise."

He pushed her shirt over her shoulders, smoothing it down her arms as he lifted first one of her hands from his waist, then the other to allow the material to fall to the floor. It was the most sensual sensation she had known in her life, his hands, calloused and warm, sliding over her flesh, removing the cloth between his touch and her skin.

"How pretty," he whispered as his gaze centered on her breasts. "So full and swollen. I can't wait to take one of those hard little nipples in my mouth, Roni."

She whimpered at his words, standing before him, her breasts straining against her lacy bra. His head raised, his eyes going over the full curves that rose and fell so swiftly. She wanted to close her eyes to escape the intensity of the feelings bombarding her. At the same time, she wanted to be certain she didn't miss a second of either seeing or feeling the power behind his sudden hunger for her.

"I'm scared." Roni shuddered harshly, fighting the overpowering lust with every beat of her heart. It wasn't natural, this need. She had always wanted him, always dreamed of his kiss and his touch, but not like this. Not this drugged, overriding demand she couldn't control. "Taber. Make it stop. Make it stop now, dammit."

Her pussy clenched with such resounding demand that it took her breath. She gasped, almost crying out as his lips stroked over the smooth flesh rising from the cup of her bra.

"It will ease soon, Roni," he promised her, his voice so rough, so harsh, it caused her to shiver in pleasure as his fingers released the front clasp of her bra. "Just as soon as I get you in that bed and slide between those pretty thighs, it will be all better."

Roni blinked in shock as Taber's words whispered around her. It will all be better? As soon as he does what?

She pushed at his shoulders, ignoring the cramps in her womb, the moisture sliding from her tormented pussy.

"I don't think so." She shuddered with need. "Taber, wait. We have to talk about this."

Oh, this wasn't good at all. Her body was overruling her mind and she couldn't seem to rein it in long enough to get a grip on the situation.

His tongue was running over the tops of her breasts. Sweet lord, it wasn't smooth and soft like any normal person's would be. It was slightly rough, hot, rasping deliciously against her skin. What would it feel like on her nipples?

"You taste so good, Roni." His shoulders tightened as he dipped his head further, following the inside curve of her breast, tracing the border of lace that still covered the swollen mound. "So hot and sweet."

His hands moved from the wall, stroking down her back until they clasped her hips, rocking her against the hard thigh insinuated between hers.

"Taber." She had to make him stop. Didn't she?

She pushed against his shoulders again, her head falling back against the wall as she fought the weakening lust surging through her blood.

"Roni, I don't know if I can stop," he whispered as his lips nudged under the lacy bra, coming dangerously close to the hard peak of her breast.

She could feel his breath on the tormented tip, every cell tightening in exquisite longing as his teeth then tugged at the material, drawing it away from the swollen curve.

"Taber. I can't... Oh God!" She arched in his arms as his tongue swiped across the hard bud of her nipple. Electricity shot from the little nub straight to her womb, taking her breath as it spasmed in pleasure. Okay, so she wasn't going to be able to say no, evidently, she thought distantly. It didn't mean she had to let him live after he was done, though.

His mouth covered her nipple, suckling at her desperately, his cheeks flexing, his tongue rasping as she began to writhe on his hard thigh. The pressure against her clit was destructive, drowning her in pleasure, in desperation.

She was only dimly aware of his hands loosening her jeans, then sliding beneath the material until he could cup the smooth globes of her ass. His hands covered the naked skin, flexing, gripping and parting her rounded cheeks as he moved her against him.

"I can't wait for the bed," he growled against her breast as his thigh moved back from the tormented mound between her thighs. "Now. Like this, Roni."

He shoved her pants down with one hand, the other loosening his jeans, freeing the thick length of his cock from confinement. He didn't take time to help her kick free of her shoes. He gave her no time to deny him. Before she could voice her shock he pulled her away from the wall, pushed her to her knees, following her down as he came behind her.

"Taber." Shocked, nearly paralyzed by the needs clawing through her system she could only whimper his name as he pressed her forward.

He held her still, her shoulders to the floor, her hips raised, opening her for him, giving him access. He didn't wait to claim what he believed was his. Roni barely had time to draw in a breath before she felt the thickness of his erection pressing against her cunt, sliding against the small slit until he found the opening to her vagina. He held her hips, he whispered her name, and then thrust forcibly inside her untried pussy.

Shock resounded through her as she felt the sudden forceful penetration stretching her, forcing past her virginity until he was lodged at the very mouth of her womb. She screamed out at the pleasure-pain of his hard thrust as he buried in her to the hilt. Her back arching as she bucked against him, straining away from the thick impalement.

Taber cursed, almost brokenly, but he didn't stop. She writhed beneath him, terrified now by the fierce contractions of her womb, the force of his thrusts, the spiraling sensations colliding inside her. It wasn't just pain. It was a pleasure so intense, so violent she could only scream against its intensity.

She could feel his cock stretching her, the muscles of her cunt both protesting and welcoming the thick intruder, clamping on it as the sounds of moist suckling flesh filled her head. She was too wet, too aroused. Her juices coated her thighs, her pussy. The sharp bite of pain should have drawn her back from her arousal, should have had her crying out in protest, but it only blended with the pleasure.

Her world centered only on the deep, heavy thrusts of Taber's erection inside her gripping cunt. The agonizing pleasure seared through her body, electrifying nerve endings, taking her breath as the sensations piled, one atop the other, drowning her in their force.

The feel of Taber, one hand pressing at her shoulder blades, holding her still, the other gripping her hip as he thrust hard and deep inside her sensitive vagina, was nearly too much to bear. She couldn't move, she could only feel, and what she was feeling threatened to destroy her.

The carpet beneath her rasped her knees, the tender flesh of her breasts, but the minute sensations only blended with the others. Lightning arced from her pussy through her womb, sizzling beneath her skin as it streaked through her body, throwing her higher, driving her closer to destruction.

He pushed her headlong in her flight to ecstasy, his cock powering into her, filling her, stroking the already blistering heat higher, hotter.

"No!" She tried to scream as she felt her womb tighten, ripple, convulse. It would kill her. Whatever the sensation, the power building furiously inside her—it would kill her.

Then there was no breath left to scream, to cry. Her eyes widened, her vision blurred. The muscles of her cunt clamped onto his cock as she felt the sudden change occurring in it. It was as though a small thumb had distended beneath the flared hood of his erection, swelling, lodging against a bundle of nerves inside her, caressing, vibrating, until she exploded.

"God! Roni! Baby..." Deep, hard, the blasts of heated semen shot into the ultra-tight channel, triggering another tremor, another explosion that left her gasping, fighting for breath as she collapsed to the carpet.

What was it? She shuddered again as Taber followed her down, groaning harshly as the small caress of the added stimulation kept shuddering through her body. As though... No. The thought was pushed away, denied. There were no physical characteristics of the animal he was. The scientists had assured the public of it. Other than the longer canines, they were human. Weren't they?

Then she couldn't think anymore. The next explosion that tore through her was nearly brutal in its intensity. She could only cry out, could only let it have her while Taber collapsed over her. His breathing was harsh, his body as damp as her own now.

"Roni." His voice sounded tormented, pained, as he fought to catch his breath.

"What did you do, Taber?" she whispered, the blurring at the edge of her vision becoming darker. "What did you do..."

Chapter Four

"She'll be fine." Dr. Martin patted Roni's slack hand as he gently settled it on the bed beside her unconscious body. He had finally finished his examination. On the table beside the bed were the vials of various samples he needed. "Remember, she's only the second known mate, and her body's been under the strain of it for over three years. Physically, it could be much different for her than it was for Merinus. I'll run my tests and we'll see how she does when she awakens."

Taber stared down at Roni from the other side of the bed, his conscience searing him with remorse. What *had* he done to her? For the first time since his childhood, the animalistic side had controlled him, rather than the human. When it had mattered most, he had forgotten he was a man.

"Is she sleeping or unconscious?" Taber almost winced at the sound of his voice and the pain seeping into it.

Doc shot him a worried glance. "She's just sleeping, Taber. The day has been quite eventful for her. Let her body rest and her mind cope. Sometimes it's all that saves a soul." The haunted shadows that lingered in the scientist's eyes gave testament to that fact. "Have her in the lab first thing in the morning. We'll run a few more tests, make certain they are coinciding with the readings we had from Merinus, and then we'll just wait and see."

Wait and see if she conceives. Taber's fists clenched with an almost murderous fury. From the moment he had seen the attack on her on that damned television his only thought had been taking her. Marking her. Assuring himself that no other could ever touch her again. He pushed his fingers wearily through his hair as he stared down at her.

She was pale. Dark circles lingered under her eyes, showing the scattering of freckles across her nose in stark relief. She looked so innocent... Hell, she *had* been innocent. A fucking virgin and he had taken her like an animal.

He turned to the window at his side, drawing back the dark curtains, staring out at the grounds of the estate. He had taken her from her home, brought her to a damned armed camp and molested her before even taking the time to explain the changes taking place in her body after his kiss.

He had known when he kissed her what he was doing. Had known what would happen, but he had been helpless to stop. He had protected her since she was a child, until the moment she had truly needed his strength. Then he had failed her. He had allowed the animal to take control and now Roni would pay the price.

"Taber, I'll need samples from you as well," Doc said softly from the end of the bed. "As soon as possible, if you don't mind."

Taber pulled back from the window, allowing the drapes to fall back in place.

"When she awakens," he said softly. "I'll come down then."

"Now, Taber. There may not be time when she awakens." Merinus stepped forward then, her voice firm. "You go with Doc. I'll sit here with Roni. Besides, she might need a more calming influence than you are at the moment when she awakens."

Taber wanted to deny it, but he knew she was right. Roni didn't need to face him when she first awoke. Hell, he was terrified of facing her. Of seeing the hatred and disgust she must surely feel for him now. How would he ever convince her how much she filled his heart when he had taken her as little more than an animal?

As he left the room, he was aware of Callan following him, sensed the strange discord in his leader, and sighed wearily.

"Shoot me," he muttered as they entered the lab on the basement floor of the mansion several minutes later.

"What would be the point?" Callan asked, a thread of amusement coloring his deep voice. "I shoot you and there goes Roni's mate. She may not thank me for that later."

Taber removed his shirt as the doctor indicated he should. He knew what was coming. Blood samples, saliva, semen and perspiration samples. The list went on and on and the very thought of them had his body tightening in distaste.

"She might kill me herself when she sees me again," he grunted, his anger building by the second. "I took her like an animal, Callan. I fucking drugged her, then raped her. Like an animal."

"Stop, Taber." Callan shook his head, crossing his arms over his chest as his golden-brown eyes narrowed. "It wasn't rape. I could smell her heat when you brought her into the house. And we both know the hormone doesn't react unless you're with your mate."

"She said 'no'." He shook his head, unable to stare his leader in the eye any longer. "She said 'no', Callan, and I ignored her."

Taber extended his arm for the doctor and his wicked needles as he avoided Callan's gaze. Son of a bitch, this wasn't how he had foreseen his first time with Roni. He had wanted — hell no, he had *needed* — to touch her gently, to ease her into the mating.

"My studies indicate that the ferocity of the mating is mutual, Taber." Doc Martin slid the needle into his arm with no more than a small prick. "Wait and see how she feels when she wakes up. The heat of lust often makes little sense when reality returns. Even if you aren't a Breed."

"She can't go back, Taber. You know that," Callan told him softly. "Besides, we have other problems. From the minute that story hit the airwaves, movement began among the Council members and their known soldiers. Her home was set ablaze within the hour and there are indications that orders have gone out to take her, no matter what, before conception. She's in more danger than Merinus ever was."

The Council. Rather than negotiating with Washington and trying to play fair, the Breeds should have slipped into the homes of the bastards running that little show and sliced their throats. They didn't deserve the mercy that had been afforded them.

In the past three months, since the discovery and rescue of nearly a hundred other Feline Breeds that Kane had located, the Council had waged a silent, deadly war against them. They hadn't been neutralized as the government had promised they would be. They weren't powerless as Kane had hoped would happen.

In the past month alone, four of their liaisons to the government and military had been murdered. The last, a young female, had been returned to them in pieces, literally. And now Roni would be in even more danger. The Council needed her to understand the mating process that had been leaked to the media. Needed her to figure out the best way to control, or to destroy, the creations that had escaped them. Taber was determined that anyone who tried to take her would die.

Taber's lip lifted in a snarl. "Let them try, Callan. I won't play nice this time."

Through the years, they had tried to be merciful. They ran rather than killed, and they killed only when no other answer was available. They had gained more amusement, more satisfaction, in seeing the soldiers running back to base in disgrace rather than in pieces. But if one dared to touch Roni, then he swore there would be too many damned pieces for anyone to attempt to collect.

"None of us will play nice in such an event," Callan assured him. "But this worries me. The Council has lain low until now, with the report of the second known mate to the Felines, and suddenly they're moving. It leaves me wondering what they've been planning while they were so silent."

Taber grunted. They had been waiting for the other shoe to drop for three months now, knowing that eventually the day would come when they had to face the monsters of their past without the public support they had garnered. But moving now made no sense.

"What do they want?" Taber shook his head. "No one has even tried to threaten Merinus since we came forward. Why now?"

"Because Kane has every damned C.I.A. agent in the world swearing vengeance if his baby sister is touched, and he has the clout to back it." Callan grunted. "The Tyler family name is protecting her, for now. I don't know if it would hold the same weight for Roni, or even if this is the reason why the Council hasn't moved yet. It's too soon to tell. At the moment all we have are questions and supposition. I need more information to be certain of anything."

"Could be the hormones the female produces during heat," the doctor spoke up as he stuck a swab between Taber's lips and poked it under his tongue.

Taber frowned down at the impatient doctor as a low growl vibrated from his chest.

"Stop that." Doc frowned back fiercely. "Remember who circumcised you. It could be castration next."

"You'd have to get the chance first," Taber snapped, ignoring the doctor's chuckle as he walked away with the saliva sample. "Is he getting grouchier or what?"

Callan shook his head as he flashed Taber a laughing glance.

"Get my jollies where I can, young 'un," Doc griped as he messed with the various vials and solutions on another table. "Now, go pee pee in the cup for the good doctor and get me some little soldiers while you're at it, and then you can run along and play again."

Taber grimaced as he flashed the doctor a killing glance.

"You're getting damned strange in your old age, Doc," he growled as he took the two small plastic containers from the doctor and stomped back to the bathroom at the end of the lab. "Hope you at least left my fucking magazines back here. A man needs more than your cackles to get the soldiers to move, ya know."

He didn't need the magazines and wasn't bothered by the cackles. Taber's libido was raging and all it took was the remembered feel of Roni, her sweet heat and the rippling contractions of her tight pussy, to bring his little soldiers spilling into the container as the doctor requested.

He returned to the lab a short time after leaving it, placing the capped containers on the table before turning back to Callan.

"What else do I have to look forward to?" he grunted. "First I rape my mate, now I'm in Frankenstein's lab jacking off. Are we having fun yet?"

Callan chuckled, though Doc Martin only grunted with the absent-minded attention of a man thoroughly engrossed in whatever the microscope was telling him.

"Come on. I have the reports in the office upstairs. From the looks of things it appears as if we have several orders going out, though we haven't busted that code completely yet. Our informants are nervous as hell, and money has started shifting around in select accounts again. Kane has his sources working overtime, as well as the brothers, but it could be days before we know what the hell is going on."

The story of their lives, Taber grimaced. The past three months had felt like years. The progress they made by revealing themselves to a sympathetic society was marked by each hurdle the Council placed before them. Even more alarming was the rise of several groups spouting a "pure blood" agenda. Breeds weren't human, they had stated. Their animal DNA canceled them from any human rights to which they would have otherwise been entitled. The bastards were fanatical monsters and growing in number daily.

"We have the perimeter fences wired for sound and ready to record," Taber told him as they took the stairs to the second floor quickly. "The animals were released last week and they're working out wonderfully. Just make certain to keep Merinus in the protected areas until we know how well Cabal's connection with them is working."

Cabal was an enigma, and often a worry. He was the only Breed so far to show a natural connection with the predatory felines that the Breed's DNA was a part of. There was a Bengal tiger, a lion and two cougars now guarding the woods. All female. All under the control of Cabal St. Laurens.

"So far, they're as tame as kittens," Callan grunted as they entered the office. "But I'm keeping an eye on things. Kane and Gray are moving into the house tonight to provide added protection for Merinus and we have most of our people back within the perimeters until we figure out what the hell is going on."

"Why would they need a mate before conception?" Taber frowned as he picked up several of the reports they had and began reading. "There has to be something they're looking for."

"I'm going to assume, as does Doc, that it has something to do with the hormones that mark them genetically," Callan reported. "It produces the pheromone that instinctively warns off all other men, including those who aren't Breeds. Combine that with the aphrodisiac qualities and it's damned hard telling what those bastards have up their sleeves."

"Anything from the Wolf Breeds?" Taber asked, frowning down at the papers.

The solitary, wary group of Wolf Breeds had made contact less than two months before. It had been assumed they had died in the lab explosions during the attempted rescue, though Taber had suspected otherwise. The Felines had laid the groundwork for contact immediately upon learning of the missing adults and several children. Everything was now in place should they need any help, but so far, none had made contact.

"They're wary, even more so than we were at first. We haven't made contact yet, but we know they're out there. In the meantime, we have the fucking Council to deal with. So, no, we're not having fun yet."

Taber cursed silently. The Council had gotten smart fast. They changed their codes and passwords often enough to drive Kane crazy trying to work them out. Soldiers were being shifted around constantly. Some were no more than distractions, while others regularly threw whatever wrench they could into the diplomatic efforts between the Breeds and the government protecting them.

"We can't stay on high alert forever," Taber sighed, shaking his head. "The men will get too complacent when nothing happens."

"Yet, we can't give them a chance to strike, either," Callan sighed. "Kane should be here tonight. We'll figure out our best course of action and go on from there. But from the looks of these reports, Roni is our main concern. Now how much of a danger will she be personally?" Callan's voice hardened as he asked this question.

Taber laid the papers back on the desk and turned to face his leader. He knew what Callan was asking. Given her father's history of illegal and less than savory business dealings, it only made sense to question the daughter's loyalty as well. At least, in most cases. But if there was one thing Taber knew about Roni, it was the fact that she was nothing like her father.

"No more than Merinus would be." There was no question of Roni's loyalty, just her love. "You've known her as long as I have, Callan. She's never betrayed a friend or a trust. But she's scared, and most likely out for my blood by the time she wakes up. I can't think she would be a danger to anyone but me."

Callan nodded. "Pretty much what I thought myself. But we have to be certain. Whatever you think you did to her, fix it. Trust me, an irate mate is more than you want to deal with."

The expression on his face was so self-mocking Taber couldn't help but laugh. He knew exactly how Callan suffered when he managed to get on the wrong side of his feisty little wife. She had a mouth that could castrate a man at twenty paces, and if that wasn't effective, then he slept in one of the spare bedrooms until she got over her ire.

"I'll have to tell her about her house," he sighed.

With her home destroyed, Taber knew she had nothing else now to hold on to her childhood or her past. It would all be gone, destroyed in a cruel, merciless act against a woman innocent of the crimes the Council laid at the Breeds' feet. But she was a mate. Any way they could hurt her, would hurt them.

"You take care of Roni, I'll take care of the rest of it." Callan pushed his fingers wearily through his hair. "We'll need to make plans to begin building cabins within the estate, though. If we don't, this house could end up filling fast with the pitter patter of little feet."

He didn't sound upset over it, merely worried.

"The children will be in more danger than we were, Callan," Taber told him softly. "Doc needs to figure out how to control this before it's out of hand."

"Merinus went out of heat when she conceived." Callan shook his head. "She hasn't suffered from it since, though my DNA still marks her." He sounded haunted. "She still carries it."

They weren't entirely certain how that happened, but Merinus still carried traces of Callan's unique DNA in her blood. It hadn't changed her body, hadn't reshaped her genetics in any way. Rather, it had marked her blood, her saliva, even her perspiration, with traces of the same hormonal variances that Callan carried.

He should have stayed away from Roni, Taber thought tiredly as he glimpsed the shadows in Callan's eyes. They worried constantly that somehow, some way, the Council would manage to get their hands on Merinus and her unborn child. During high alert times, Callan rarely slept and would re-check their security on the hour — damned near every hour.

"I can't let her go," Taber whispered. He only wished he could.

"I know." Callan wiped his hands over his faced wearily. "I know exactly how you feel."

Chapter Five

Roni came awake, bathed in perspiration, her flesh feeling irritated and achy. Her breasts swollen, her nipples throbbing. Between her thighs her pussy clenched, wept, as she remembered the hard driving thrusts of Taber's cock inside the narrow channel.

It hadn't been the romantic interlude she had always fantasized about. There had been no candlelight, no Taber on his knees begging for forgiveness, instead, there had been blistering heat, intensity, and some unnamed desperation clawing between both of them that refused to be ignored. The orgasm that ended it had blown all her preconceived notions of what an orgasm could be, right out the window. Now, if she could just get him to do it again.

She would have to find him first, though. She looked around the room. Night must have finally fallen. The room was dimmer than before, lit only by the soft glow of the lamp beside the bed. The heavy dark wood of the furniture gave the room a protective feeling. Sturdy, uncluttered, and yet uniquely Taber's.

On the far side of the room a large picture of him standing in front of the garage he had owned in Sandy Hook hung prominently. Several trophies he had won in shooting contests were displayed on the dresser beneath it. Taber hadn't been an excessively public person, but he had been well known. Well known and well trusted.

She tried to get her bearings, to fight the insidious arousal building in her. He had said she was in heat. That she would be unable to deny him. Unable to deny his touch. This went beyond denial — this was a beast clawing at her womb, screaming out in demand for the explosive orgasm he had given her before.

She moaned weakly as she turned to her side, wondering at the tight cramps in her lower abdomen. With each spasm her vagina pulsed and throbbed in accompaniment. With each twisting contraction her anger grew. Taber had done this to her. Where before her arousal and need for him had been only a hypersensitive irritation, it had now become an agony.

"God, it could only happen to me," she whispered into the silent room as she stared at the wall across from her.

"Not exactly." A sympathetic female voice spoke behind her, causing Roni to jerk over in the bed, clutching the comforter to her bare breasts as her eyes widened.

She remembered meeting Merinus the day before, though only vaguely. Her mind was consumed with the memory of the heat, the driving need that had tormented her. And Taber. Fierce, savage, determined to claim her despite the fact that he had been the one to walk away years before.

The other woman watched her with deep brown eyes filled with compassion. She was slender, about Roni's height, with long, light brown hair and compassionate eyes. Her expression was calm, sympathetic, and brought a lump to Roni's throat. She had never truly had friends, at least not once they met her father, and this woman's gentle manner made her realize all she had given up over the years.

Merinus, despite the luxurious surroundings of the estate and what Roni remembered of this house, didn't appear to adopt a "lady of the manor" attitude, though. She was dressed in faded jeans, a loose cream-colored cotton shirt and sneakers. She seemed the type more at home camping in the great outdoors than supervising a mansion.

"Where's Taber?" She looked around the room to be certain he wasn't there.

"He's with Callan at the moment. He's head of security here at the estate, and some of the new measures they were putting in place required his attention." Merinus stood up from the chair she had been sitting in and padded over to the bed.

"I have some clothes that should fit you laid out in the bathroom if you would like to wash up and get dressed. I'd suggest a bath for now. It seems to ease the worst of the mating effects for a short time."

Roni felt heat rise in her face as the other woman mentioned the insane desire that had held her in its grip earlier. She could handle wanting the man until she ached, but this was ridiculous.

"For a short while?" she asked her fiercely, frowning. "No." She shook her head at that one. "Something has to stop this. Now." She couldn't accept anything else.

She could feel the heat rising in her body once again. Her skin felt irritated, sensitive, her breasts swollen, her clit throbbing in demand. She couldn't handle this. It had been bad before, but this was worse than she could have imagined.

She wondered if Taber was even suffering from it. More than likely not. And if any man deserved to, it was he.

Merinus sighed. "The effects are temporary, Roni, but not without a certain price. Take your bath while I call down and have your dinner brought up. We'll talk when you're done."

She turned to leave the room, leaving Roni with too many damned questions and no answers.

"Wait." Roni wrapped the comforter around her as she slid from the high bed. Dammit, did Taber think everyone was as damned tall as he was? "Tell me how to stop this now."

The look on Merinus' face when she turned back was somber.

"You can't stop it now. It has to run its course. Now go bathe. The time you can stand to wait for Taber is limited. I know you have questions, and some of them I can answer. But not until you're more comfortable."

Roni drew in a rough breath, staring at the other woman's implacable expression. She looked more than determined, and Roni had a feeling she was used to getting her own way.

"This bites," she snapped, turning away from Merinus. "If I wanted to bathe first I would have asked." But she stomped to the bathroom anyway, determined to get it over with and get her questions answered as soon as possible.

Merinus had been right, though. The bath did seem to ease the building heat that had already begun tormenting her. Of course, Roni opted for a cold bath, shivering in the coolest water she could stand on her skin and gradually adding more until it became tolerable.

The bathroom was a dream. Italian marble floors, a porcelain sink set in a cherry cabinet. In the center of the room was a large sunken tub big enough for three grown people. A shower was set in a far corner.

Against the wall opposite the door was a sky-blue print Queen Anne chair, and beside it, an antique cherry table. Cabinets were set within the walls, and decorative nooks held a variety of expensive knick-knacks. It was opulent and comfortable at the same time. And unlike anything Roni had ever experienced.

When she felt as though she could stand to walk without being fucked first, she got out of the large tub, dried her hair and hurriedly dressed in the long gown and robe the other woman had provided. There were no panties, but she didn't want to tempt her luck at this point by allowing anything to touch her overly sensitive cunt.

Dinner came next. It was waiting on her in the sitting room, on the small glass table positioned beside the sliding balcony doors. It was a light meal and Merinus stood guard over her every second, making certain she finished it before covering the tray and then sitting back in the chair and watching her silently.

"Okay, answers," Roni reminded her. "What did he do to me and how do I get rid of it?"

The answers better come fast too, she thought, because the small contractions in her womb were about to drive her crazy.

"Conception." Roni froze at the other woman's words. "It's the only thing that stills the heat. But you won't be free of Taber, even then. Nature is a little smarter than we've given her credit for here. You and Taber will never be able to separate. You'll always be a part of him, through the child you conceive as well as the hormone that will never completely leave your body. You're his mate. Forever."

Roni stared at the other woman for a long, silent minute. If Merinus didn't look so serious, Roni would have laughed in her face. Unfortunately, this just didn't feel like a good time to find amusement in a situation rapidly bordering nightmare quality.

"Like hell I am." Roni jumped to her feet, paying little attention to the chair that flew out behind her, turning over on the carpeted floor.

This was not good. She stared at Merinus' calm expression, feeling panic well inside her as the other woman watched her almost pityingly.

"Roni, you need to understand…"

"No, *you* need to understand," she retorted furiously as she pushed her fingers desperately though her hair. "I did not ask for this. I didn't ask him to leave this stupid mark on me and I sure as hell didn't ask him to kiss me. I won't accept this."

A child? She had to get pregnant first? Bring a baby into the world that would have every mercenary and low life criminal looking to steal it. To take it from her arms and turn it over to a group of monsters who would do only God knew what to it.

Horror welled up within her as her hands pressed against her stomach and her mind fought to reject any such conclusion. She couldn't do it. God help her, she wouldn't survive it.

"Roni, denying it won't help." Merinus came slowly to her feet. "I've been where you are. I know how confused you are and how pissed you are. But they didn't ask for this, either. Not in any way. You can work this out with Taber."

Roni stared up at her, unblinking. She could feel hysteria building inside her mind as she fought to accept what she considered the unacceptable.

"Work what out with him?" she finally snarled furiously. "Spread my legs so he can knock me up and leave again? Oh yeah, let's talk about that one. His track record sucks, Merinus, and I'm not willing to face the consequences of this alone. And sure as hell not with a child whose very existence will be in danger from the moment it's conceived."

Merinus frowned. "Taber would never leave you, Roni."

She laughed. She couldn't help it. Merinus looked so sincere, so very certain of Taber's honor, that it was all she could do. "So tell me, Merinus, how did I get this mark? Where the hell has he been the last year or so?"

"Taber didn't know about the mark…"

"So they can mark whoever they want to and then like any old tomcat just jump and run to the next." Roni clenched her fists as her fury nearly overwhelmed her.

"Roni, you have to understand…" Merinus tried again.

"Wrong." Roni's hand slashed through the air as she rejected Merinus' plea. "I don't have to understand shit, Merinus. This is my life. Any child conceived will be mine. I won't let him do this to me. And I sure as hell won't let him get me pregnant and then decide he needs someone who is more woman than I am again."

The thought of Taber touching another woman made her insane with grief.

"Roni, Taber wouldn't do that," Merinus protested. "You will be protected and your child even more so."

Roni snorted in disbelief.

"Callan might be more of a man than that, Merinus, but I've seen Taber's work first hand. No thanks. No babies. No Taber. Where the hell am I and how do I get home?"

"What home?" Taber's voice, pitched low and furious, growled from the doorway. "It was burned to the ground before we even landed here at the estate. Looks like you're stuck with the tomcat, baby."

"Taber!" Merinus' voice was distant, though the thread of shock was readily apparent. "That was uncalled for."

Roni didn't give him time to apologize, though. She stomped over to him, fury and rage blending with a pain so resounding she felt as though it would destroy her.

"Did I ask you to bring me here?" she screamed at him furiously as she shoved at his broad, immoveable shoulders. "Look what you've done, Taber. You made my own body turn against me. Now some bastard has burned my house down because I wasn't there. You let them burn my house down." She couldn't believe it, couldn't process the fact that she would never see her home again.

Conception was something she couldn't consider. Her home was real. Her home was all she had left when Taber decided he no longer wanted her. That he needed someone older, or more experienced, or whatever else she wasn't that someone else would be.

The pain building inside her would kill her. Not just the physical, womb-ripping pain of the agonizing arousal tearing through her, but the soul deep pain of losing her last link to her own peace of mind.

"Look what you've done," she screamed again, her fist flying for his face, violence surging inside her like a tidal wave of overwhelming emotion.

"God, Roni…" He jerked her into his arms, tightening them around her, holding her still as she struggled against him, fighting him, because God help her, there was nothing or no one left to fight. "I'm sorry, baby. I'm so sorry."

Silence filled the room. Roni fought to stay on her feet. He held her against his body, a steady weight, as he had always been. A comfort she knew could be taken away from her all too soon.

"Let me go." But she didn't fight for release.

One hand held her head to his chest, the other wrapped around her waist, cushioning her from the violence raging through her system.

"I just bought a new chair," she whispered. She trembled and fought the reaction. God, it was all gone?

"Roni, I'm sorry," he whispered into her hair. "I shouldn't have told you like that, baby. I'm sorry."

She flinched as she pushed back, moving away from him, desperate to escape the pain echoing through her soul. There was nothing else they could destroy now, nothing left for anyone to take away from her. Nothing except the child, if she allowed its conception.

"Well," she breathed out roughly. "Hell." She didn't know what to say, what to do. She felt fragmented, dazed by the events that were happening too fast to allow her to catch her breath, to make sense of what was happening.

She breathed in roughly, pushing her fingers into the pockets of her robe, fighting the panic blooming inside her. Okay, she couldn't kill him. She was sure the others in his family would consider that a no-no. No matter how damned bad she needed to shed his blood now. She was okay. It was just a house. She was going to have to leave it behind anyway. She should have expected this.

The little pep talk wasn't helping. She could feel something inside her chest thickening with pain at the thought of the home she had slowly been creating. With her own hands, blisters and blood she had made it worth living in, made it something worth having rather than the eyesore it had been when she was younger.

"Roni, you have a home here now..." Taber's voice only fed her fury. It was soft, remorseful. As though her pain was breaking something inside him. The loss of her home had been nothing compared to the agony she had faced when she had lost him before.

"Do I?" She fought the surge of adrenaline that cried out for a fight as she turned back to him, watching him with brooding fury. "With you, I presume?"

"With me." His expression hardened as he said the words.

"Poor Taber." She sneered. "Stuck with me after all. Not exactly what you envisioned for a future mate, am I?"

He watched her with a slight frown and no small amount of heat in his eyes.

"I actually never imagined anyone else." He finally shrugged, confusing her further. "Though I can tell you aren't exactly pleased." And why did it seem to bother him so much, that she wasn't pleased?

So where was the man who decided he needed more of a woman than she was? His attitude wasn't making sense to her. Unless it was just the hormone or whatever the hell it was driving her insane. The thought that a drug, no matter how natural, was their only bond broke her heart.

"Not exactly pleased would be a little mild for my reaction." She made certain her smile was all teeth and no warmth. Her pussy was hot enough to make up for it, though she had no intention of letting him know that any time soon. The adrenaline thundering through her system seemed intent on building the arousal that much higher. "Where are my clothes?" She ignored the cramps building in her womb as she turned away from him.

She didn't even have a home now, and she couldn't allow herself to believe that anything she could have with Taber would last longer than it took for her to become pregnant. Where would she be then? She had to leave, had to run, or she would never be free of him.

Taber sighed heavily behind her. "I know you're scared, Roni."

"I'm not scared." She fought back a shudder of pure sensation as heat sizzled between her thighs. Then made sure the look she gave him glittered with her need for retribution. "I'm mad. So get the hell away from me before I take your head off like I should have done when you put this damned mark on me. Where the hell are my clothes?"

She re-entered the bedroom, determined to ignore the man stalking behind her. She could feel him and he wasn't even touching her.

"Your clothes are being washed," he told her, his voice too soft, too carefully controlled as he came up behind her. "Roni, you're in pain. It doesn't have to be this way."

Roni stopped at the bottom of the bed, gripping the footboard with desperate fingers as her stomach clenched almost violently. She closed her eyes, fighting the man, fighting the knowledge of what was happening to her with everything inside her. God, she was so weak, because she knew that despite the unnatural height of the arousal, she would have still found it hard to resist him, to maintain her fury. His voice was soft, regretful, reminding her of the years he had always been there for her. Reminding her how much she had loved him, how much it had hurt when he suddenly wasn't in her life any longer.

Even the fear of conception couldn't dim the needs rising in her body like a flashflood of sensations. How was she supposed to deny him? How could she fight her body, its needs and her heart as well?

"I'm fine." She forced the words between clenched teeth. "Find me some clothes. I want out of here."

If she could just get away from him, she thought desperately. It hadn't been this bad, this intense, until he showed up in her life again. If she could leave, maybe it would ease, settle back to the mild irritation it had been before.

"It won't go away, Roni." His hands settled heavily on her shoulders, his thumbs smoothing over the taut muscles as she fought the shivers of pleasure his touch evoked.

The calloused pads of his thumbs rasped over her skin, heating her flesh, making her moan with the pleasure that streaked through her body. It was exquisite, his touch, the scent of him wrapping around her with a warmth that seared her to her soul.

"I can't do this," she whispered, fighting the tears that thickened in her throat. She had needed so much more from him. "Everything's happening too fast."

"You don't have to do anything, baby," he promised her gently, his lips whispering over the mark he had made so long ago. Making her shiver in longing. "I'll take care of everything, Roni. I promise."

Every cell in her body screamed out in pleasure when his tongue stroked over the small wound. She would have denied him, she assured herself, if she could have fought past the web of arousal and need that tightened about her, leaving her breathless beneath his touch. How could he do this? How could nature have been so cruel as to give him this advantage over her?

"I can smell your heat," he whispered at her ear. "Like warm, sweet cream. It draws me, Roni. I want nothing more than to go to my knees, draw the gown to your hips and bury my tongue in your hot pussy."

She shuddered violently at his words, a whimper of longing escaping her throat as he drew the robe from her shoulders. She felt weak, dazed, unable to fight him when she wanted him with every breath in her body.

"You're so warm, so soft and tempting, you make me lose any semblance of control. You make me desperate, Roni, so hungry for you I can barely think of anything except tasting you."

His tongue licked over her shoulder, raspy, slightly roughened, drawing a gasp of pleasure from her lips at the sensation. His hands drew the thin straps of the gown over her shoulders as his lips trailed hot kisses down the slope of her arm.

"I lost control before." The gown slipped over her hardened nipples, but she had no chance to miss its dubious warmth.

Taber's hands covered the swollen mounds, his palms cushioning the elongated points, rasping them gently as she moaned in rising pleasure. That was good. Too good. Too hot.

She stared down at his hands, amazed at the contrast between his dark skin and her paler flesh. It was so erotic, watching him touch her, seeing the differences between his hard, muscular body and her softer one.

"I won't lose control now. I'll show you how good it can be, baby."

His voice was rough, a sensual caress to her senses as the gown slid to her hips, caressing her as it slipped lower and finally pooled at her feet.

"See, all you have to do is relax," he assured her, his voice at once soothing, stroking her senses as carefully as his hands stroked her breasts. "Let me show you what we missed out on all those years ago."

"You left me." She fought to breathe, to find the strength she needed to refuse him. But it wasn't there. Her body was overruling her mind, stealing her objections, her fears.

"You left me no choice, Roni." His hands cupped her breasts, his finger and thumb gripping her nipple, making it hard for her to think, to speak.

She left him no choice? She had loved him, needed him, until the sheer intensity of those needs had nearly destroyed her. And yet he claimed that she had left him no choice? She wanted to rage, to scream at him, but it was all she could do to breathe beneath his demanding touch.

The pads of his thumbs rasped over the tops of the swollen peaks, then with the help of his index fingers, gripped them with firm, exact pressure as he tugged at them slowly.

"Taber." She cried out at the sharp, streaking pleasure that arrowed from her nipples to her vagina, causing her to arch against him, her hands to reach back and tighten on the outside of his hard, muscled thighs.

"Do you like that, baby?" He did it again, and Roni thought she would explode from the building heat. "I'll use my teeth next," he whispered at her ear. "As I grip and pull, I'll stroke them with my tongue, suckle with my mouth and make you come from that sensation alone."

And he could. She knew he could. Her climax was already building, the pleasure threatening to peak inside the tormented depths of her pussy. Then he stopped. Roni whimpered at the loss of sensation on her tormented nipples. Then she groaned in pleasure as his teeth nipped at the mark on her neck a second before he placed his mouth over it and began to suckle, much as he threatened to do to her nipples.

Her head fell back against his chest. She was distantly aware of the fact he was undressing behind her, removing first his shirt, then his shoes and jeans. His chest caressed her back, making her shiver with the sensation of the tiny, almost invisible hairs that covered it. She had noticed those years before, but had forgotten how sinfully sexy they felt against her skin.

"That's right, baby," he whispered, his breath sighing over the mark, making her shiver in reaction. "Just enjoy. Feel how damned good it can be. You're so sweet and soft, so tight and hot when I thrust inside you. Just touching you is the most pleasure I've ever known in my life."

"You're killing me." Her chest was tight with emotion, aching with the need for more than just his physical touch. "How will I stand it when you're gone again?"

He growled, a fierce, animalistic sound that nearly made her climax from its impact on her senses. God help her, how could something so feral sound so damned sexy?

"There's no way in hell I'll let you go now, Roni," he told her, his voice dark, his hands gripping her hips and pulling her tightly into the cradle of his thighs.

His cock was strong and thick, hot and hard. It felt like warm steel as it pressed against the crease of her ass. She ground her buttocks against it, her hips moving, forcing the shaft to part the rounded globes and press deeper between them.

Behind her, Taber breathed in sharply a second before a rueful chuckle vibrated through his chest.

"Don't tempt me," he warned her, his voice vibrating with arousal. "I'm already at the edge of my control, Roni." She could almost imagine that sexy grin she heard in his voice. The one that made her heart clench at the wicked thoughts it inspired. The little quirk to the side, the flash of teeth as his green eyes sparkled with humor and warmth.

"Why should you have control?" She fought to breathe, to hold back her pleas that he take her now, fast and hard, as he had before. "You haven't cared about stealing mine."

"Ah, baby." He moved slowly, his arms coming around her thighs, her shoulders, as he picked her up. "But my control will bring you more pleasure than you could ever imagine."

She gasped, her arms circling his neck as she stared up at him in surprise. No one but Taber had ever carried her in his arms. She had missed that. It made her feel too feminine, too desired to have him hold her like this now, though. His eyes were dark and glittering with hot, naked lust as he carried her the short distance to the bed.

He had no problem holding her as he maneuvered them both into the bed. But he held her close, secure, until he lowered her slowly to the mattress beneath them.

"I want to lick every inch of your body," he growled. "But I don't know if I'll make it past your lips before I've got to have you."

He knelt beside her, his gaze possessive, brilliant with his rising needs as it raked over her. His body was a work of art. His chest and arms flexed with power, his tight abdomen rippled with strength, and his cock... She swallowed tightly as she allowed her hand to smooth along his thigh toward it. Like silk-encased steel, the dark head throbbed with life. The sight of it had heat and moisture spilling from her hungry cunt.

"No." He caught her hand before she could touch him. "Touch me, Roni, and I'll lose all control. Just relax. Let me show you how good it can be."

It was too damned good. Roni's hands clenched in the sheets beneath her as Taber lay beside her and drove her to the edge of madness. His lips were at one breast, toying delicately with the hard peak while his hand tormented the other.

His tongue stroked confidently around the sensitized nub, the rough rasp causing her to cry out at the building sensations weaving through her body. When his mouth covered it, drawing on it with deep, hard pulls of his wet mouth, she nearly climaxed in reaction. Her womb spasmed with such force she flinched from it and nearly screamed out her pleasure.

"Yes!" he hissed, his voice rough as he moved over her, settling between her thighs, his mouth continuing to torture the swollen tip. "Let it go, Roni. Let me have it all."

He moved to her other breast, repeating the caresses there as her hands clutched at his shoulders. How much more could she stand? She writhed beneath him, her hips arching as she pressed the aching mound of her pussy against the hard planes of his stomach. Oh, now that was good. Her clit throbbed in pleasure as it raked across his flesh.

At the same time his teeth gripped her nipple, pulling at it, his tongue stroking across it, creating a vortex of sensations that rippled through her womb. He stared up at her, his eyes so brilliant, so hot, it hurt to stare into them. His expression was intent, savagely hungry, yet softened with gentleness. How many nights had she dreamed of him touching her this way, holding her?

Her fingers tightened on his muscled forearms. Something was rising inside her that she didn't know how to contain. Something too primitive, too powerful to make sense of.

"I need to touch you." She was restless, a heat and a yearning blooming inside her that she wanted to fight — wanted to and yet couldn't.

It was that look in his eyes. Despite the lust, despite his pleasure in touching her, there was a sadness she barely glimpsed. She wanted to wipe it away and replace it with something more. With a pleasure as destructive as what he was giving her. Something beautiful, something so soul-deep it would wipe the shadows from his gaze.

He licked her nipple again, purring — oh God, he was purring — his chest vibrating with such a sexy sound that her pussy gushed with the force of her excitement.

"Not yet," he whispered, his breath whispering over her flesh as he moved farther down her body. "Let me touch you, Roni. Let me drown in your taste. You have no idea how much I've needed this."

His voice was tormented, hoarse. As though his only thought, his only need, was the hunger for her. But in his eyes she saw another need, one that came much too close to what she had seen in her own eyes over the years every time she looked in the mirror.

When he moved again she couldn't think of anything more.

"Taber." Her voice was a squeak of dismay as she felt his breath between her thighs.

Startled, she looked down her body then moaned weakly as she watched and felt him spread her legs further, opening her to him, his eyes locked with hers.

"Cats love cream, Roni," he whispered wickedly. "And I bet you have the sweetest cream in the whole damned world."

The breath locked in her chest as she watched his tongue distend then disappear within the curl-shielded slit that guarded her sex.

"Oh God!" She tried to scream but the sound was weak, breathless, as her hips rose from the bed, her body shuddering at the feel of the long slow lick that parted her feminine lips and delved to the secretive opening into her vagina.

His hands cupped the cheeks of her bottom as he lifted her from the bed, angling her to the stroke of his tongue. Then he began to lap at her, small, hungry licks through the thick essence of her desire. He growled as he ate her, his tongue dipping into the furnace of her pussy, drawing yet more of the frothy sweetness into his mouth.

Roni stared unseeing up at the ceiling, wracked by a pleasure so exquisite she feared it would destroy her mind. His tongue was ravenous, merciless. It plunged into the small channel, stroking sensitized tissue, driving her to the edge of madness as she writhed beneath it.

He slurped at the cream he drew from her, the sounds of the moist excess joining his rumbling groans as his tongue fucked her with slow, even strokes.

It went beyond her most desperate dreams. The pleasure filling her was like nothing she could have imagined, nothing she could have dreamed of ever sharing with him. The intensity began to build. The rippling in her womb strengthened, the convulsive tightening of her vagina became spasms of almost painful pleasure.

"Taber," she panted, shuddering in his grip, her legs tightening against his broad shoulders as she fought the rapidly building sensations streaking mindlessly through her body.

He growled again, the sound vibrating against her clit as he lifted her closer, his tongue stroking deeper, his nose grinding against the little bud in a caress that devastated her.

She screamed. The sound echoed around her as he destroyed her. Her orgasm exploded through her, ripping the world apart as light and color splashed behind her closed eyelids. Her hips gyrated, grinding her pussy against his mouth, intensifying the excruciating sensations as every muscle in her body trembled in protest against the strength of her release.

"Mine!" Taber's hoarse shout was the only warning she had before he rose to his knees, lifted her, and buried his cock into the snug depths of her tightening channel.

Death couldn't be as painful, as exquisite, as completely shattering, as the feel of his heavy erection separating her, forcing its way into the ever shrinking depths of her pussy.

Roni shattered. Everything inside her collapsed around the desperate penetration, the hard, almost brutal thrusts of his cock inside her gripping cunt. He fucked her like a man gone mad, but even worse, her body accepted it, screamed out for more. She couldn't believe that was her voice she heard. Shattered screams. Pleas for more. Deeper, faster, oh God…

"Harder…" Her hands were locked around the tight muscles of his forearms, her nails biting into his flesh, her legs lifting, her ankles crossing above his driving hips. "Harder… Fuck me, Taber. Fuck me harder…"

Not her, she thought distantly. She wouldn't scream such words. She wouldn't plead so desperately…

"God! You're too tight! Too tight, too hot…" He was gasping, sweat dripping from his body to hers, his cock stroking inside her, pistoning desperately until he threw her higher, harder into yet another orgasm.

She felt the change in his cock again—the locking, the stroking against the most sensitive area of her quaking cunt— and lost all sanity. She didn't know what she cried out. Didn't know she could have the breath to voice a word. The sounds echoed around her, guttural, primal, as a roar exploded from his chest and she felt the deep, heavy pulses of heated sperm shooting hard and hot inside her.

Roni was only barely aware of Taber collapsing over her. His breaths were hard, gasping, his voice rough as he whispered words she could make no sense of. Their bodies were damp, locked together, and loath to separate. They could have stayed that way for eternity and she wouldn't have protested. Her eyes were closed and as the last violent pulse of her climax shuddered through her body, she allowed exhaustion to capture and take her away.

Darkness swept around her as Taber's body blanketed her, warmed her. She sighed, for the first time in years sated, replete and safe. She allowed herself to sleep.

Chapter Six

Taber was aware when Roni slipped into an exhausted sleep. Her body relaxed beneath him, becoming boneless, accepting of his weight as he struggled to learn how to breathe once again.

His hands were clenched in her hair, his face buried at her shoulder, his teeth still locked into the mark he had given her so long ago. He could taste the sweet essence of her blood in his mouth where the skin had broken and he had lapped at it like a man dying for the taste of ecstasy.

Moving away from her was the hardest feat he had ever attempted in his life. Pulling away from the fisted grip her pussy had on his cock was torture, an agony of pleasure nearly as intense as achieving the soul-destroying release that had ripped through him.

The animalistic barb had receded, drawing back beneath the head of his cock, releasing him from the sweet heat he had been locked inside. He dragged his body off her, amazed at the incredible weakness that had overcome him.

God, he felt as though he were dying and would be more than willing to give himself to the arms of the Grim Reaper. Anything to stay there just another second, to relish the sublime pleasure he had found locked inside her heat.

It was unlike anything he had ever known. Every cell in his body had gloried in touching her, making her scream, making her beg as the rush for release came upon her.

He moved from the bed almost drunkenly, a wry grin tilting his lips as he forced his legs to hold him up, albeit a bit unsteadily. Then he made the mistake of turning back and gazing at the woman responsible for it all.

His chest clenched. A brutal ripping agony swept over him as he stared into her pale face, the gentle line of brow and cheek. Her lips were slightly parted, kiss-swollen. God help him, she was his life. He stared at her as though seeing her for the first time, realizing what he had forced himself to deny for years. The woman had the ability to destroy him. Hell, she had already nearly killed him with her first rejection. What would it do to him now if she walked away? How could he force her to stay if she conceived and being with him wasn't what completed her heart? Would nature be cruel enough to have mated him with a woman who couldn't—or wouldn't—love him?

Taber reached out, pushing back a thick strand of golden-brown hair as he slowly pulled the sheet over her body before turning quickly away from her and walking to the bathroom. As he did, he remembered the first time he had ever laid eyes on her, over ten years before. He had found her huddled in the woods, her arms wrapped around her small body. Her eyes were gazing into the wilderness, though he had known it was something inside her, not without, that she was focused on.

He knew that feeling. He had been a young age, but the brutality of the labs and the horror of their escape had forever wiped away a part of his humanity. How can you miss something you never remembered having, he wondered as he braced his hands on the sink and stared into the feral expression staring back at him. He had been no more than an animal in those days. Furious, wounded, unwilling and unable to fit into the carefree lifestyle Maria had tried to give them.

He had been stalking the woods, escaping, allowing the savagery that filled him to release itself in the hunt. Until he found Roni. Her face was tear-stained, her knees scraped, her eyes vacant as she lost herself in whatever horrors filled her young mind.

He had imagined they saved each other that night. He had picked her up and taken her to Maria, holding her against his chest, feeling a sense of rage, of protectiveness that anyone so fragile, so innocent and pure, could be forced into such pain. The look in her eyes had reminded him of his sisters, their minds as violated as their bodies had been before their escape.

Roni hadn't been raped, rather, she had been terrorized. Left alone, with no food, no one to care for her, and her father's enemies stalking her, striking out at her when the bastard who sired her couldn't be found.

From that day on, Roni had been his. At first, it had been friendship, a protectiveness, a need to care for her. Later, it had grown, terrifying him with the depth of emotion and desire she inspired in him.

He drew in a hard, deep breath. The child had grown into a woman before he could make sense of his own changing feelings for her. Her smart mouth and wild ways had worried him incessantly, but he had always known what she was thinking, what she was feeling. The woman whose screams had rocked his lust moments before was not the woman who had sworn her love to him three years before. This Roni was too quiet, too self-contained, shut down. As though life had dealt her one blow too many and now she refused to trust or to try again.

He breathed in tiredly as he pulled a cloth from the small shelf beside the sink and wet it with warm water. She would be sore, and wouldn't rest comfortably with her thighs slick and damp from their mating.

Taber moved back to the bed, feeling his cock harden, lengthen, as he stepped closer and drew in the faint, distinctive scent of their combined releases. It was reminiscent of a wild wind after a summer thunderstorm, untamed and earthy.

He drew the sheet back from her slumbering body, grimacing at the effort it took to keep his hand from trembling as he began to clean her. From her neck, along her arms, her full, firm breasts — rosy from his earlier suckling attentions — down to her slender torso, her delicately rounded tummy to her thighs. He swallowed tightly as he spread her legs, ignoring her pleasured moan as he cleaned the slick, inner juices from her body.

He was breathing hard and heavy by the time he covered her once again and dragged his own weary body into the bed beside her. Dawn was approaching and it felt like weeks since he had slept.

He pulled her close to him, ignoring her first instinctive move to pull away from him, shushing her gently, wrapping his arms around her and tucking her against his chest.

"What happened, Roni?" he whispered into her silken hair before bestowing a soft, gentle kiss to her forehead. "What the hell happened to you?"

* * * * *

"You can't bathe yet, Roni." It was late afternoon before Taber awakened, drawn back to consciousness by Roni's furtive escape from the bed.

She paused, gripping the footboard as her body tensed.

"I'm sore." Her voice was low, but he could hear the vibration of anger. It sure as hell beat the confusion he had heard the night before.

"I know you're sore, baby." He flipped the blankets back, rising and padding over to the chest at the end of the room.

He drew a soft, blue, cotton button-up shirt from one of the drawers, which would make it easier for Doc Martin to check her out while maintaining her modesty.

"Put this on." He walked back to her, handing her the shirt as she stared at him suspiciously.

"I stink of you," she snapped, raising her head, her blue eyes so filled with anger he almost flinched. "I want a shower."

Taber frowned down at her, uncomfortably aware that her fury was only sparking his lust. His cock was beginning to stiffen, to pulse in hunger.

"Put the shirt on, or get your ass back in bed where I'll fuck you until you're too damned tired to argue with me. It wouldn't be wise to push me right now, and you know damned good and well once I touch you, you won't deny me."

She was breathing hard, her breasts rising and falling sharply, her nipples peaking at the harsh sound of his voice. His mouth watered as his gaze flickered to them.

"Stop." She jerked the shirt from him, drawing it roughly over her arms and holding the edges tightly together. "Do you think I don't know just how little you do want me, Taber? Do you think I'm just going to willingly accept what you've done to me?"

Well, if he had, he guessed it was time to change his mind, he thought sarcastically.

"Doesn't look to me like you have much choice." His cock was insistent now. Damn, Doc said to be in the lab first thing after Roni awoke, not after another hour or two of fucking her silly. "Button the shirt, Roni. We have to go down to the lab and I'll be damned if I'll let you flash that pretty ass for whoever is standing around outside this room."

He stomped back to the dresser, jerked a T-shirt and sweat pants from the drawers, and hastily donned them.

"Lab?" At least she was buttoning the shirt, even if her voice did pulse with disgust. "Do I look like a fucking rat to you?"

He turned to her slowly. Her voice was harsh, guttural, the scent of her building heat reaching him effortlessly.

"Don't push me right now, Roni." He was holding onto his temper and his arousal by the thinnest thread. "You won't like the consequences."

She eyed him with brooding fury and a bitterness that confused him no small amount.

"You mean it can get worse?" she asked with vicious sweetness. Damn, that smile could cut a man in two without even trying.

He stepped closer, his hand reaching out, catching in the long strands of her hair before she could jerk away from him. He watched her eyes widen as he exerted just enough pressure to force her head back, to look into her face, fighting instincts he hadn't even known he had.

"It can get worse," he snarled, allowing his lips to pull back, the lethal canines at the sides of his mouth to flash dangerously. "I warned you years ago, baby, I was more than you could ever imagine. You should have heeded that advice."

She didn't show fear as he had expected. Fury leapt into her gaze—hotter, stronger than before.

"And I thought I had." She mocked him with a sneer. "What are you going to do now, Taber? Take me to the floor and mount me again? Is that the only way you know of to make your women submit to you?"

He leaned closer, inhaling the sweet scent of her arousal. "The good thing about taking you to the floor is how much I know you would love it." He allowed the growl building in his throat to escape with his words.

Instantly, the smell of her heat intensified.

"Unwillingly." Her lips thinned, her nostrils flaring as she tugged at the grip on her hair.

She liked it. The knowledge pierced his anger like the sharpest sword, making him damned near desperate to have her now.

"Unwillingly?" He backed her against the bed, watching her eyes darken and her cheeks flush with lust. Oh yeah, that's how he wanted her. Hot and hungry for him.

"It's a drug, Taber." He stilled against her as she spoke with chilling emphasis. "Otherwise, I wouldn't allow you within a mile of me. You drugged me. I can't stop it, I can't control it, but I'll be damned if I'll let you sugarcoat it."

She spoke as though there had never been natural desire between them. As though the hunger and the heat were something she would have never felt otherwise. It sent a surge of anger crashing through his system, ripping aside his natural control as he faced his mate's defiance.

"You wanted me before," he snarled, furious that she would deny the bond they once had. "I hadn't kissed you then, Roni. Before the mark, before the kiss, you still wanted me."

He dared her to deny it, staring down at her, praying she wouldn't because he knew if she did, his control would break.

"I was a child, remember?" A flash of pain, quickly covered yet so deep it seared his soul, shadowed her eyes. "I grew up and I grew up fast, thanks to you. Now either fuck me, or let's get these tests the hell over with because I need a shower. I told you, I stink."

He released her slowly but watched her more closely than ever before. She looked angry, sounded furious, but beneath the smell of her arousal, the scent of fear and pain surrounded her.

She thought she was so tough, standing up to him, hating him for only God knew what, when he could sense the agony slashing at her soul. She was a part of him, more than she knew, more than she could ever understand.

Taber's hand reached out, his fingers touching her cheek despite her instinctive flinch.

"You were mine when you were eleven years old, and mine when you turned into a woman. You're no less mine now, Roni." He kept his voice soft, fought back the beast roaring to make her submit and to do it now. "You can fight it all you want to, for now. But I won't let you go. Don't deceive yourself there."

She inhaled slowly, deeply. He could see the moisture shimmering in her eyes. Not tears, but close, though she maintained the disdain in her look.

"You must enjoy deluding yourself, Taber. If so, that's fine. But I won't play the game with you. Not this time." Her voice trembled on the last word.

Taber stepped away from her carefully. He could feel his fragile hold on his control weakening.

"We'll take the elevator to the lab." He refused to comment on her statement. Let her believe as she wished. For now. "Doc was impatient an hour ago, I'm sure he's less than pleased by now."

He gripped her upper arm lightly, needing to touch her, no matter how small that contact was.

"I don't need you to lead me like a child." Her voice was low, pulsating with a mix of anger, arousal and fear as she tried to pull her arm from his grasp.

"Stop fighting me, dammit." He turned back to her, jerking her against him, allowing her to feel the erection that was throbbing like a raw, open wound. "Give it up for now, Roni. Let it the hell go before I do something we'll both regret."

Déjà vu swirled around them. *Would I regret it?* She had once asked him.

"I already regret it," she snapped out, trembling with the excess of emotions that seemed to be tearing her apart. "Don't you understand, Taber? I regret it all, more than you can ever imagine."

He clenched his teeth as an unbidden rumble of warning escaped his chest. He was rock hard. Every instinct he possessed screamed out that he show her differently, that he force her to admit that it wasn't just the hormone causing her need, that it wasn't something her heart and soul regretted. The animal was roaring for submission, the man was screaming out for more.

"One day," he snarled softly, "you will admit differently, Roni. Pray, baby, that you haven't pushed me too far to hear the words by then. I'm not one of those civilized little boys you used to date. I'm your fucking mate, and by God, you're testing my limits right now. Stop, before I hurt us both."

Fear flickered in her eyes. Taber thanked God that she stayed silent as he slowly released her, that she didn't protest further as he gripped her upper arm once again and began leading her from the room. Because if she had, he had a feeling he would have showed her more of the animal than either of them wanted her to see.

* * * * *

"Just how many more needles do you own, anyway?" Roni snapped as Doc Martin inserted yet another in her vein and began drawing blood.

Her skin was crawling, the touch so sickening she wanted to vomit right there on the pristine floor beneath the small gurney she sat on.

"I have several boxes actually," he said drolly as he withdrew the needle, then stared down at her with a kindness that brought tears to her eyes. "I know how hard this is on you, Miss Andrews. I promise, I'm trying to hurry."

She glanced over at Taber where he stood propped against the wall beside the door. He was tense, his expression savage as his gaze watched her with a hungry fury.

"Take your time. I have plenty of blood." She drew in a deep breath, determined to get through this. "So tell me, have you come up with a cure yet?"

Taber growled. The doctor glanced over at him a bit worriedly, though she caught him smothering his chuckle.

"No cure that we know of." He finally moved back, giving her a chance to breathe in air that didn't smell male. "I've run every damned test I can think of and we now have over two dozen other scientists working on it. The only answer is conception."

"As if!" Roni allowed all the pent up anger and fear to power the small exclamation. "I need my birth control pills. I've already missed one." It was the only answer. She had taken them before to keep her cycles timely but now she needed them desperately. "You're a doctor — get them for me."

"Doesn't work." He shook his head as Taber snarled, a low, dangerous sound that rocked her body, not with fear as it should have, but with excitement.

"Excuse me?" She lifted her brows, fighting back her shock. "What the hell do you mean it doesn't work? Fine, give me a Depo shot, an IUD. I don't give a damn, but do something."

Having a child was out of the question. She had no intention of becoming pregnant, not by Taber, not by anyone, and especially not amid the danger she was beginning to realize lurked outside the estate Taber and his family were working frantically to secure.

"Depo doesn't work." The doctor stuck a swab in her mouth, swirling it around quickly as she nearly gagged.

She pushed her hands through her hair as he moved away, fighting back the rising panic welling inside her and the pain blooming through her body. Every bone and muscle felt as though it was on fire, blistering her insides with heat. Perspiration dotted her skin and no matter how she fought it she couldn't hold back the small wracking trembles that attacked her body.

"I need a vaginal sample." The doctor's voice lowered, filling with regret. "I'm sorry. I know this isn't easy."

Taber paced closer.

"Get back, Taber!" She was amazed at the fury that echoed in her demand. "If you come near me I'll shove one of those damned needles into that black heart of yours."

"Dammit, Roni, you can't do this alone," he retorted. "I'm only trying to help you."

"You've helped enough," she sneered, dragging several deep, strengthening breaths before turning back to the doctor. "Why is this so hard?" she demanded of the other man. "Tell me what the hell's wrong with me before you do anything. I feel like fire ants are eating away at my insides and I'm getting damned sick of it."

She could handle it, she assured herself as she watched the doctor, keeping her expression fierce. It seemed neither he, nor Taber, responded to anything other than complete determination and more than one threat of physical violence.

Doc Martin heaved an impatient breath. "Young woman, let's get these tests completed first..."

"You touch me and you may not be walking straight for days." She cocked her leg back as he watched it warily. "I want answers before you stick another needle, swab or whatever the latest device of torture is at the moment." She sure as hell didn't like the looks of that damned speculum he was holding in his hand.

"Roni, I told you what was wrong." Taber stepped closer.

Roni turned her head slowly, watching him with all the pent up violence raging through her system. He stopped again, only feet from the gurney this time.

"A mating does not a relationship make," she told him with false sweetness before turning back to the doctor. "Answers, if you please. In English would be nice, too," she ventured, unwilling to try to understand whatever doctor's jargon he used.

"In a nutshell," he sighed. "For the time being, your body is addicted to the hormone contained in Taber's saliva as well as his semen. The effects are intense, bringing violent illness and pain, which only goes away after, uuhh...relations are attained." He flushed before her shocked gaze. "The best we've been able to figure is that it's nature's way of ensuring the species. Normally, the minute amount of normal sperm the Feline Breed males possess makes them virtually impotent. But the hormone infecting you forces your body to ovulate every three days. To further ensure procreation, it strengthens normal arousal to the point that it cannot be denied."

Roni cursed her own stubbornness. She could feel the blood draining from her face as her stomach pitched and her mind fought to reject the diagnosis.

"It ends with conception?" Her voice was thready as she fought to speak.

"The symptoms left Merinus upon conception," he agreed. Sympathy filled his voice. "It is something that, so far, seems to occur only with a woman with whom the emotions of the Feline

Breed are involved. A natural mate, in Callan and Merinus' case. It has never occurred before."

She pressed her hands to her stomach, swallowing tightly, refusing to allow herself to be sick.

"Prevent conception." Her voice was shaking.

"Roni..." Taber's protest was ignored.

She stared up at the doctor, fighting the rage rising sharply within her. She would not allow this. She couldn't.

"I don't care what you have to do, or how you do it, but stop it."

Taber stood still, refusing to speak despite the pain lodging in his chest. He could hear the terror shaking in her voice, the pain rocking through her and would have given his own life then and there if it would save her from this.

He couldn't bear the stark agony resonating through her voice. God help him, he would give anything to go back, to take back the mark, to make this easier on her somehow.

"I'm sorry, Roni." Martin's voice echoed his own regret. "If I could do this for you, I would. IUD won't work. The body will reject it. The hormone is affecting every organ, working to ensure conception. The same for the Depo shot and the birth control pills. We've found no way to prevent this. Not yet."

It was then she turned to Taber. His soul shattered with pain as he glimpsed her eyes. They were deep, shadowed wells of misery that had every animal instinct inside him demanding that he protect her. She was terrified and he had no idea how to help her.

He stepped to her before she could speak, his hand weaving through the tangled strands of her hair as the other caught her close. And in that second he damned his own soul. His lips took hers, his tongue plunging into her mouth, forcing her to accept him despite her instinctive cry of rejection.

She would never make it through this while everything inside her clamored for him, the hormone attacking not just her mind, but her body as well. Her hands caught his shoulders as a whimpering cry whispered from her throat. But her tongue stroked his, her lips drawing on him as her breath hitched on a sob.

He held her tightly, easing her, stilling the instinctive rejection of the tests the doctor needed to perform. When he pulled back, her eyes were nearly black with emotion, tear-filled and hazy with arousal.

"With my life, Roni," he pledged to her. "With everything I am, I swear to you, I will protect you and any child that comes of this. Whatever you want I will give you, baby, as God is my witness. Anything to make up for what I have done to you."

He could barely hold back his own tears. He who had never cried, who had fought emotion since he had first learned of its effect on him. He would give her anything she desired, if only it could ease the pain he knew was flaying her soul.

Her arms tightened around him, her face pressing against his chest, her shoulders quivering as she fought her own sobs. He tightened his hold on her, bending protectively over her, rocking her, hating himself with every cell in his body.

Finally, she drew in a deep, hard breath. Her nails clenched at his back and he felt the dampness of her tears on his shirt.

"No more tests," she whispered.

"Taber, I need those tests. All we've had to go on were Merinus' samples..."

Taber snarled in fury. His head turned, his gaze locking on the doctor's as he fought to protect her from any further pain.

"A swab only," Martin demanded. "For God's sake. This isn't just her, Taber. It's the future."

He tensed, intending to pull her from the table and stalk from the room.

"No. He's right." Her arms tightened around him as shudders quaked through her. "He's right. I can do this. I can." But she didn't release her hold of him.

"I'll hold you, baby." He lowered her slowly to the gurney, remembering Sherra relating how Callan had been forced to do the same for Merinus. "Just hold on to me, Roni. I won't let you go."

It was hell. Roni forced back her screams as everything inside her protested the doctor's touch, his tests, his soothing voice. She knew she was leaving deep marks in Taber's back from the grip her fingers had on him, but couldn't seem to care. It was that or scream. That, or fight to be free.

She breathed in hard and deep. She could do this. She wasn't a quitter. She could fight. She had forgotten that since Taber's desertion. She knew how to hold herself together when the fear was like a beast clawing at her stomach.

One second at a time. One minute at a time. One hour at a time. It had saved her before. She could think later, when the pain had eased, when the terror had lessened and her mind had absorbed the rushing change that had fallen into her life. Then she could find safe ground. Then she would think.

"You leave me again and I'll kill you!" She jerked violently as the doctor used his demon's tools to examine her. "I swear to God, Taber. I may not be woman enough for you, but if you leave me after this, I'll make you pay. I'll cut your black heart from your chest myself and then I'll carve your cock into so many tiny pieces you'll never find them all."

And she would, she promised herself as she throttled the scream wanting to break free from her throat. She could feel the tension in Taber as well, the furious growls coming from his chest, his protective, fierce hold on her body. He was hers for now. She would deal with the future when she had to.

* * * * *

Confusion was a state of being that Roni was becoming accustomed to, albeit reluctantly. As she stood on the balcony of Taber's suite that evening and watched the men moving around the estate grounds, she wondered if the world had suddenly gone insane.

Men. Living, breathing, walking on two legs and possessing exceptional abilities, moved about the place with automatic weapons and suspicious gazes. There were no dogs in sight, but she had watched one of the Breeds as he moved into the tree-line, flanked by two cougars.

The animals bodies were sleek and well muscled, powerful killing machines that acted like overgrown kittens until the Breed walking with them entered the forested mountain. She watched until they disappeared out of sight, seeing the subtle shift of motion in the large animals, the prowling, dangerous stance they took.

For all its gracious beauty inside the house, the estate was an armed camp. In an age of supposed civilized behaviour, these people were forced to live with the constant knowledge that they were never safe. That no one or nothing could protect them but themselves.

An hour before she had watched as a van moved into the clearing across from the house while a group of men rushed from what appeared to be bunkhouse of sorts. They had stood back, faces reflecting weariness and rage as two young women slowly stepped from the opened doors.

One had supported the other, watching the surroundings warily, stepping slowly into the sunlight before helping the other girl into the building. The men stayed a careful distance from them, their expressions closed, their attitudes one of careful distance as armed guards watched more diligently than before.

There had been something about the two as they stepped from the protection of the van and made their way to the open door of the building. Something heartbreaking. Something that made Roni all too aware of the danger surrounding not only herself, but every man and woman who now lived within the estate.

"Roni?"

She turned at a familiar female voice, surprise filling her as she stared back at the young woman who had stepped into the room.

"Dawn?" She blinked, shocked at the younger girl's appearance.

She was dressed in army fatigues. A dull green tank top and the multicolored earth-toned pants. Boots laced to mid calf, and a holster and weapon were strapped to her lean waist.

The younger girl of the Lyons extended family had always seemed to melt into the shadows, hiding, even when in full view. Quiet, shy, with dark brown eyes and hair the color of the cougars Roni had seen disappearing into the forest earlier.

"You need to come off the balcony." Dawn moved to the wide doors, closing them behind her and pulling the shades in place before she turned back to her. "We're not one hundred percent certain of security at the moment. Taber should have warned you to be more careful."

He had. She had just opted to ignore him.

This wasn't the girl Roni had known before. Something had changed within her, had hardened, grown cold.

"It's good to see you again, Dawn." She watched the other girl closely as she turned.

Roni had always been closer to Sherra. The blonde Breed had a more natural affinity to others, Roni supposed. And though Dawn had always held herself back, it had seemed at the time that shyness had been the root, rather than this harder, bleak pain that she glimpsed now.

Dawn watched her quietly, the odd, hazel-flecked brown eyes cool, almost an amber in her sun darkened face.

"It's good to see you too, Roni," she finally said, her voice stiff, almost formal. "Stay away from the windows and off the balcony until we have more security in place. We don't want to take a chance that you could be harmed."

She turned, moving slowly, her body movements reminding Roni of the animals patrolling the forests now.

"This is a change from living in Sandy Hook," Roni commented before Dawn could reach the doors, watching the other woman, fighting to make sense of the change she sensed in her.

"Is it?" Dawn pushed her hands into the pockets of her pants, her eyes wary. "It's not much different, Roni. Just, instead of hiding, we're securing. Hiding never really helped us anyway."

There was an edge of cynical pain that had Roni's chest tightening in response. What the hell had happened to Dawn?

"I was sorry to hear about Dayan's death," she extended the condolences she had been unable to say during the funeral.

Something flashed in Dawn's eyes. Something primal, dangerous.

"Thank you." The words seemed forced past her throat. "If you'll excuse me now I need to get back to work. I'll remind Taber to outline the safety measures to you again when I see him. He should take better care of his mate."

Roni's brows snapped into a frown.

"I don't need Taber to remind me of anything, Dawn. I can't live in one room forever without looking outside."

"It beats a cell where everyone watches you." Dawn shrugged then, her words sending shock waves vibrating through Roni's mind. "That's what will happen if you're kidnapped, Roni. Placed in an open cell, even things as private as bathing or using the toilet watched and analysed, noted and discussed. Unless they just kill you outright. A bullet to the brain doesn't really hurt, but it's pretty final. I would think this suite, or the rest of the house would be preferable to either."

Roni swallowed tightly as she glimpsed the haggard pain that shadowed the other girl's eyes.

"Dawn..." What could she say? Were there even words to let her know how much Roni hated the life she had obviously led?

"No words needed, Roni." A bitter smile shaped her lips. "I've learned the hazards of burying your head in the sand and praying things will change. Things won't change, all you can do is protect yourself as best you can. At least for Taber's sake, protect yourself, even if you care nothing for your own safety. He's lost enough, just as we all have, don't take this from him as well."

"This?" She shook her head then, uncertain what the other girl meant.

"This," she reiterated. "The chance to be more than an animal, even as he's more than a man. The chance for a family, a child, a mate to hold him when the dark, bleak horror of the nightmares haunt his nights. He deserves that, whether you believe it or not."

Roni refused to allow the anger blooming inside her to fall on Dawn's head. She could sense the pain, savage and overwhelming, that swirled around her. There had always been something different about Dawn, something sad, almost broken.

"But he is a man, Dawn. And as so, he's responsible for his actions, good or bad," she reminded her with a snap in her voice that she regretted being unable to hold back. "Taber isn't unaccountable, no matter the demons that haunt him."

Dawn's eyes flashed, then cooled once again. As though the anger surging within her had nearly had its say. Roni almost wished it had. The silent, haunted eyes were nearly more than she could bear.

"Taber, more than others, deserves some happiness," she finally said. "I have to get back to work. Stay away from the balcony, Roni."

Roni watched her leave the room, her frown deepening as anger surged inside her. Not anger against Dawn, whose quiet strength seemed more bitter now, harder, less forgiving. But the world in general. The cruelties of humans could, at times, be terrifying. What had been done to these people? How were they supposed to live, always aware, always knowing that their lives could be taken at any time? That outside the security of this compound, no more than a prison itself, that they were hunted?

She pushed her fingers through her hair, still damp from her shower, and gritted her teeth in fury. A fury she knew by now only pushed the arousal closer to the surface. She could feel it building in her, moving through her system, making her want to scream out in frustration.

Moving her hands from her hair, she smoothed them down her stomach, pressing them against her abdomen as she felt the sensitivity of her body there. Conception. To ease the heat, she had to conceive. What then, if she did conceive, after the child was born? Would it begin again? A never-ending cycle of heat and conception, birth and danger from those who would take those children from her?

She swung around, pacing the room, fighting the horrifying thoughts that began to attack her. There had to be answers. There had to be a way to live in this suddenly alien world she found herself in, with some measure of peace. And there was only one person she knew, that could have that answer. Merinus.

Chapter Seven

"I will assume you're pregnant." Roni fought to keep her voice calm as she came to a stop at the small glass table Merinus sat next to on the back deck of the house. "What's next? What do I have to look forward to?"

The other woman was watching the construction of a high fence an acre from the sheltered porch, her expression pensive. The men worked on the twelve-foot high barricade being stretched from post to post with an almost fanatical vigor, as though nothing were more important than getting the steel-linked barrier in place.

"You know," Merinus said softly, sighing with aching regret, "this estate was so beautiful when we first saw it. Stately, graceful, despite the horrible experiments that were practiced in the buildings that once stood where those men are working. Everything was peaceful, as though its very elegance distanced it from the horror those who owned it practiced."

Merinus tapped a perfectly manicured nail on the glass top restlessly. "Now look at it. Fences everywhere. Wild animals turned loose for protection, and nightly attempts to break the security Callan is trying to enforce. The bastards will never stop until they're put out of their insane misery, like rabid dogs."

With each word, anger pulsed and throbbed in the other woman's voice as she turned her head, her gaze meeting Roni's fiercely. "Yes, I'm pregnant, by a man I would have gladly given my life to save, Roni. A man who has faced more horror than you can ever imagine in your life. Daily, he faces his worst nightmare. Nightly, he awakens in a sweat after having dreamed the child and I were taken. Who is suffering more? Me, who he protects? Or Callan, who knows the consequences should it happen?"

Awareness pulsed like a hidden ache in Merinus' voice. Her love for Callan throbbed in every syllable. Her fear for him and her unborn child was like a living fire in her eyes.

"It would seem to me both of you are suffering. You don't sound unaware of the dangers or the consequences, Merinus." Roni tilted her head to the side as the brown eyes watching her warmed only marginally.

"No, I'm not, but you are." She waved her hand to the vacant seat across from her. "Share some coffee with me. Decaf, unfortunately." Her lips twisted with a hint of self-mockery. "I so miss the caffeine." The last words were drawn out, dripping with an almost palatable thirst for something that didn't even have a taste.

"Decaf doesn't stress you." Roni shrugged as she took her seat. "And whatever the hell those men do to your body, the caffeine only makes it worse. I found that out after Taber decided to do the marking thing on me."

"The marking thing?" Merinus laughed in delight, a bit of the strain easing from her face. "That's as good a word for it as anything. But damn if it can't be fun."

Roni glimpsed the remembered fire in Merinus' gaze. Her eyes were soft with the memories, her lips curved as though they brought her comfort.

"You don't...burn anymore?" Roni asked her hesitantly, wondering if she would ever sit outside Taber's presence again and not ache for him.

"Oh, I burn." Merinus sat back in her chair, her gaze flickering to the men working once again. "But it's natural now, Roni. I wanted Callan when he was no more than a picture, a story, a man who had suffered. I wanted him like nothing I had known before in my life. A compulsion. A need I wasn't about to deny. The hormone only kept me from denying it. When I conceived, it was done after I had admitted and realized how much we were a part of each other. It wasn't something I felt was forced on me."

Roni looked away. Hadn't she wanted Taber just as well? From the time she had been eleven to the minute her soul had shattered with that letter he sent her, hadn't she dreamed, longed, loved?

"I was at Dayan's funeral," she whispered, remembering how desperately she wanted to go to Taber at the time, to ease the grief that lined his face. "It was after Taber marked me. But I remember how desperately I hurt for him, not sexually, but because I could see his pain."

"Dayan's death changed them all," Merinus told her quietly. "You don't know what happened to Dayan, do you?"

Roni nodded hesitantly. "He was killed saving you..."

"Oh no." Merinus shook her head, her tone harsh. "That was what we told the media, Roni. Dayan died by Callan's hand when he tried to kill me. He killed Callan's mother, Maria, years ago because she had nearly talked Callan into going to the press, and he was determined to kill me for the same reason."

Roni didn't disbelieve her, and wasn't entirely shocked. Dayan hadn't been completely sane. The day he had brought her Taber's letter, he had pinned her against the wall of the bedroom over the garage, his breath rasping, his eyes burning with lust as he offered to train her to satisfy Taber.

"When he brought me Taber's note, letting me know Taber didn't want me, he tried to attack me," Roni whispered. "It felt like knives going into my skin when he held me. I had never hurt so bad."

"Taber's note?" Merinus leaned forward, shaking her head in confusion. "I knew you two had a history, but I was unaware of what it was."

Roni pressed her lips tightly together before licking them nervously. She had never told another living soul what had happened. Briefly, bitterly, she told Merinus the whole story, including Dayan's part in it.

It was humiliating, remembering how much she had depended on Taber over the years, knowing he would save her, take care of her, rather than forcing her to take care of it on her own. She had learned, though, that she could care for herself. She had lived and worked, and had slowly been making a life for herself. At the moment, that small salve to her ego was in much demand.

"I hadn't seen Taber since," she finished, breathing in deeply. "Not until he jumped out of that damned helicopter and made the situation that much worse. Now if I'm going to get through this, I at least need to understand what the hell is going on, Merinus. I'm terrified because my body is tying me to a man who can destroy me. Who *has* destroyed me."

"Whew." Merinus breathed roughly as she pushed her fingers wearily through her hair.

"What are you going to do?" Merinus asked her. "This doesn't sound like Taber, Roni. I know him. He would have never touched you—period—if he hadn't been dying for you. But his need to protect you would have gone deeper than the hunger driving him. Which could have made him react more hurtfully."

"That excuse doesn't help much." Roni shook her head, knowing that Taber would have indeed been capable of trying desperately to protect her.

He had shown it in the doctor's lab. His voice had been hoarse, his body so tight, so filled with fury on her behalf that he had trembled with her. The tone had been a rumbled, primal sound, the words barely recognizable as he promised her everything he could think of in return for what was being done to her.

"I need to trust in him, Merinus," she whispered painfully. "I need more than some damned addiction to his sperm or his kiss. I need his love…"

Merinus leaned slowly back in her seat. "Surely he's told you." She shook her head. "Roni, he has to love you, otherwise that hormone would not have kicked in as it had. It's more than just a chemical or biological urge. Dr. Martin has tracked that much himself. Hormones that are only released through emotional impulses begin the process in the male, spreading it to the female. He has to love you."

Yeah. Right. That one was easy to believe.

Roni gave her a mocking, half-angry look. "Would I be worried if he had told me he loved me?"

The other woman's eyes narrowed. "Assholes. I swear to God if all men aren't the most hardheaded, stubborn, exceptionally dense assholes. I swear they all need to be…" She jerked as wood exploded mere inches from the side of her face, catching her cheek and temple as it sprayed violently around them.

Shock had no time to rush through Roni's system. Instinct, fear and desperation kicked in all at once.

"Gunfire!" Roni screamed out as she came to her feet, throwing the table out of the way and pushing Merinus to the floor of the porch as fire seared her shoulder. "Taber!" She was screaming his name as hard pings began to vibrate around the porch. "Gunfire!"

It was hell. There was no sound, only the ping ping of the bullets hitting the porch around them, shattering wood, coming much to close to them as they fought to find cover. For a moment, Dawn's warning echoed in her head with savage fury.

Men were screaming now, a roar of a lion echoed in the distance. Lion? Good God, was it one of the Feline Breeds or a real lion? For a moment, hysterical awareness shattered her system at the sound. Who the hell could tell?

Cement splattered inches from her, a hole tearing into the floor as she pushed Merinus deeper into the shadows of the porch and the dubious protection of a woodpile that had been stacked to the side. There wasn't a chance in hell of making it to the door, and from the angle of the gunfire even less chance of making it around the side of the house.

"Taber!" Her screams joined the frantic cries from the yard. "Taber, where are you?"

She fought to cover Merinus, to protect her and the unborn child she knew the other woman carried. Nothing could happen to them. She knew Callan as well as she knew Taber and she knew nothing or no one would be safe in this world if anything happened to the other woman.

"We have one down! One down!"

Roni turned back to look into the yard, watching the workers scatter, one of them hauling a wounded man on his back as they rushed for shelter. There was very little. Dirt and wood was exploding in clumps around them as the silent ping pings turned into deadly explosions.

Gunfire rattled off then. The *rat-a-tat-tat* of automatic weapons, the single sharp bursts of revolvers. And still, wood and cement flew around them as she sheltered Merinus' unconscious body. Oh God, where had she had been hit? She was breathing. At least she was breathing. That was all that mattered.

She could smell her own blood, feel the tearing pain in her shoulder from a bullet, the crawling of her flesh as she lay over Merinus, fighting to keep the deadly little missiles from tearing into Merinus' body, harming her or the child she had spoken of so tenderly.

Men were everywhere, but none close enough, or in position to reach them and drag the other woman to safety. Roni heaved a sobbing breath, screaming out Taber's name again as another volley of gunfire came much too close for comfort. She felt the wood tearing loose from the side of the porch just above her head, raining into her hair as she hunched protectively over the other woman.

"Roni!" Nothing had sounded sweeter than Taber's voice at the moment.

She lifted her head, watching in amazement as he came sailing over the low rock wall that separated the grounds from the outer working area. In his hands he carried a lethal, powerful M-16, spraying a round of gunfire over the heads of the fleeing workmen into the area the enemy fire was coming from.

At the same time, the terrible roar she had heard earlier sounded again. Behind Taber, Callan cleared the fence as well, but he came unarmed, his expression savage, rage echoing through the animalistic roar as he caught sight of his fallen wife.

Simultaneously the back porch became a haven rather than a trap. Feline Breeds, male and female, placed themselves between the porch and danger, guns blasting as Taber and Callan rushed for them. A wall of human bodies, weapons blasting into the forest, a simultaneous neverending sound of warfare that seemed unrelenting, unending.

Taber snatched Roni from her position in a surge of strength that amazed her, keeping her off her feet as he threw them both into the open doorway of the kitchen, skidding across the floor and cushioning her body as he forced her down. Callan was no more than a half second behind him, Merinus' unconscious form cradled in his arms as he bent and ran. He covered the distance with long, powerful legs before going down like a homerun king, all the time, holding his fragile wife from further harm as he slid to the doorway before coming back to his feet in a powerful surge of motion.

"Doc!" Callan's enraged, grief-stricken scream echoed around the house as he seemed to fly by them, his expression horrified, savage.

"Are you hurt?" Taber rushed behind him, half-carrying Roni as he forced her farther into the house.

"No…"

"Fuck, you're lying to me!" He must have seen the blood. "Come on. Downstairs. You'll be safe there."

Safe. Her head was swimming, her shoulder was throbbing like hell and all she wanted to do was have him throw her to the floor now and fuck her until she screamed. She moaned in defeat. At this rate, she would be pregnant before three days were up.

* * * * *

Well, it was official. Morphine didn't ease the mating heat either. But at least the symptoms were a shade more bearable. The good doctor was able to check her shoulder and dress the flesh wound quickly as they all kept a careful eye on Merinus.

The other woman had finally awakened, none the worse for wear. The force of the wood that had hit her temple had merely rendered her unconscious for a while. There was minor bleeding but no complications that the doctor could see.

Callan wasn't listening, though. He sat beside the small hospital gurney, his body hunched over the bed, arms wrapped around his wife as he held onto her protectively. His large hands ran over her tangled hair, her back, the slight mound of her abdomen where, the doctor assured them, the babe rested safe and sound.

His voice was broken, hoarse with emotion as Merinus tried to soothe the fury trembling through his body. Twice she had been forced to whimper, a more than obvious fake sound of pain, to keep him from rushing back outside when news came that the assassins were contained. Two were dead, another was alive but wounded. Doc Martin had not yet moved to treat the mercenary locked in one of the empty supply sheds.

"Matter of priorities," he had said calmly when she asked him about the doctor's oath he had taken. "Besides, if that one dies, there'll be more to take his place."

There was a hatred so unforgiving within the older man that Roni shivered at the force of it.

Taber had said very little. He had held her as her shoulder was bandaged and still hadn't moved but inches from her side as she lay on her stomach, fighting exhaustion and arousal. He smelled too damned good and she was so tired.

"Take your wife to her bed, Callan," Doc finally said wearily as Callan's head rose, his body still trembling in reaction. "She needs to rest. And you need to assure yourself all is fine. The danger is over for now. Same for you, Taber." He turned back to Roni. "Take her upstairs and care for her. Tomorrow is time enough to worry of other things."

Martin's shoulders were slumped, his voice tired and so filled with sadness Roni wanted to weep for him. As he moved away from the bed, Callan rose from the chair he had pulled to Merinus' bed and approached Roni slowly. As she looked into his eyes, she knew this was a man she never wanted to cross.

The golden-brown orbs were almost full amber, glittering with an animal savagery that assured her he wouldn't hesitate to kill.

"I know I can't touch you," he sighed as he approached her, going to one knee in front of her as she stared back at him in surprise. "I know what you did, covering her body with your own. My men were screaming the information at me as I ran for that damned porch. If I could hug you, I would. If I had riches, I would bestow them upon you. If I had anything to show you the gift you gave me in saving her life, then it would be yours. If you hadn't dragged her to safety I would have lost her forever."

His voice was soft, throbbing with all the pent-up emotion that he was fighting.

"Morphine's a great little drug," she whispered conspiratorially, lying through her teeth. "I didn't even feel a twinge when the doc dressed the wound. You can hug me if you need to."

A small smile tilted his lips, involuntary and chastising. "You are still the little imp you always were," he told her gently, shaking his finger at her. "I know better. I could smell your pain as the doctor worked on you, and it flayed my soul to know that it had happened. She would have been defenseless..." He swallowed tightly.

"She's fine." Roni knew she was feeling a little giddy from the drugs when she gave Callan a mock frown. "But I want a gun now. I know how to use it."

"It's yours." He nodded firmly, not even bothering to glance at Taber to be certain, as she had expected. "Side arm or rifle?"

She felt a thrill of satisfaction. "Rifle. Like Taber's."

Taber groaned behind her.

"Lessons," Callan muttered, shaking his head at her. "Let Taber teach you the use of it and it's yours. If you like, you can pick your own."

He rose to his feet then, a small smile lighting his eyes. "Just don't shoot Taber, huh? He has his good points."

"I'm sure he does," she drawled. "I just haven't found them yet. I promise to look harder before making a firm decision to take his head off, though."

"Thanks, buddy," Taber retorted sarcastically to Callan. "Appreciate the help and all."

Callan winced. "Yeah. Welcome ole son." He smothered his laughter as he looked over her head at Taber. "I have confidence in you, though. I'm sure you can convince her to let you live, at least for a while yet."

Taber snorted, but by then Roni was bored with their male amusement.

"I need a bath." She eased herself from the bed, testing the strength of her legs, which really wasn't so good at the moment. "And food. I need food. Pizza is definitely called for in this situation."

Taber scooped her up in his arms, his grip fierce as he strode quickly from the room.

"I can walk," she sighed, wrapping her arms around his shoulders, enjoying the brief respite from her worries that the drugs had provided.

"Of course you can." He glanced down at her, his lips much too distracting as they curved up into a smile. "But I like carrying you."

He had always carried her, every chance he had, she remembered. He had carried her when he first found her, huddled in the night, terrified of the sounds of darkness and the men who had run her from her home. Every chance after that, he had carried her whenever the opportunity presented itself.

"Do you have any idea how good you feel in my arms?" he asked her as he strode quickly up the stairs into the suite he claimed as his own.

He kicked the door closed behind him, but didn't make it to the bedroom. He collapsed on the couch, his arms still firm and hard around her as he lowered his head, his lips covering hers demandingly.

Roni wasn't willing to just be a participant this time. She had faced death earlier. Had faced the knowledge that at any moment, she or Taber could cease to exist. She wasn't willing to fight the needs clamoring in her body. Or those in her heart.

She rose in his arms, ignoring his little growl of warning until she was straddling him, staring into his surprised gaze.

"Mine!" Her whisper, despite its softness, resonated with the sense of possessiveness and power filling her now.

His eyes flared. The jade-green color darkening, the pupils expanding as her fingers went to the buttons of his bloodstained shirt. The cotton, though she was sure it was soft enough, rasped her palms as she smoothed it across his shoulders then down to the first button. It slipped free easily.

"Roni." He swallowed tightly, emotion echoing thick and intense through his hoarse voice.

"You marked me," she told him softly, determined. "But you didn't mark me the day you placed your mouth on my neck, Taber. You marked me when I was eleven years old and you carried me to safety. When I was sixteen and you arranged my first birthday party. When you placed that little, all too innocent kiss against my lips. You marked me a little more every time I saw you, every time you touched me. Now, I'm going to mark you."

She smoothed his shirt back from his chest, over his broad shoulders, and laid her mouth at the point where his shoulder and neck met. There, in the thick, pulsing muscle, she bit him. Not enough to draw blood, just enough that his body tightened, his hips arching and grinding his cock into the cradle of her thighs as his hands gripped her hips with bruising strength.

She bit down, laved the area she held in her grip with her tongue, suckled it deeply, repeated the erotic, sexually charged caress he had given her so many years ago. The effect on him was no different than it had been for her, it seemed.

He tore the shirt from her back as her attention stayed on the tight flesh she caressed with a force that would vary between pain and pleasure. He shredded the cloth then pulled it from her body before his fingers moved to her snug jeans.

"Take them off." His voice was feral, rumbling, as he pushed the material over her hips, midway over the curve of her buttocks.

Roni murmured a soft sound of pleasure as his hands pushed beneath the jeans, cupping her rounded flesh, his fingers flexing against the firm muscle as he moved her roughly against his jeans-covered cock.

She wasn't in a hurry, and she had no intention of allowing him to rush her. She needed to touch him, to taste him, to know he was safe and in her arms and that this wasn't just another desperate dream.

"You're killing me." He was panting for breath now, his head tilted to the side, giving her complete access to the strong line of his throat.

Roni realized she had never felt as confident or strong, sexually, as she did at that moment. He was helpless beneath her touch. Rough groans vibrated from his throat, every muscle tense, his erection grinding desperately against the cloth that shielded her hot, damp pussy.

Her nails raked over his chest, the corded planes of his abdomen then back to his tight, hard male nipples. When she was satisfied she had left at least a small mark on his tough skin, she released the flesh she held then ran her tongue slowly along his neck. She nipped him lightly under the hard line of his jaw, then licked her way down his throat, feeling the flexing of his skin as he swallowed tightly.

"I love your taste." She moved back from the erotic, mind-destroying movements of his cock pressing into her sex. "So wild and untamed. Can I tame you, Taber?"

A short, sharp laugh, devoid of humor, was an exclamation of primal lust as he fought to answer her. "You already have. Years ago."

"Mmm. My own wildcat. Can I stroke you? Or will you devour me before I can show you all the ways I've dreamed of pleasing you?"

His eyes were heavy-lidded, glowing with such a staggering heat it warmed every corner of her soul. For now, this small place in time, nothing or no one existed in Taber's world but her. She nearly climaxed from the heady knowledge that she held such power over him.

"Show me," he whispered, though his voice was as tormented as any man's could be.

She gave him a slow, deliberately provocative smile as she gazed at him from beneath lowered lids. Watching him carefully, challengingly, she rose slowly from his lap, ignoring the bestial sound of protest he made.

"Stay there," she told him softly as he moved to stand as well.

Taber leaned back against the couch as she instructed, but she could see his muscles flexing, everything inside him demanding that he take her now.

"Oh, so controlled," she murmured, pleased. "I wonder how long you can hold on to all that power."

"Not long." His fists were clenched at his sides as his gaze followed her hands.

Roni slid the straps of her bra carefully over her shoulders, fighting back any fear or modesty that would have held her back from the enjoyment of this moment. He had seen her naked more than once, and evidently the sight didn't displease him.

He licked his lips, the movement slow, hungry, as she reached back, unclipped the lacy fabric and drew it away from her swollen breasts.

Her nipples were erect and hard, pleading for his touch. Roni touched them instead. Watching him, she gripped them between her thumbs and forefingers, tugging at them, massaging them as she watched his gaze darken further, his expression becoming heavy with the intensity of his arousal.

"I can do that." He swallowed tightly.

"I know you can," she agreed, her breath catching as a bolt of sensation shot from her nipples to her cunt. "Take your jeans off, Taber. Let me see if I arouse you." He began to rise. "No. Don't stand up. Remove them while you watch me."

He hesitated, obviously fighting for breath, for control. Roni lowered her hands from her nipples, smoothing her palms down her stomach until they came to the loosened front of her jeans.

Quickly, Taber loosened his own. She smiled back at him, loving the game they were playing, wondering who would lose control first. She pushed at the material, allowing them to slide leisurely from her thighs, then down her legs. She kicked the material from her feet, her mouth drying out as she watched Taber do the same.

She had made an error in judgment. Each time they had come together she hadn't had time to truly look at the amazing organ that brought her to such pinnacles of pleasure. But now she did.

It rose to his navel, nearly as thick as her wrist, as bronzed as the rest of his body and throbbing with a life of its own. The mushroom-shaped head was tapered for maximum penetration, flowing to a wider base and heavily veined shaft. No wonder he drove her crazy with the edge of pain that followed the rapturous pleasure. His cock, like his body, was built for endurance, and right now, she wanted nothing more than to endure its presence within her steamy cunt.

But she was going to wait. Taber stared at her with a challenge glowing in his eyes as his fingers wrapped around the erect stalk. Roni licked her lips as he massaged himself, his fingers stroking from the heavy hood to the base of the shaft.

"Come here," he whispered, his voice dark, rich with sexual demand.

"No," she drawled softly as she went to her knees before him. "I told you, Taber. I want to stroke you."

"Damn." He jerked in reaction as she leaned forward, her tongue licking over the hot head of his erection.

His hips flexed, driving it against her lips as a strangled groan ripped from his chest.

"Roni. God. Baby." His chest was rising and falling violently with the force of his breathing. Perspiration gleamed on the powerful muscles, making his skin look satiny, warm and vibrant.

She licked the head of his cock again, slowly, easily, watching his eyes, his expression as he grimaced in rising need. The sharp canines at the sides of his mouth gleamed wickedly, giving him a decidedly sexy, dangerous appearance.

"Roni, I won't make it," he panted, his voice tight, regretful, tortured. "I'm going to lose my control, baby. I can't stand it."

"Can't you?" She brushed his fingers out of the way, her own hand attempting to surround the burgeoning flesh of his cock. "Poor baby. Then how will you handle this?" Her mouth covered the thick head, stretching over it, sucking him inside as her tongue began to rub, stroke and tease the ultra-sensitive, hard throb of flesh just beneath the hooded crown.

The throttled, animalistic growl that tore from his throat had her womb clenching, her sex flooding with moisture and heat. The man within had always stayed in control, had always maintained a delicate balance in their sexual encounters. Roni knew she was tempting, daring the animal to break free. And she couldn't wait to show him he had met his match in her.

She was beautiful. There were no other words to describe the soft glow of passion in Roni's blue eyes, the flush of need on her cheeks, her reddened lips stretching around his erection. Too beautiful. Too damned innocent and too hot for what she was tempting. But there was no way in hell he was going to push her away.

He kept his hands bunched into the cushions of the couch, his eyes narrowed as she watched him with a siren's gaze, his body tortured as her tongue continued to tempt the primal barb hidden just under the skin into revealing itself.

He could feel the presence of the unnatural extension. It throbbed, pulsed, fought to be free even as he fought to hold it back. God, he wanted it to last forever. From the seductive, lingering caresses of her mouth, it appeared she did as well. There was no frantic suckling, no indication that she wasn't enjoying every second of touching him, as he did touching her.

"Oh yeah," he moaned as her tongue rimmed beneath the flared head, stroking and probing, learning every curve and rise of his straining flesh. "Good, baby, so good."

He flexed his hips, pushing his flesh farther into her mouth. Her moan vibrated around it, her fingers tightening as her tongue flattened and stroked what she could of his turgid cock.

Heat surrounded him. Moist, slick heat. Her tongue was like a silken demon running rampant, her lips a snug, gripping pleasure. Heaven, because nothing had ever felt so good. Hell, because the fight to restrain the explosion building in his scrotum was nearly more than he could bear.

"Damn, Roni." He could feel the sweat building on his skin as snaking fingers of pleasure wrapped around his cock and the tightened sac beneath it. Tingles of sensation chased up his spine, enclosing his scalp with static sensitivity.

He groaned weakly as her lips dragged back up the small amount of flesh she held in her mouth, caressing over the head then leaving it entirely as her tongue swirled over the tip. Taber pushed up to her mouth, groaning with the need to have her envelop him again.

The little tease. Her teeth scraped gently, adding a sharper sensation, but no less pleasurable before her tongue laved over it again. He couldn't stand it. His cock was throbbing like a wound, his scrotum tightening, pulsating with the need to release the built up sperm. Beneath the head of his erection, the barb flexed, desperate to lock inside the hot depths of her pussy as he spilled his seed.

But not yet. He wasn't ready to come yet. He wanted to feel her mouth again. Hot, liquid fire, her tongue a stroke of seductive agony. Taber lifted his hands to her head, fingers spearing into her hair, gripping the silken strands, relishing the dominance of his hold on her.

He stared into her challenging gaze, his own narrowing as the man willingly gave over to the animal in that single, undefined second. She was his mate. She could challenge him, tempt him, but he was too close to the edge for her teasing little games now. The flare of excitement in her gaze and her expression assured him that it affected her just as deeply.

"Suck it." The hard growl accompanied the slow slide of his cock back in her mouth. She enclosed it firmly, willingly, though she strained against his hold just enough to satisfy the need he had to maintain the edge of dominance.

She moaned again. The sound echoed around the portion of his erection trapped within her mouth, causing the entire shaft to pulse, the hidden barb to press closer to revealing itself.

Spearing shards of pleasure shot into his balls as the muscles of his abdomen clenched in spasmodic reaction. Sweet heaven. He fucked slowly into her mouth, holding her hair in a firm grip, relishing the snug drag of her lips, the flickering whip of her tongue. And all the while, he watched her. Watched her eyes darken, her cheeks hollowing out, her lips sliding over his cock.

"Oh yeah. There you go, baby," he groaned as he rocked slowly back and forth, every muscle in his body tightening as he fought his release. "Suck it, Roni. Suck it deeper, baby."

He pushed back, filling her mouth, fighting not to breach her barrier of comfort in taking him. Her tongue flattened further along his cock, rasping tissue so sensitive he wanted to roar with the pleasure of it.

Her moan of protest as he slid a bit too far had him pulling back in regret. She could take more. He knew she could. God help him, he needed her to.

"Breathe through your nose. Relax." He panted roughly, staring down into her wide eyes, gauging if it was fear or excitement lighting them. He prayed he was right and it was excitement.

He felt the hot depths of her mouth relax marginally, her tongue losing a bit of its desperate tension.

"Yesss," he hissed in pleasure. "You can take more, Roni. Just relax, baby. Relax." He slid slowly inside her mouth as he chanted the word to her.

She took the smallest amount more. Enough to have him shaking, shivering in quaking pleasure as he watched his shaft sliding into her mouth. God, how much more could he stand?

"More." His demand was rough, rough enough that for an immeasurable second he fought the need rioting through him.

Then he sank in further, nearly to the convulsive swallowing at the entrance of her throat. There he was. God yes. That was it. He couldn't see his cock fucking into her mouth now, but the sensations of it were so extreme he decided he could do without it.

He rested his head on the back of the couch, fucking her mouth with short desperate strokes as the suckling moist sound of it enclosing him had him groaning with each breath, fighting his orgasm with everything inside him.

"Roni," he whispered desperately, unable to hold back the words, the sensations tearing through him. "God, yes. Suck it. Suck me, baby, just like that."

He could smell her heat now. She was so aroused the sweet, earthy scent of her lust wrapped around his senses, drowning him in it. Her moans were another caress on his cock. Her fingers gripping him, stroking the shaft, were pushing him past his limits of control. The barb was a fierce, agonizing throb that he knew he couldn't hide forever. But not yet. He didn't want her to know. Didn't want to chance her fear and disgust.

"Enough." He pulled her back, ignoring her protesting cry, fighting his own need to surge back inside the exquisite heat. The moist clamp of her mouth was paradise, but he knew it was one he could not yet fully enjoy.

"Taber." Her voice was a thready, needy sound that had his erection twitching in barbaric demand.

"Fuck me, Roni." She was kissing his abdomen, her tongue licking as he held her back from the surging strength of his cock. "Now. Damn it, I can't wait, baby…"

He pulled her back into his lap, spreading her legs over his, lifting her, holding her close, then pushing her relentlessly down onto his raging cock.

"Ah, God." His cry joined hers as he worked the thick shaft into the ultra tight recess of her blistering pussy. "Hot. So hot. So sweet and slick." He pushed deeper, holding her as she arched in his arms, fighting to take more, her cry echoing through the dim room.

Her cunt was a vise of slippery, flexing, torturous pleasure. The muscles clamped on him, fighting to accept him, to relax around the girth spreading them apart. Nothing had ever been so erotic, so filled with lust and tempestuous sexuality.

"Take it," he growled, pressing her closer, feeling the protesting tissue grip and convulse as she fought to accept him. "All of it, Roni. Now. Take it, baby."

He thrust harder inside her, spearing into her, feeling her pussy part, take, accept, until he had buried every throbbing, desperate inch of his cock inside the fist-tight grip of her suddenly shuddering, exploding cunt.

It was too much. Too much heat, too much need welling up inside him, tormenting him. He heard his own cry shattering the air, felt the emergence of the barb, the scalding pulse of his semen, and died in her arms. There was no other way to explain it. His soul exploded with the tip with his cock, spewing out an emotion, a need, a compulsive hunger as thick, hot and life-giving as the semen winging its way to her fertile, hungry womb.

Chapter Eight

"When are you going to tell me what's wrong with your cock?" The lazy tone of Roni's voice didn't fool him for a minute. He could hear the steely determination in her voice that had marked more than half his conversations with her over the years. The word "cock" whispering so seductively from her lips had that particular portion of his anatomy twitching in interest.

"Hmm, you didn't seem to think anything was wrong with it when you were screaming and clawing at me earlier," he grunted as he glanced down the line of his body, frowning at it in disapproval, as though that would somehow ease the effect of her words.

"Don't try to distract me, Taber." She was draped halfway across his chest, her breath a warm caress against his skin, stirring senses better left resting for the time being.

He had hoped to still this conversation for a while yet. He could pretend male outrage, he figured. It wasn't every day a man was accused of having a problem with that particular portion of his anatomy. But he had a feeling Roni wouldn't be fooled. His instincts warned him to step lightly where this subject was concerned, or at least in his deliberate attempts to avoid it.

"When are you going to go to sleep?" he mumbled, ignoring her question as he lay back on his pillow and closed his eyes, determined to sleep himself.

"You didn't answer me." Her voice was reflective, the very softness of it warning him that soon it would breach the anger point.

Her temper was like lightning, striking fast and hard, but rarely lingering. That first hard strike was rarely comfortable though, and he would prefer not to tempt it now, while he was lying there lazy and replete from loving her.

Her fingers danced over his chest, her nails scraping lightly, the pads of her fingers feeling, he knew, the tiny hairs that covered his body. Nearly invisible, soft as down, the light pelt was yet another reminder of his DNA.

Taber opened his eyes, staring at the ceiling as he breathed in deeply. How many years had he longed just for one day to forget who and what he was? Yet the knowledge was always there, never far enough away to give him the ease he often prayed for. And now, Roni needed answers, which he was more than reluctant to give her just yet. He didn't know if he was ready to face the possible consequences and her horror of learning just how closely he resembled the animal his genetics had been mixed with.

"I know I didn't answer you," he finally said softly, curving his arm under her body so his fingers could play absently with the long waves of silken, golden hair.

He loved her hair. It was thick and soft, curling gently around her shoulders and framing her heart-shaped face seductively. He noticed with distant amazement that it was rather comforting to smooth it between his fingers, to feel the cool, gentle weight of it.

She was comforting. She always had been. She could still the rage and the nightmares inside him as no one else ever had. Her laughter lit up his world, and each touch from her, even as a child, as innocent as her touches had been, had been filled with caring and warmth.

"Are you going to?" Taber glanced over as she sat up in the bed, pulling her hair free of his fingers as she tucked the sheet around her until she could shield her full, naked breasts.

His lips quirked at her modesty. He knew every inch of her body, yet still she would blush the prettiest pink if he saw her nude while not engaged in their lusty play. The pressing subject of her sudden need for answers weighed on him, though. Answers he had no intention of giving her yet.

"Let it go." He sighed deeply, moving to rise from the bed. Dammit, he wasn't sleepy. He was fooling himself thinking he could rest now. "I need to check security outside..."

"You're avoiding the question now, Taber," she snapped, her eyes glittering with blue fire as he glanced back at her.

She sat on her knees, watching as he moved to the bottom of the bed. He was more than aware that by refusing to answer her, rather than feigning ignorance, was a dangerous proposition. He could avoid her questions, but he'd be damned if he would lie in response to them. He had little else to give her but honesty, in those areas where he could answer at all.

"Guess you're right." He shrugged, trying to appear unconcerned, to hide the aching loneliness that rose in the pit of his soul.

She had every right to know the answer, and yet, he couldn't bring himself to say the words, to explain to her the animal that found such satisfaction in the tight depths of her rippling pussy.

"And you think you're just going to walk out of here with no explanation?" she asked him, her voice rising with anger and an edge of hurt.

Taber stared back at her, steeling himself against her pain. She needed so much more to hold on to than she was being given, and he knew it. Everything in her life had been stripped away from her in one blow. Her home, her job, a chance to be free and safe, and he couldn't even give her answers. There was no fairness in it, and yet neither could he bring himself to fix it.

"Let it go, Roni." He padded to the bathroom door, intending to pull a change of clothes from the walk-in closet in the other room.

As he reached the bathroom door, with no warning whatsoever, the shattering of a crystal bowl from the nightstand had him stopping in disbelief. The dim lights of the room gleamed dully on the crystal shards, mocking him with his belief that she would have allowed him to walk away so easily. If nothing else, his Roni could be a tempestuous little spitfire. Had she been Feline, she would have made a perfect wildcat mix.

"You leave this room and I'll take your head off with the next one," she snarled.

His cock leapt to life. Taber glanced down at the heavy erection with a sense of resigned amusement. It said a lot about a man who got a hard-on from such an event. It said even less about him that his female's rage could trigger it. Damn. He wanted nothing more than to turn around, go back to that bed and fuck her silly. His skin itched with the need. In a single second every cell in his body was screaming for hard, driving sex.

He turned back to her, watching her broodingly as he crossed his arms over his chest. Her gaze flickered to his erection, and damned if she didn't blush again. That added color only seemed to make him harder.

She had moved from the bed. In one hand she clutched the sheet to her chest, in the other she held the matching bowl from his nightstand. Evidently the state of his arousal held no bearing on her determination for answers. It figured.

"You know, those came with the house," he sighed, nodding at the small, decorative item. "I imagine they cost quite a bit."

"Who gives a damn?" She was spitting mad now. "I'm sick of you running out on me, Taber. I'll be damned if I'll be tied to you while you waltz on your merry way, avoiding me whenever you feel like it."

He watched her in amazement. Emotion, thick and hot, colored her voice while her eyes snapped with fury and stubbornness. Her slender body vibrated with emotion, her frown darkening her brow, thinning her full, luscious lips. She was tempting him to mount her there and then.

"I have never run out on you, Roni..." Her words finally sank past his lust-crazed brain and in the next second, his eyes widened as he jumped out of the way of her next flying missile. "Son of a bitch, Roni."

He sprinted toward her, jerking her back from the heavy candlestick that sat on the table as well. His arms wrapped around her waist, pulling her against him, restraining the violence he could feel shuddering through her body.

"What the hell's wrong with you?" He released her as he tossed her to the bed, but he didn't attempt to follow her. He was tired of this. Tired of the fury that filled her—the distrust, the shadows that haunted her eyes. "I'm sick to damned hell of you accusing me of leaving you when it was your own decision to break off whatever relationship was beginning."

She scrambled across the bed, landing on her feet on the other side. Better, he thought. The further she was from him, the more of his common sense he seemed able to maintain.

"Oh, come on, Taber, I never took you for a liar, too," she yelled back, a sneer on her lips. Something else he was tired of, that sneer. Condescending, offending. "Stop playing so innocent. You don't have to pretend with me. Not here while we're alone. The only reason I'm here is because of this damned mark you put on my neck. Otherwise, I'd still be sitting in Sandy Hook wondering why the hell you changed your mind so quickly."

He stilled, his instincts kicking in as logic began to take over. What couldn't be understood must be examined. Studied, stalked or hunted. And he sure as hell didn't understand this.

"Why *I* changed *my* mind?" he asked her carefully, his chest tightening at the pain that had been reflected in her voice and her expression. It came much too close to the pain he had felt when he received her letter, mere hours after he had placed that mark on her neck.

And yet, by her own furious words, she believed he had broken off the relationship, new as it had been, himself. Roni wasn't a liar. She didn't play games and she didn't pass the blame on something she was responsible for herself.

His body had been a mess that day, he admitted. Arousal unlike anything he had ever known, a hard-on damned near strong enough to split his jeans, and here came Dayan with…he stopped. Dayan. Son of a bitch. He wiped his hand across his face, staring over at her, fighting a betrayal he had prayed had been over with the death of his brother.

Dayan's determination to destroy the rest of them had nearly killed Merinus and the child she now carried. His death was too well remembered. His betrayal burned too deeply into Taber's brain to discount his senses. Dayan had lied. And Taber had fallen for it.

"Don't answer that." He hated the hoarse, tired sound of his own voice as he stalked over to his dresser.

He opened the middle drawer, pushing back several thick envelopes and a few mementos. In the back, near the corner, was a small wooden box. He removed it, flipped it open and removed the folded square of paper.

I'm quitting the garage and you, Taber. I've realized, after that scene in the truck, how easily you'll try to take me over. I won't be a puppet for you any longer. You're too blunt, too crude, too rough. I need someone who touches me softly. Someone I don't have to be frightened of. Someone closer to my own age. You'll be old while I'm still young, and I just don't want to deal with it. Please afford me the courtesy of staying the hell away from me. That's surely not too much to ask! Roni

He had the letter memorized. He was barely eight years older than she was, but at times, it felt like centuries.

"Read this." He handed her the letter, watching her confused expression closely.

Taber kept his gaze locked with hers as she took the folded square, watching her closer, his soul bleeding. Instinctively, he knew she hadn't written that letter now. Knew that the past three hellish years, needing her, aching for her until he thought he would die from the need, had all been for nothing.

She unfolded the letter, her gaze moving to the words. Her eyes widened. Her lips trembled. The pain that crossed her expression tore at his soul.

"I thought I was respecting your wishes, Roni," he whispered, feeling wearier now than he had in years. Dayan had been a trusted, much loved member of the family. "I will assume you received a letter as well, since I know Dayan's only true gift was that of forgery."

She crumpled the note in her hand, tears shining in her eyes, spiking her lashes as her gaze returned to his.

"I didn't write this," she whispered bleakly, trembling. "But I received one as well." A fine shudder rippled over her body as she stared back at him. "It was your handwriting." She looked at the letter again, her breath hitching as she fought a sob, realizing as Taber did, just how close to her handwriting that letter was.

"And I didn't write you one, either," he said gently. "I was fighting desperately to give you time to think, to know what we were about to do was what you wanted. I knew what I was, Roni. I knew the danger I was putting you in. I was trying to be certain, beyond all doubt, that I could protect you if somehow my existence was revealed to the Council. As far as they knew, I was long dead. I had all intentions of returning to you."

"When you didn't show up, I waited." There was so much pain, so much regret in the dark depths of her eyes that he wanted to scream out in rejection of such misery. He had fought for so long to protect her, only to have one he considered his brother deal her the final blow to her confidence. "The next morning, he brought the letter. He pushed me against the wall with his body..." She broke off painfully, swallowing tightly before continuing. "He offered to train me for you."

Rage ate at his soul and Taber knew that if Dayan weren't dead then he would have killed him personally for daring to touch Roni in any manner, let alone saying anything so hurtful to her. He remembered well the bright dreams, the need and emotion that sparkled in her eyes when she looked at him all those years ago. That letter, and Dayan's attack, had nearly destroyed a part of her soul.

Taber reached out, unable to keep from touching her, from needing her. God, he needed her like he needed to breathe. Or worse. His fingers smoothed over her satiny cheek, his thumb caressing her lips. She had the softest lips he had ever known, and eyes that pierced every corner of his soul with sunlight when she was happy. Yet when she hurt, as she did now, it was like a knife plunging into his chest.

"I would have given my life to be with you that night," he swore, knowing it was no more than the truth. "At the same time, the Council's mercenaries were moving in on Callan, and rather than let that rage loose where you might see it, I let it loose on them instead. I should have come to you." He had known that then. It had taken all he had at the time not to do exactly that. "I should have fought for what I knew was mine."

A tear slid down her cheek. "I loved you," she whispered, breaking his heart with the aching emotion in her voice. "I still love you, but I'm not pleased with you, Taber."

His hand dropped as she moved away from him, frowning in surprise. "I had no idea you hadn't written that letter, Roni," he argued.

"Oh not that," she snapped as she tossed the wadded-up ball of paper across the room before casting him a dark look. "I'm as guilty as you are in letting that bastard trick me." She turned back to him, the anger slowly returning. "I haven't forgotten my original question, and don't you think I have. Fine, we were tricked. We'll deal with it. But we have other things to deal with as well. I'll ask you once again. What happens to your cock when you climax? And I want to know now."

Thankfully, blessedly, strange as that thought was, the security alarms began to blare.

"Get dressed." He picked her up quickly, ignoring her gasp of surprise as he strode around the glass by the bathroom door and carried her to the walk-in closet.

"What the hell is that?" she yelled over the din of the sirens, catching the clothing he threw her way as he jerked his own jeans and T-shirt from their hangers.

They dressed in seconds, pulling on leather sneakers then rushing from the room. Taber worriedly eyed the revolver she insisted on carrying. To be honest, he wouldn't blame her, or be surprised if she turned it on him. And he knew damned good and well her aim was almost fucking perfect. He had taught her how to shoot himself.

Chapter Nine

"Can't a man even come visit his goddamned daughter without being attacked? She's my kid, I have a right to know if she's alive or not."

Roni flinched as her father's booming voice echoed up to her, coarse and blustering, causing her to come to an abrupt dead stop halfway down the stairs that led to the entrance hall. Taber stopped behind her, still and silent, watching her carefully.

She was too tense, almost frightened, wary. Like a deer sensing danger but not certain which direction it was coming from.

Reginald Andrews was one of the worst fathers Taber had ever known. His only saving grace, the only reason he still lived, was the fact that he had never laid a hand on Roni. Otherwise, Taber would have killed him years ago.

"Mr. Andrews, that doesn't explain why you were trying to sneak into the grounds. Why not just press the call button on the gates?" Callan's voice was as cold and crisp as a winter night. He was flat furious.

Reginald was, as always, making excuses. Loudly.

Taber watched as Roni drew in a deep hard breath. He could almost feel the distaste that filled her and the reluctance that held her still and silent. But he could sense more than that. The morass of emotions that seemed to rush from her overwhelmed him, made him move closer to her, determined to protect her.

He laid one hand at her waist, leaning close to her, his chin settling against her shoulder. "We could go back to the room.

Ignore him. If you don't go down there, Callan will take it as silent permission to have the bastard thrown out."

He whispered the words so softly that only she heard him. He kept his body close enough to be certain his warmth and silent security enfolded her. He would protect her, no matter what it took.

She swallowed tightly and he could literally feel her fighting for the strength to face the man raging in the hallway.

"No." She finally shook her head as she reached back, tucking the revolver he had given her into the waistband of her jeans. "I'll deal with him."

But she didn't want to. Taber was getting the distinct impression that there was something about her father that literally terrified her now. Before he could question her about it, she was moving gracefully down the stairs, her hand retaining a light grip on the balustrade, her shoulders straight and erect. As regal as a princess and so determined to be strong it brought a lump to his throat, made him want to shelter her that much more.

"Why are you here, Reginald?" She had to raise her voice to be heard over his furious tirade concerning the welfare of his beloved only child. The sound of it made Taber sick.

Reginald had aged severely in the time since Taber had last seen him. His dark hair was almost fully gray and thinning. He tried to make up for that fact by growing one side longer than the other and combing it over the opposite side, giving him an off center, clownish appearance.

His brown eyes were dull, his cheeks ruddy from drink and overweight. He was barely six feet tall, and not nearly as muscular as he had been even five years before.

As Roni stepped into the entry hall, all eyes turned to her. The Feline Breeds filling the marbled entrance to the house were on alert, their hands on their weapons, their eyes sharp and missing not a move that the older man made.

"Roni." Reginald's smile was more calculating than loving.

Callan had noticed it as well, if the narrow-eyed look of dislike was anything to go by.

Taber watched him closely, seeing the flash of hatred the other man tried to hide as he glanced at his daughter. Taber moved quickly then to insinuate himself between Reginald and Roni, every instinct inside him screaming out that he protect her from whatever threat her father represented.

Roni stopped as he stepped in front of her, confronting her father rather than allowing her to.

"Taber." She laid her hand on his arm as he pressed it back, stilling her attempt to move in front of him.

At his movement, the others stepped into protective positions as well, their eyes narrowing on Reginald, hands now gripping their weapons in preparation.

"Why are you here, Reggie?" Taber didn't bother with the formalities. Roni was upset, his own instincts were kicking into overdrive, and he would be damned if he would allow it to continue.

"Well, she's my daughter." Reginald's voice softened, but he couldn't hide the stench of his own lies. He wasn't there to assure himself of Roni's safety, which made him an immediate threat to her.

"Fine time to remember that," Taber growled, making certain to show the canines that he knew would gleam menacingly at the sides of his mouth. He was pleased to see a bit of the ruddy color dim in the other man's face as he paled at the sight. "I don't remember it bothering you overmuch before."

"I can handle Reginald, Taber." Roni pushed at his heavy body, attempting to get him to move aside. There was no going around him as the other Breeds had aligned themselves in a way that would keep her clearly out of the other man's reach.

"Taber, you should at least let me see my little girl." Reginald's voice was too soft, too intentionally non-threatening for Taber's peace of mind.

"Taber, dammit, I can handle this." Roni kicked his shin. And it sure as hell wasn't a love pat. The damned woman had dangerous feet.

He turned back to look at her warningly.

"Don't you give me that look," she snapped, frowning back at him in determination. "Get out of my way so I can deal with this, then you can send him packing."

She was going to kick him again and he knew it, he could see it in her eyes. Damn, he loved it when she got physical with him. He smiled at her. A slow baring of his teeth, a sexual reminder of retaliation. He was pleased to see the slight widening of her eyes, the ripple of response that was barely detectable, the scent of sweet, clean arousal that suddenly bloomed from her body.

He stepped back slowly, his arm going behind her, his hand clasping her hip to be sure she stayed close and well out of reach of the threat he was sensing.

She had tucked her gun in the small of her back, anchoring it in the waistband of her jeans. She was taking no chances, and it infuriated him that her father could make her feel so threatened.

"Hmphf. I can see you're getting along fine." Reginald couldn't hide the small telltale hint of vindictive displeasure in his voice. The insult that had Taber flexing his muscles in preparation to take the bastard apart, limb by limb.

"Broke already?" she asked him softly. Her voice was smooth and mocking, but Taber sensed the anger he could feel building inside her.

Reginald grunted. "They burned the house. Your mom's pictures, the quilts, everything's gone."

Roni flinched noticeably. Taber speared the man with a look that promised retribution, a rumbling growl of warning sounding from his chest. He was deliberately hurting her now, choosing his words carefully, striking where she was most tender. Reginald eyed him warily.

"You used to be nicer than this, Taber," he sighed as though the reception he was receiving disappointed him.

"And you used to be smarter than this, Reggie," Taber retorted softly, barely restraining his violence. If only he could figure out why the other man was sending his instincts off the scales, then he would feel more comfortable. "You've seen her. She's fine. You can leave now."

"Roni, you gonna let them throw me out?" Reginald turned to his daughter, the whine in his voice grating on Taber's ears. "Things are real tough right now. With our pictures flashing all over the television screens and your association with this..." Reginald paused insultingly, "...man being reported all over the world. I can't even get a decent job from the old sources anymore."

The "old sources" no doubt being illegal.

"You should have spent your last payment more wisely, Reginald." She tried to sound unfeeling, cool under pressure, but Taber could hear the pain in her voice. "This isn't my home. Mine burned to the ground. Remember? I have no right to determine who stays and who goes."

Reginald cast Callan a calculating look. "You gonna throw her daddy out on the street? You know how much trouble this has caused me, Callan?"

Callan watched Roni as closely as Taber did.

"You have family," Roni reminded her father almost desperately. "I'll give you the money, Reginald..." She stopped. Taber could hear her breathing in harshly. "I don't have my purse, but I'll call the bank. I'll get you the money..."

"No, Roni honey, you know none of those brothers of mine are going to let me bed down in their fancy-assed houses. You know how they always turned their backs on us."

It was no less than the truth. Just as it was no less than Reginald's own fault that his family had literally disowned him.

"The house is full at present, Reginald." Callan finally stepped forward. "We can put you up at the barracks on the other side of the house grounds. There are a few empty bunks there."

Reginald's gaze never left Roni's. He stared at her the way a snake did an intended meal. Cold, deliberate, unflinching.

"That's right friendly of you, Callan," he finally said softly. Taber felt a chill chase down his back as Roni stilled a flinch.

She was frightened. He could feel it, almost smell it radiating from her body. She tensed, holding herself rigidly erect as she stared back at her father.

"Don't make trouble here, Reginald," she finally warned him, her voice low, resonating with throttled anger. "I won't be held responsible for what they do to you if you try to."

Taber looked down at her, holding back his surprise. He had never heard Roni threaten anyone other than him personally. And certainly never her wayward, mercenary father.

"Why, Roni, shame on you, making these good people think I'd cause trouble." He hadn't even blinked at he stared at her. "You know I'm a right social person. They won't have a peep of trouble out of me."

Taber tensed at the veiled threat directed at Roni. It pulsed in the air around them and caused the fine hairs on the back of Taber's neck to lift and bristle in response.

Taber wanted to order the son of a bitch off the estate, cast him out into the streets and tell him to fend for himself. As long as Roni had been old enough to hold down a part-time job the bastard had leeched every penny she could make. There had been no protecting her from him then, but by God, he could do it now.

"Escort Mr. Andrews to the workers' bunk shed, Merc," Callan ordered one of the burly guards.

Mercury was six and a half feet of muscle with a face so closely resembling that of a cat that there was no way the man could walk down a public street without inciting riotous panic among the citizens now. He was stern, cold, a killing machine and one of the most loyal, honorable men Taber had ever known.

"He can have the bunk nearest mine." Thin lips spread into a cold smile as eerie amber eyes glittered with cold knowledge. Merc wasn't a fool.

"We need to talk soon, Roni." Reginald smiled thinly as Merc gripped his arm firmly. "Catch up on things, ya know?"

"I think we said enough last week, Reginald," she answered him firmly, her voice cold enough to chill an iceberg. "Enjoy your stay. But I doubt I'll have time to visit."

"You might want to make time." Reginald tried to pull his arm back from the soldier escorting him from the house. "Think about it, Roni. Think hard."

The door closed on his parting words.

Taber continued to watch his mate closely, his mind working, turning over possibilities and threats and only coming up with more answers.

"You want to explain that little meeting to me, Roni?" he asked her softly, aware that all eyes had turned to them.

Her gaze lifted to his slowly, but not slow enough for him to miss the flash of fear that she fought to hide.

"Sure, Taber." He didn't like that slow, tight smile that crossed her lips. "I'll be more than happy to, the very minute you answer my earlier question. Turnabout, baby." She nudged his waist with her elbow in a deliberately forced playful mood. "You just let me know when you're ready to talk."

She turned then, moving quickly for the stairs again and taking them with quick, almost running steps. She was fighting to escape, to hide, just as she had always done when she was younger and rushed into the night with only her senses to guide her. More often than not Taber found her lost and frightened each time. He wondered what he would find when he followed her this time.

"Taber, we might have a problem." Callan stepped closer, pulling a small, ultra-sensitive receiver from the pocket of his slacks. "I picked this up from the office when Merc informed me who he had." The receiver was a handy little bug locator given to them by the U.S. military. "Good old Reginald was wired for sound to hell and back. Our only problem now is figuring out who hired him."

Roni paced the bedroom after leaving Taber, her hands clenched in her hair as she wondered what her father could have been talking about. As though he had some secret, some information she could possibly want.

Or maybe, something he was finally willing to tell her?

She knew nothing of her mother's family, not their names, where they lived or who they were. She remembered, when she was young, how her mother spoke of her parents, of perhaps one day taking Roni to meet them. But it had never happened.

Reginald was blackmailing her, she realized. She would do as he wished, give him whatever he wanted, if she wanted that information.

She sat down on the prettily patterned chair by the bed and lowered her head wearily. She had gone without them this long, she wouldn't betray Taber for that knowledge now. Knowledge that she had a feeling she would never live to use, if her father got whatever he was here to attain.

Once again, betrayal.

* * * * *

"The best way to figure out what he's up to is to keep him from Roni as long as possible," Taber told the men assembled in the large office downstairs early the next morning.

Callan, Tanner, Merc, Kane and several of his brothers were watching him quietly.

"You knew him better than we did." Callan shrugged. "What do you think he's up to?"

Taber grunted. "Reginald is low-level sleaze. He doesn't have the brains to mastermind anything but a good drunk and some petty theft, so I'm going to assume it's one of two things. He wants to weasel money out of us, or someone has him on a chain. He doesn't do too badly when he has instructions, but he doesn't improvise well."

Taber frowned as he considered the scrapes he knew Reginald had been in throughout the past decade. He had been his most wily, his most dangerous, when working for others.

"It would be my guess he's on a chain then," Kane spoke up. "I pulled his record last night after Merc took him to the barracks. After that, I pulled in some favors and got a little added info from my own sources. Mr. Andrews has worked with some very heavy hitters in the past. Men who wouldn't care a bit to use him to gain access to his daughter. If they got hold of her, I doubt it would be pretty."

They were all aware of the fact that the Council was now desperate to learn the importance of the mark Merinus carried on her shoulder, and the significance of the tests they had managed to attain from the scientists who had examined the Breeds after their surprising announcement to the world three months before. The hormonal changes that had shown in Merinus and Callan's blood work and other tests had thrown the scientists into a tailspin. The discovery that she could conceive, despite the small amount of human sperm Callan's body normally produced, had shocked them further.

The truth their own doctor had found would have astounded them even more. It wasn't the sperm contained in the ejaculation of his cock that was so potent. It was the sperm contained in the small, thumb-like barb that only became engorged during sex with Merinus that allowed the conception.

"For some reason, he must think he can gain her cooperation." Merc sat stiffly in his chair and Taber could sense his impatience, his discomfort. Merc had been trained in almost complete isolation. There had been no Pride to sustain him, no friends, no confidants in the lab he had been found in. Being closed up in the office with the other men wasn't easy for him.

"What makes you say that?" Taber asked him carefully. It was no more than he had sensed himself the night before.

"The man is pretty impatient to get to her. Keeps demanding to see his little girl." The Breed sneered the last two words. "He's not her father, by the way."

Taber stared at him in surprise. "He told you this?"

"He didn't have to tell me." He snorted. "You can smell it if you take the time to try. There's no relationship there. Scents are all off."

Taber looked at Callan. His leader hadn't mentioned this ability the newest member of their Pride had. Callan only lifted his shoulders in reply and gave a short shake of his head. Evidently, he hadn't known either.

"How are the scents off?" Taber asked, watching him curiously.

The other man leaned forward in his chair, a frown crossing his lion-like face. "Anyone born of the same blood shares a unique scented bond with their most immediate family. You just have to be able to detect and separate the varied smells to understand it. Reginald Andrews does not share this with the woman he claims as his daughter. He is no relation to her."

It made sense. Suddenly, more pieces of Roni's life were beginning to come together.

"So he's no relation, which means there's not a chance in hell of any bond keeping him from harming her," Kane pointed out.

Taber snorted. "There never was. Reginald would sell his own mother to slavers if it would bring him enough money. His only bond is the one he has with his wallet and the bottom of a liquor bottle."

He rose from his chair, pacing along the room. He was aware of Callan's gaze following him and the concern from the other members of the meeting.

"How is your relationship with her working out?" Callan asked.

Taber shook his head. He wasn't about to discuss that with any of them. Hell, he wasn't sure he understood it himself.

"She didn't seem too pleased with him last night." Tanner chuckled. "Sounds like he's holding out on her. Let me guess, you didn't tell her about the little buddy your cock has."

Taber shot his younger brother a withering glare.

Tanner wiped the smile quickly off his face but it lingered along the edges of his lips.

Kane chuckled. The damned man was working quickly at getting on his bad side. He was finding too much amusement in this situation.

"Whoever has a leash on Andrews wouldn't be far away," Callan spoke up, bringing the conversation back on track. "They would have to be somewhere close."

"And he'll have to make contact pretty often without the little bugs that shirt of his carried." Merc's voice was hard, lethal. "Those buttons were state of the art, let me tell you. Too bad it got thrown in the wash. Guess he shouldn't have left such expensive material laying around."

"Yeah, shit like that happens." Taber smiled coldly. He would have liked to see Reginald's reaction to that one. "Keep a close eye on him. I want a report on everyone he talks to, on and off the estate grounds. Let's see if we can't figure out who his handlers are."

"I have some men on it," Kane spoke up. "One of them we can possibly use to get close to him. Sometimes, my men can come off as real cat-haters."

Taber sighed deeply. There were times a few of Kane's men could have convinced him of it.

"Then we just sit back and wait," he sighed. Waiting had never been difficult for him before—he was considered one of the most patient of the three males that made up his original pride — but he'd be damned if that patience wasn't wearing thin now.

"Wait and see how far we can push him." Kane shrugged as he came to his feet. "We have some contractors coming to the estate today to finish up that fence around the grounds. Keep the women in the house and the curtains closed until they're gone. I don't want to take any chances with them. I'll post guards at all the entrances to be certain no one slips in. Other than that, it's business as usual."

Business as usual was becoming a fight to stay alive.

"What about our little gun toting friend?" Taber asked him, wondering about the assassin they were still holding. "Has he talked yet?"

"Not yet." Kane shrugged. "Pretty soon it won't matter. We're running background checks on him now and should have answers soon. When the report comes in, I'll know every dirty little secret he ever thought he could have hidden. He won't be a problem for long."

If Taber or Callan got their hands on him, he wouldn't be alive long either.

"Okay, everyone knows their jobs today..."

Callan was interrupted when the door to the office was rudely jerked open. Taber turned in surprise to see Roni standing there, a short little sundress gracing her slender body, a frown etched on her brow as her eyes blazed furiously.

That dress was going to drive him insane, Taber thought. The soft cream color was a perfect foil for her skin, bringing out the blue in her eyes, the flush on her cheeks. He wanted to jerk it to her hips and take her there in the doorway, pounding into her pussy until she screamed out her pleasure.

"Look at it this way," Kane muttered behind him. "At least you have a reason for being pussy-whipped. No need to be ashamed."

Taber eyed him in irritation. "You know, Kane, when Sherra finally decides to show you what you keep daring her to,

I'm going to enjoy giving you back every smart-assed remark you've ever made. Count on that."

"Meow." Kane chuckled. "Good luck, Garfield. Catch ya around."

"Roni?" Taber questioned her when she didn't move from the doorway. "Is everything okay?"

It wasn't. He could smell the desperate heat coming off her body, but mixed with that, he could sense the pain she was fighting so hard to tamp down.

She glanced at the other men. "I'll come back. I didn't know you were busy."

"That's okay." He shook his head in response. "We're pretty much finished up here."

He moved to her, amazed at the sensitivity of his own flesh as he neared her. As though a part of him longed for nothing more than her touch. It was a strange feeling for a man who had never known such a weakness before.

He watched the way she glanced at the others uncomfortably, her gaze flickering to them before lowering. A light blush stained her cheeks and the soft color only added to the beauty that never failed to amaze him.

"What's wrong?" He nuzzled her cheek gently as his hand cupped her hip, moving her against him just enough to feel the warmth of her body.

"You know what's wrong." Her voice was tight, tense with the heat he knew traveled through her body, through his own. "And don't think for one minute I'm pleased about it. Now let me talk to Reginald so we can get him the hell out of here. Tell your guard dogs to back down."

"Cats, Ms. Andrews," Kane laughed. "Wrong species."

Various snarls greeted his words, not the least of which was Taber's. He was running out of patience with his loosely related brother-in-law.

"No." He finally turned back to her, regretting the anger that flared in her eyes. "Not yet, Roni. Not until I know how dangerous he is. I won't allow you to see him."

He watched the fire that snapped in her eyes, his cock thickening in arousal as he felt her preparing to defy him.

"Won't allow me?" she snapped furiously. "You won't *allow* me? Since when, Taber Williams, do you have the right to allow me anything?"

He smiled tightly, tamping down the need to show her, rather than tell her, exactly what gave him that right. She was tempting him. Daring him. Pitting her stubbornness against his own, and he was about to inform her who would win. In no uncertain terms.

"When I took you to the floor and mounted you, I took the right to protect you as well," he informed her coolly. "Mate."

Chapter Ten

The office cleared out rather quickly after Taber's words seemed to echo around the room. His voice pulsed with ire, with lust, setting her nerves on edge, causing the blood to thunder through her veins. She couldn't figure out how he managed to do it. It had to be that damned hormone he kept infecting her with. To say his kiss was addictive would be an understatement in his case.

"You have no right to tell me what to do, or how to handle my own father," she snapped, slamming the door behind her. "And you sure as hell don't own me just because you managed to infect me."

"Infect you?" he snarled. "Goddammit, Roni, it's not a disease."

Offended fury reflected in his voice and in his expression. As far she was concerned, she was infected. Someone needed to produce a vaccine to combat it.

"Bet me," she dared him recklessly, her anger and her lust merging. "It's painful, Taber. And I don't like the reaction it produces." The lie nearly seared her lips on its way out. There was nothing she liked more than the results of the searing heat they shared. "And I sure as hell don't like this possessive attitude you seem to want to take."

"Too bad." He crossed his arms over his chest as he stared back at her furiously. "Guess you're just going to have to live with it, aren't you?"

Her eyes narrowed dangerously, her lips thinning with her rising anger. Now, if she could just get her breasts to stop swelling and her vagina to dry up, maybe she could really blast into him. It was hard to be pissed when all she wanted was to be fucked.

"Taber, I'm about to lose my patience with you." She sighed roughly, pushing her fingers through her hair, hating the sensual feel of it sliding along the bare skin of her upper back. She knew better than to let Merinus talk her into wearing this damned dress.

"Why?" He laughed in surprise. "For God's sake, Roni, all I'm trying to do is protect you, not lock you up. As soon as we figure out what the hell he's up to I'll let you run him off personally."

She gave him a resentful look. "No you wouldn't. It might be too *dangerous*." She drew the last word out mockingly.

Taber sighed. The sound of it pricked at her conscience. He seemed tired, sad. She had always hated it when Taber seemed saddened, the weight of the world seeming to drag at his shoulders. No, not the weight of the world, she amended painfully. The weight of survival.

"Is it so bad, Roni, to need to protect you?" he asked her softly, watching her with a heated, lust-filled gaze. Mixed with that hunger though was a gentleness, a need that went beyond the sexual and made her heart clench in desperate hope.

Her eyes flickered to his hips, then back to his face. She ignored the glimmer of amusement she saw there. His cock filled out the front of those jeans in a way that sent her pulse hammering and silky heat sliding from her vagina.

"In a way, it is," she finally answered him as she moved closer, drawn to him, her body demanding his touch. "I don't like it, Taber, not having a choice."

She saw his grimace as her hands touched his chest. His larger, calloused hands covered hers, his eyes closing briefly before he opened them, allowing her to see the haunted depths of his own fears.

"I know this isn't easy for you." His whisper stroked over her nerve endings like sensuous silk. "It's not easy for me either.

But I can't take the chance that he'll hurt you. I can't risk you, Roni."

And she knew he wouldn't. She had known that the moment she realized her father was the reason those alarms had went off. That just as he had betrayed her, he would betray the Breeds, and there was nothing she could do about it unless she could get face to face with him. Somehow, someway, she had to convince him to leave. Sometimes it was actually possible to appeal to his sense of self-protection. It was the only chance she had.

It was a chance Taber wasn't going to allow her yet though, she realized. All she could do was hope and pray that with so many suspicious Breeds watching him, that Reginald wouldn't have the chance to cause too much trouble. Definitely not the chance to actually hurt anyone.

For now, she was close to Taber, his heat enveloping her, his fingers caressing her hands with a strength she had always dreamed of feeling. Beneath his touch, she allowed her fingers to move, to caress his chest, to feel the building heat in his body. She loved the look on his face when she caressed him, touched him as a lover. His eyes became heavy-lidded, his lips a bit fuller, his high cheekbones flushing darkly.

"Being horny makes me cranky, Taber," she attempted to apologize as she leaned against him, cushioning the hard ridge of his cock against her lower stomach. "It makes me want to take a bite out of someone." She leaned forward, her mouth opening over his flat nipple as she allowed her teeth to sink into the muscle there.

His groan shattered the silence of the room as his hands moved to her hips, holding her against him with almost bruising strength.

"Go ahead and bite me all you want to." He was nearly panting when her tongue peeked out to rub against the hard little nub beneath it. "Damn, Roni. God, yes."

She felt the material of the dress inching up her thighs, pulled by Taber's gripping fingers as she rubbed against his chest. She could feel the heat of his flesh radiating through the soft cotton shirt he wore, the building lust that simmered just under the skin.

"I need you," she whispered as she lifted her head from his chest and licked her lips nervously. "Now."

An involuntary moan escaped her throat as his hand cupped the bare globes of her rear, clenching the firm muscle, lifting her closer to the cradle of his thighs. Her fingers moved to his shirt as desperation speared through her like wild lightning. She didn't take time to unbutton the material. Her fingers gripped the parted edge and pulled, ripping buttons free, tearing cloth as he growled in sexy approval.

"Whenever you want it, baby," he whispered. "However you want it."

He pushed the material of her dress to her waist before his fingers hooked in the waistband of her thong, tearing it casually from her body. There was now no barrier between his touch and her flesh as his fingers slid between her thighs.

She was so wet, so slick from the juices seeping from her pussy that his fingers slid easily along her cunt lips. He circled her clit slowly as his arm tightened around her waist, holding her still for the erotic manipulations. She was drowning in heat, in sexual desperation.

Roni couldn't still the twisting of her hips as she fought to get closer to the tormenting fingers driving her insane. Her mouth opened on a soundless moan of exquisite desire only to have his lips cover hers, his tongue plunging in demandingly, twining with hers, silently demanding she take what he offered. Her lips closed on the intruder with a desperation that she knew should have horrified her.

The sweet, honeyed essence of the unique mating hormone surged through her system. She could feel it. The taste of him filled her first, then within seconds she could feel her blood heating, burning through her veins, surging to her nipples, her sensitive pussy.

"Good girl," he whispered thickly as he drew back from her long moments later, staring down at her, his gaze hot as two fingers spread her inner lips before plunging inside the gripping depths of her pussy.

Roni rose to her tiptoes as a harsh exclamation of near orgasmic pleasure rushed past her lips. His fingers thrust ruthlessly inside her once again, spreading her apart, working in and out with a fierce, controlled rhythm that had her pussy gushing.

"Taber." Her fingers struggled with his belt, desperate now to release the hard wedge of his erection from the confining material of his jeans.

She needed him with a hunger she couldn't control, one she didn't want to control. Hard and fast, slamming into her pussy, driving her to the edge of madness and beyond.

"I can't wait to sink into this tight little pussy," he whispered, his voice guttural, vibrating with the animalistic growl that never failed to make her cunt clench. It did so now, causing him to groan against her lips as he licked them hungrily. "Come for me, baby. Let me feel you come on my fingers."

His voice stroked over her senses. His fingers fucked into the tormented depths of her gripping cunt, driving her insane with the whiplash of pleasure that tore through her body.

Roni was gasping for breath as she felt the heated coil in her womb tightening with spasmodic intensity. She fought for breath as his fingers took her ruthlessly, driving deep, stroking nerve endings that were throbbing in desperation from each plunging thrust.

"Taber, I can't stand it…" She was drawn tight, hips thrust forward, gyrating on his fingers as he pushed her closer to the brink.

"Take it." He held her tighter, his fingers working inside her tormented pussy, his thumb stroking the swollen bud of her clit. "Come for me, baby. Let me feel your pussy explode, Roni."

The sounds of hot, wet sex filled the room. The plunge of his fingers slapping inside her, her moans tearing through her chest, his explicit, exciting words pushing her over the edge as nothing else could have.

Her back arched as she felt the end rushing for her. Fingers of electricity danced over her skin, struck her womb, seared her cunt until it came together in a flash of blinding, rapturous sensation. She felt her entire body explode, her pussy tightening until he was groaning with the effort to continue thrusting inside her. Her release poured through her, convulsing her body as she drove herself repeatedly on the hard digits invading her.

"Hell, yeah," he moaned, holding her close as she shook against him. "There, baby. So good. So good. Come on my fingers like a good girl, baby."

Roni felt the tears on her cheeks as she trembled in his arms, the wicked forks of sensation flaying her body in repeated aftershocks as she felt him move her.

Her buttocks met the cool wood of the desk as a small measure of sanity began to return to her. She was weak, shaking with a release she couldn't have anticipated, couldn't steel herself against. Her gaze was heavy-lidded, her mind sluggish until he spread her thighs wide and gazed down between them with hot, greedy eyes.

"I want that sweet pussy so badly I can't think straight," he growled as he worked at his belt and the metal buttons of his jeans. "All that matters is pushing my cock so deep and hard inside you that we both scream with the pleasure."

Taber was burning with a fever of lust so deep, so strong, he felt as though every cell in his body was going to explode with the need. His fingers shook like a youth's as he unbuttoned the small pearl closures on her dress, spreading the edges apart, revealing the full, tempting globes of her aroused breasts. He didn't know what to do first. Latch onto one of those spiked nipples like a starving man and fuck her until they were both dying of it, or eat the thick cream that lay tempting and sweet on the swollen lips of her pussy.

He licked his lips, staring up at her as his cock throbbed its insistent demand to plunge inside the little slitted opening of her cunt. His mouth watered for the taste of her.

"Play with your clit." He held her legs up, spreading her, staring down at her with a building need he didn't know how to answer.

She whimpered. A low, desperate sound that had his cock jerking in response.

"Play with it, baby," he crooned gently, watching as her trembling fingers slid down the soft roundness of her stomach. "There you go. Feel how wet and hot you are."

It was the most exciting thing he had ever seen in his life. Her fingers, slender and graceful, moving to the soft, soaked fleece that surrounded the swollen bud of her clit, parting the swollen lips, circling the hard little nub.

"Oh yeah, sweetheart," he encouraged her, almost panting from excitement. "Slide your fingers down, Roni. I want to see you fuck yourself. See you part that pretty cunt with your own fingers."

She was whimpering, flushed, her soft blue eyes dazed with lust as her hips jerked.

"Oh, that's a good girl." His hands tightened on her thighs as he watched her fingers slide down the narrow cleft, two of the slender digits sliding to the first knuckle inside the tempting depths of her cunt.

"Feel how hot that sweet pussy is." He could barely force the words from his mouth. "I'm going to fuck it so hard and so long you'll never forget what it's like to have my cock owning you." Her hand jerked, a cry tearing from her chest as more of her juices coated her fingers.

His cock was an agonizing throb now. Propping her small feet on the edge of the desk, he used one hand to spread her pussy apart, the other to grip his cock, to ease the mindless rush to shove it so far inside her that he merged with her very soul.

"I'm dying." Her cry echoed with a touch of fear, thickened with lust, emotion and desperation.

Her fingers sank into her vagina again. Pulled back. Thrust in as her hips lifted from the desk in response.

"Yeah, baby," he groaned. "Get your fingers nice and slick with that sweet pussy juice. Because you're going to feed it to me, allow me to suck it from your pretty fingers while I fuck you crazy."

She came. He watched it, the way her clit swelled further, pulsed and glistened. The flesh stretching around her fingers clenched, spasmed, as her desperate mewl of release whispered past her lips. Taber could wait no longer.

He gripped her wrist, pulling her fingers free, grimacing in painful pleasure at the sound of her tight cunt sucking at her departing fingers. Pressing closer, he tucked the head of his cock at the little opening as his eyes met hers. He brought her fingers to his lips, dripping with the swirls of her rich cream, and sucked one into his mouth as he plunged his cock deep inside her pussy.

"Oh hell." His back arched. The tight, gripping muscles of her sex sucked him in, closing on his erection like a silken vise, milking it rhythmically. "Sweet Roni," he groaned around her fingers. "That's a good girl. Oh yeah, good, baby. Milk my cock."

Her cries were constant now, mewling little sounds, the whisper of his name, the erotic plea that he fuck her hard, deep. But he wanted to stay just like this, his cock spreading her, the lips of her pussy nearly flattened from the width of flesh shoved inside her.

"So pretty." He licked her fingers of the last drop of erotic cream before laying her hand to the desk, pressing it there firmly, a silent demand that she not move it.

She stared back at him, her eyes wide, her lips moist as she tried to breathe past the excitement building in the air around them.

His gaze dropped back down to her thighs, a primal rumble of conquest escaping his chest.

"My pussy." He pulled back then, watching his cock slide nearly free of her, glistening with the slick inner juices that flowed from her. "My pretty, hot pussy." He worked the desperately hard shaft back inside her, loving the fierce grip, fighting his orgasm with every breath so he could relish the nearly painful clenching of her muscles on his flesh.

His balls had contracted tight and hard beneath his erection, pulsing with the need to release their hot load of sperm into the silky depths of her cunt. His body was raging. Sharp talons of sensation streaked up his spine as he pulled free of her again, only to re-enter her slowly, groaning at the sheer pleasure of watching his cock fuck into her, feeling her grip him, her pussy weep for him.

"Ah baby, so good." She tightened on him again as the head of his cock sank to the entrance of her womb, pulled back, stroked in. "That's my sweet baby. So tight and hot around my cock. God, I love fucking you, Roni."

But he couldn't fight the need clenching every cell in his body much longer. Her sex was an inferno around the thick flesh fucking into her, tightening on him with every thrust as her keening pleas rocked his mind.

He was unable to stop the building speed of each penetration, his mind consumed by the sheer exhilaration of burying his cock inside her, feeling the tender flesh glove him, tighten on him. His release was only seconds away. He could feel the barb beneath the head of his cock beginning to lengthen, to prepare to lock him inside her, to release its silky semen along with the load ready to erupt from the head of his cock.

"Baby." He moved inside her hard and deep now, the moist sounds of his cock penetrating and her cunt suckling, filling the air.

He couldn't plunge into her fast enough, hard enough, couldn't get enough of the feel of her pussy tightening on him. Tighter. Tighter.

"Fuck yes. Yes." He gripped her thighs harder as he felt her vagina quake, ripple, then lock down on him with a force that had him roaring in pleasure as she unraveled beneath him.

He couldn't hold off any longer. He threw his head back, sweat dripping from his hair, his face, as he lost his hold on reality. The barb extended its full length, locking him inside her as it pressed firmly into the back of her pussy, holding him in as it released its own precious load into her fertile body.

The sensitive extension prolonged the exquisite agony of his release, making his body tremble, convulse, as another roar tore through him. The animal was triumphant, the man awed by the sheer power of emotion that poured from him. His. His woman. His pussy. All his.

Chapter Eleven

God, he was handsome. Roni sighed in utter disbelief as the incredibly sensuous man used a damp washrag with gentle precision to clean the silky, thick excretions of their combined climaxes from her thighs and the tender folds of her pussy.

His actions did nothing to detract from the sheer masculine grace that was so much apart of him. Power and honor, strength and courage. She had never really analysed all that Taber was. To her, as she grew up, he was just Taber, the center of her world, her protector, her advisor, her friend. He had the same unhurried drawl of most Eastern Kentucky inhabitants. Used the same slang and though he kept mostly to himself or his family, he had been social enough not to be suspicious.

Now, he was one of the most widely known men in the world. Hell, one magazine had even dubbed him one of the most sexy men alive. Him, Tanner, Callan and any other Breed unfortunate enough to have their pictures plastered within the media.

She had always known there was something different about Taber though. Something she couldn't put her finger on or fully explain. Something undefined. It was a something she well understood now.

She watched as he disposed of the cloth then stared up at her, a small, half amused quirk tilting his lips. Dammit, it should be illegal for a man to look like that. Impossibly sexy, totally erotic.

He inhaled deeply then, his smile edging higher.

"Whatever you're thinking is making you hot again, baby." She loved how he called her baby. How his voice softened, his gaze becoming hot and possessive.

Rather than carrying out the sensual threat she heard in his voice though, he gripped her hands and helped her sit up on the desk as he straightened her dress.

His fingers were quick and adept as he refastened the tiny buttons.

"Yeah well, it's all your fault. I told you, you infected me." She snorted when he finished, moving back from her enough to allow her to test her legs and stand upright.

"I didn't infect you. I *affect* you," he corrected her with a fierce scowl.

"Yeah. Right," she drawled with a smile. "However you want to excuse it. Comes out to the same thing I bet."

He grunted at that. "You need to be spanked."

"So you keep telling me." She shrugged nonchalantly, though the cheeks of her rear clenched in excitement. "When you start feeling man enough to do the job, then you just let me know."

A chuckle vibrated in his chest then. A rough, almost happy sound that filled her heart with warmth.

"You are a troublemaker, Roni." He shook his head as he chastised her. "Do you have to think of ways to drive me insane, or does it just come naturally."

She tilted her head, watching him with mock-consideration. "I think it probably comes naturally," she announced with a suggestive lift of her brows. "But I can start of thinking of ways if you want me to."

"Lord forbid." He laughed at that one, shaking his head at her as he bent, picking up his discarded shirt and pulling it on.

It should be criminal to cover that body. It was tight and hard, a true work of art. Well-defined muscles, smooth, strong flesh. Every movement of his body caused something to ripple with power. It was enough to make a girl stare at him in dreamy surrender.

She shook the dazed look she knew she must have on her face, away. Dammit, she wasn't going to act like a star struck kid forever, surely. But the way her vagina was already creaming in demand for him, she wasn't so certain. Some men just had a power that wasn't fair when it came to mesmerizing the opposite sex. Taber had that power. And it equally infuriated her and amused her.

She moved across the room to the closed curtains of the window, wishing she could draw them back and stare into the bright sunlit expanse of the estate. She wasn't used to be locked in, denied the outdoors she loved so much.

"Is it always like this Taber?" she asked then. "Even before you revealed who you were?"

She turned to him slowly, watching as the amusement left his face, leaving his expression resigned. Regretful.

"It wasn't so bad before." He shrugged then. "But only because Callan drew most of the danger and kept the soldiers away from the rest of us. They knew he was alive, but they had no idea we survived the explosions that were set in the labs at his escape. Our safety came with a price."

It was a price she could tell weighed heavily on his pride.

"What about Dayan?" She had tried not to talk about him, to mention him, but the impact she was learning he had on her life, made questions necessary. There was so much she had to understand, needed to know to survive in this world.

Taber shook his head. "I never understood Dayan. Doc Martin swears he was like he was because the human elements were stronger in his DNA than the animal. It seems the stronger the animal genetics are, the less likely they are to turn in such a way. Very few animal species turn on their own kind. Humans are the most likely to do so," he ended with a large measure of mockery.

How could she refute it?

"So there's like an honesty gene?" That one was hard to believe.

"I wish," he sighed. "No, it just seems to be the nature of the beast I guess. I'm sure there are rogues, just as there are good people and bad people in the world. But for the most part, what we're finding are Breeds with an innate code, one that parallels the animal world more than the human. It's one of the reasons the scientists used the extreme measures they did to train us. Brutality will turn an animal. Beat it once too often, and it turns mean. They had hoped that same thought would hold true with the Breeds."

"Did it?"

He paced over to the small refrigerator at the bar across the room and pulled out two bottles of water. Opening both, he returned to her, handing her one.

"In some cases," he finally admitted. "Until they killed their trainers and escaped. We're finding a lot of reports in the Council records detailing some of those instances. There are a lot of Breeds, of many species, still unaccounted for. The Wolves and even a few Coyotes as well. As of yet, we've found none of them though."

She should know better than to let curiosity ask the questions that rose inside her. The world the Breeds lived in horrified her.

"What now?" Her voice was faint as she asked the question.

Taber grimaced. Now, we try to stay alive, to survive. For the moment, we have world sympathy on our side, but the crackpot organizations against us are growing. Pure Blood groups, the Council soldiers using guerrilla tactics to attempt to prove us to be the no more than the animals they created. Every day is another battle, another test."

Weariness edged his voice. How did they keep fighting? Roni could feel tears thickening her throat, behind her eyes, as the true depths of their fight became clearer by the day.

"What can I do to help you?" The question was ripped from her throat as he stared back at her in surprise. "I don't know how to help you, Taber."

He reached out, his hand cupping her cheek as thumb smoothed over her trembling lips.

"I would have never brought you into this willingly." He shocked her with his declaration. "If I had known what was going to happen, how you would be affected by this, I would never have touched you. I would never have given nature the chance to endanger you like this. But I have to say Roni, having you with me, holding you, knowing that if one thing in this world is mine, then it's you, brings me more peace than you could ever know."

His voice throbbed with conviction. With the power of emotions he never spoke of.

"Strange sorta peace you like then." She gave him a watery smile. "I'm not exactly at the peak of rationality here."

"Were you ever?" His eyes glowed with warmth. "Roni, darlin', if there's one thing I could ever say for certainty, it's that rationality was never your strong suit. You proved that every time I had pull your tight little ass out of jail."

"Hey." She frowned in mock offense. "It was never my fault."

"Yeah. So you always said." He wrapped his arm around her waist, pulling her to him. "Come on, vixen, I'm starving to death. These demands you're putting on my body requires energy. I need food."

She leaned against him, luxuriating in his warmth for a second before pulling back to stare up at him somberly.

"You have to let me see him sometime," she said softly, reminding him of her father. "You don't know him like I do, Taber. You can't get the truth from him, all you can do is read between the lines. And no one can do that like I can."

He sighed, frustration flashing in his eyes. "Not until I know you'll be safe, Roni, No matter what. Not until then."

Chapter Twelve

"Taber, we have movement outside the house. I'm sending Dawn and Sherra to protect Merinus and Roni in their rooms, but I need you out here." The call came in after midnight, mere hours after Taber and Roni managed to fall into an exhausted sleep.

They had returned to the suite after a large dinner spent with Callan and Merinus. There, he had proceeded to love her again, to assure himself, to reinforce to her, that she did belong to him.

The drowsiness fled his brain at Kane's abrupt announcement. "I'm on my way," he said quietly as he moved from the bed. "How close are they?"

"Too fucking close. I have men securing the outside of the house. You and Callan take care of the inside. There are still too many holes we haven't managed to plug yet. I'll keep you updated."

"Fuck," Taber cursed as he jerked his jeans from the floor and rushed for the weapons he kept in the large walk-in closet in the bathroom. Roni was only steps behind him.

"This is turning into a bad habit," she muttered as she pulled on a pair of sweat pants and a loose T-shirt he threw her. Merinus was going to run out of clothes soon if she didn't manage to get her own.

"Stay in the room. Dawn will be up here in a minute to stay with you," he ordered her softly. "Keep the curtains closed and stay away from the balcony doors. You'll be safe here. I don't want to chance moving you through the house right now. Dawn knows what she's doing, baby. Just scream if you need me."

He handed her the pistol he had taken from her the night before and extra clips before jerking the automatic rifle from the gun rack mounted on the wall.

"I shoot first and scream later. Remember?" She pulled her sneakers on and laced them quickly before following him into the room.

He moved carefully, his body tense, poised for action. Roni didn't speak, just followed his lead as he moved through the bedroom, paused at the door that led to the sitting room and stared into it intently.

"You'll be safe here." He turned, his lips pressing into hers for a hard quick kiss before he moved for the door. "Lock the door behind me and don't let anyone in, Roni. No one but me. Do you understand?"

She gazed up at him intently. "I understand. No one but you."

"Good girl." His voice was seductively approving. She frowned at her own reaction to it. "Lock the door now."

He opened it slowly, moving with a smooth, graceful slide of his body that drove home the fact that he had lived his entire life enmeshed in danger. He was so used to it that he unconsciously moved with care, no matter where he was or what he was doing.

He slipped through the door, then held it open as the small, silent figure of his sister entered the room. Glancing at her one last time, Taber closed the panel gently behind him. Roni turned the lock quickly, then slid the steel deadbolt into place. They locked their bedrooms here tighter than some people did their homes. She laid her head against the thick panel of wood and fought her tears at the thought.

She couldn't hear anything or anyone outside the door. She knew the heavy carpeting would have muffled most things, but she also knew the number of men who slept in the house just for safety's sake. The Breeds weren't taking any chances with their leader's wife and the mother of the Pride's first child. All precautions were taken to protect Merinus and Roni from any threat.

"He'll be fine." Dawn's voice was a soft, gentle sound, almost purring as she spoke behind Roni.

Roni drew in a deep breath, pushing herself away from the door as she turned to face the other woman.

Dawn shifted uncomfortably as Roni gazed at her through the dim light that barely filtered from the other room.

"Thank you for staying with me," Roni said softly, moving to the couch, trying to still the nervous shaking of her hands. She laid the gun on the cushion beside her as she curled up in the corner, watching the other woman.

Dawn followed suit, though she took the chair opposite her, propping the rifle against her knee as she watched Roni with shy curiosity.

"Taber's one of our best fighters," she said in that soft, melodic voice. "He won't let anyone get up here. And if they did, I wouldn't let them past the door."

A thread of steel ran beneath the last statement. There was barely enough light to see by, but Roni glimpsed the flash of rage in her eyes.

"The estate here is gorgeous," Roni finally said, desperate to keep the other woman talking. She needed to concentrate on something other than the possible dangers Taber would face outside. "How did you find it?"

A mocking little smile played about the lush fullness of Dawn's lips. "The estate was given to us, actually, along with a nice little lump sum of money to help aid the other Breeds being found in various locations. Several of the Council members were high-ranking heads of our government." Her voice sang with an earthy, haunting quality.

"How many are there so far?" Roni asked her curiously.

"So far, we have nearly a hundred Feline Breeds on site working to secure our place in society in Washington. More come in monthly..." Her voice trailed off, as though the thought of those coming in struck a chord of resounding pain within her soul.

"I'm sorry." Roni didn't know what to say.

A gentle smile crossed Dawn's lips, filled her expression. "Don't be sorry, Roni. We are alive and isn't that what matters?" It was obvious that Dawn asked herself that question often.

What was it about her? Roni had never understood the quiet aura that always surrounded the other woman. She had seen the men of the county when they were around her. Rough, hard-edged men suddenly softened, their smiles gentling. Men who would have often made lewd advances to any woman as beautiful as Dawn had cast their eyes to the floor, shame marking their expressions.

Her looks weren't so unusually striking as to stop traffic. She was slender, delicate, with thick silken hair and large brown eyes that always seemed so haunted. And perhaps that was it, Roni thought. Her eyes seemed to tell a tale that Dawn never whispered.

"Everyone looks at me like that." Dawn shook her head in apparent confusion as Roni watched her.

The strength Dawn had displayed in their earlier encounter was still there, the pain and razor edge of danger. But she seemed more inclined now to talk, to renew the fragile friendship they had shared before she left Kentucky.

Roni sighed deeply. "I'm sorry. You seem...so sad. I guess before I never realized why."

"And you do now?" There was no insult intended in her voice, just weary acceptance.

"I don't think so." Roni shook her head slowly. "I think it's more than the situation, more than your entrance into society. How old were you when Callan brought you out of the labs?"

And there was the answer. Her eyes flashed. Nightmare, memory and terror.

"I was fifteen. Sherra was eighteen. That was more than ten years ago. It seems only yesterday sometimes." She shook her head, a weary smile crossing her face. "They made us tell them about the labs during the Senate hearings and the closed trials of some of the Council members. Sherra cried." Her voice dropped. "Like she did in the labs, before Callan took us out. She has never cried like that since our escape. Callan picked her up out of the witness stand and carried her out of the proceedings. It was weeks before she could awaken without screaming."

"What about you?" Roni asked her gently.

Dawn shook her head, lowering it before giving her a soft, broken smile. "I just don't sleep, Roni. Not for long and not very deeply. What's the point when the monsters can take you again and again and again?" She shuddered and came to her feet, her head tilting, her eyes suddenly narrowing as the gun fell naturally into her grasp.

"What...?"

"Shhh," Dawn hissed softly. "Listen."

She heard it then. A scratch, a scrape at the balcony doors. Her eyes widened in horror as she grabbed the pistol, moving along the wall, careful to stay as far to the side of the glass doors as possible.

Dawn moved like a shadow then. She jerked the comm. link down from its position on the back of her head, adjusting the mic as she listened intently. The scratching came again, followed by a careful shuffle of the doors.

"Alpha one. We have a breech." Dawn's voice was so soft Roni barely heard it as the other woman moved to her, covering her as she motioned to the bedroom.

Keeping her weapon at her shoulder, Roni moved quietly around the room, her breath nearly strangling her as she fought to keep the fear to a manageable level.

She got as far as the bedroom door and stopped. The slow slide of the balcony door had her eyes flying to Dawn in alarm.

"Fuck. Get up here!" Dawn's voice was soft as she spoke into the comm. link, carrying no further than Roni as the other woman motioned to her and they headed quickly to the bedroom door. "We're evac. We're evac." She slid the locks free, opening the door as she checked outside quickly before moving from the room.

Roni followed quickly, her finger caressing the trigger of the gun as she held it ready, checking behind them often, fighting to hear above the pounding of her heart. The hallway was dark, silent, as they moved quickly along the corridor.

"We're heading to Merinus' room, Taber. Get up here. They're on our asses now." Dawn opened another door and they moved through it as a sudden curse echoed from the open door of Roni and Taber's room.

Dawn locked the door with a silent movement and turned back to the room. Merinus and Sherra were waiting, both armed, both watching the darkness from the side of the balcony doors that room held as well.

But Merinus and Callan's room wasn't a suite. It was one large bedroom and completely open except for the attached bathroom.

"They're moving toward us," Sherra hissed into her own mic as she and Merinus moved into the center of the room. "They know the location of the bedrooms and we're sitting ducks. Goddammit, Kane, get me some help up here."

"Taber and Callan are on their way," Dawn reported as they all moved quickly for the only shelter left to them.

The bathroom was as large as Taber's, but still, it afforded few places that could be used to stop a bullet. Roni placed herself in front of Merinus instinctively. Dawn and Sherra pressed them back, though, shielding them from anyone who would attempt to come through the doorway. Priorities, Roni thought sadly.

Sherra and Dawn considered themselves expendable in the place of the only two mates to the brothers they had fought beside for so many years. Just as Roni considered herself expendable against the life of the child Merinus carried. And yet, they were all pawns as well, because someone knew the Breeds' weaknesses and they had found a way to strike.

* * * * *

Taber had promised Roni she would be safe. He had told her to lock the door. Not to leave the room. No one would get to her. The acrid taste of failure coated his mouth. He had been wrong.

He entered the back of the house at a low crouch, his rifle held ready as he swept through the kitchen then stood aside to allow the other half-dozen men who followed him entrance. His blood pumped with the demand that he rush upstairs, that he blow the bastards to hell and back, but he knew the risk to Roni would only be greater.

Kane's men were moving on the balconies to trap the bastards. Now Taber and his men would move up the stairs to catch them on this end. Rage burned low in his gut, making it a fight to maintain control and proceed, as he knew he had to.

"We have a breech." Dawn's voice was low, steady and calm, but Taber could hear the horror that backed each word. "We're compromised, Taber."

Each man had received the same transmission. Silent as the night, as deadly as the animals their DNA mixed with, the men surged up the stairs. They caught the first four outside Callan's room as they were opening the door. The assassins never knew what hit them.

Taber wrapped his arm around the neck of one and twisted with a sharp, deadly move that resulted in the muted satisfying crunch. The others fell the same way, only to be pushed aside as Taber opened the door slowly.

He went in at a crouch, throttling his roar of triumph as they met the other group of would-be assassins in the middle of the room. Their eyes widened in surprise at the force they met as they turned to make their escape. At the same time, Kane's men stepped through the balcony entrance.

"Oh look, Callan, they want to play," Taber drawled as one raised his weapon. It was shot out of his hands before he could pull the trigger.

"Keep the women in there, Sherra." Callan's voice was cold, deadly, as he stepped farther into the room and smiled the cold smile of death Taber had rarely seen on his face. "Hello, gentlemen. If you had knocked, we could have conversed civilly," he stated a bit too mildly. "Your entrance into my home has left much to be desired."

Taber lowered his weapon as Callan handed his off to him. "Tell me, Taber, what should we do with such rude guests? Make nice, or have a late night snack?"

Taber allowed the snarl curling his lips to rumble through his chest. There was no mistaking the wary looks the assassins were now giving them.

"I missed dinner," Taber said clearly. "How about a snack?"

The four men jumped in startled surprise as twelve fully grown Feline Breed males growled in hungry menace.

"Wait." One of them spoke nervously, holding his hands out, his gun held in a clearly non-threatening manner as he laid it on the floor. "No harm, no foul…"

"No harm, no foul?" Callan asked mildly as he eyed the gun on the floor before raising his head to stare at the man with brooding fury. "Wrong. You broke into my home, attempted to harm my woman, and you think you're just going to walk out of here?"

"We're just doing our job." One shook his head desperately. "Come on, Lyons, you've always let us go before."

Taber recognized the voice. One of the mercenaries who had been sent home in defeat years before, smarting from the lazy, amused chase Callan had given him.

"The rules changed, Brighton," Callan snapped. "You don't just walk away anymore."

"Callan, we question them first." Kane moved into the room, watching the Breeds warily. "You know the score."

"I know they're dead." It was as though the very air itself stilled with that announcement.

There was no mercy in Callan's voice, no weakness. "We'll send them back to their owners in pieces. Isn't that how they sent back our scout last month?"

Taber's jaw tightened at the memory of it.

The four assassins shifted nervously within the room. Taber could see the whites of their eyes, the fear that no filled them. They thought they were going to continue to float on the old rules. The ones where they struck and if they failed, Callan let them go. They couldn't seem to understand the fact that Callan was no longer playing.

"Come on," Callan dared them, lifting his hand as he turned it, gesturing at them to bring on their worse. "Show me what you're made of. Personally, I smell the stink of a coward."

"Callan..." Taber warned him carefully. "Step back, man. This is no time for mistakes."

The mistake being an accidental death. "Think of Merinus and the babe. She would have to go on without you."

Callan tensed, flashing Taber a furious look.

"Callan?" Merinus's voice whispered from the bathroom, faint, frightened.

Callan snarled silently, casting the soldiers a look of promised retribution.

"Kane, get this shit out of here. Lock them up with the other bastard you're holding until the garbage runs. We'll send them out then. Maybe in pieces."

It was a threat that pushed the intruders into action. A flare of brilliant light pierced the darkness, blinding them as the assassins made their bid for freedom. Weapons were dropped as the Breeds used senses well honed from years in captivity. They couldn't see, but they could smell, hear and taste the evil flowing around them.

Taber's knife cleared its sheath at his side as he reached the first man. The weapon sliced through flesh, severing the jugular vein. Blood sprayed around him as he dropped his enemy to the floor and turned for another. The brilliancy of the light had dissipated and he came face to face with Roni's horror-filled expression.

Rage and grief filled him because he knew what he looked like. He knew, because he had seen Callan in a similar rage. His canines were bared, blood covering the lower part of his face, his chest. Another man's blood. The animal gloried in the scent of it, the feel of his enemy's defeat, the knowledge that this time, Taber had been victorious. But the man he was screamed out in rage against the fates, the cruelties, and the single instant that his mate had seen the carnage and the animal within.

The agonized roar that echoed through the house was one of rage, pain and a protest against the realities of a life never asked for, never imagined. A protest against the loss of innocence he glimpsed in Roni's eyes.

The roar was unlike anything Roni had ever seen or heard. She stared at Taber in shock as his head went back, his chest expanded and the primal sound of rage and anguish ripped from his throat.

Everyone stilled. The assassins lay dead. There had been no mercy. Roni hadn't expected any. But neither had she expected to see the bitter, raging pain in Taber's eyes as he dropped the assailant, either. Blood covered him, staining his cheek, his neck, the black cloth of his shirt, and running in a rivulet along the hardwood floor beneath his feet.

God help her, how was she to ease so much pain? She wanted to run to him, to clean the blood from him and whisper how thankful she was that he lived, but she was held rooted to the floor, tears whispering down her cheeks as she witnessed the one thing she knew Taber would not have wanted her to see.

As the sound of his fury echoed around them, his head lowered, his green eyes glittering with an intensity she had never witnessed before and an expression that terrified her. His legs ate the distance between them as he moved to her, gripping her wrist and jerking her along behind him as he headed for the door.

"Taber..." Callan's protest was cut off when Taber turned back to him with a snarl so threatening, so demanding, that the other man stood back, shaking his head in regret.

"Dammit, Callan, stop him." Merinus' voice was filled with fear as Roni was pulled from the room.

No one would stop Taber. No one could stop him now if they wanted to. Violence and lust swirled around him, tightening his body as the animal surged ever closer to the surface. Roni didn't even try to stop him. She followed him, nearly running to keep from being dragged behind him, her heart thundering in her chest, shock ripping its way through her body.

He had barely caught the assassin before the other man let loose on the trigger of the submachine gun he held. The bullets would have ripped through the bathroom at that angle, possibly killing them all. She remembered all too clearly watching the knife slice through human flesh, the hatred and surprise on the other man's face as his gaze locked with hers.

Taber pulled her into the bedroom, slamming the door behind them before he turned to her. She didn't have time to gasp before he ripped the shirt from her back, leaving her breasts bare, nipples hard, as he worked at the closure on his jeans.

"Taber..." She didn't know what to say. What to do.

"Mine." He bared his teeth as he pushed his jeans over his hips, freeing the thick, desperate erection they had contained.

She whimpered as he reached for her. The sweatpants were stripped from her, the legs ripping as he managed to free her from the material. He braced her against the padded arm of the couch, lifted her leg and thrust hard and heavy inside the sensitive depths of her pussy.

Roni arched in his arms, a strangled cry tearing from her throat as pleasure seared her body, even as pain lashed at her heart. Her gaze was locked with his and in it she saw the bitter fury and anguish no man should have to bear. Blood stained his face, his neck. His eyes glittered with remorse, with hunger.

"Roni..." His voice was strangled as he paused, buried to the hilt within her, a small measure of sanity replacing the bleak horror in his eyes. "Roni..."

She covered his lips, her fingers trembling.

"Feel how wet I am for you," she whispered with a sad smile. "How much I love you inside me, however you need me, whenever you need me."

Tears filled her eyes as he blinked down at her. Part of the feral intensity had faded, leaving instead an overwhelming sadness.

"He would have killed me and possibly Merinus as well," she whispered a second before he moved, his hips jerking convulsively, causing his cock to stroke the tender depths of her pussy with hard demand. "I love you, Taber. All of you," she cried out then. "I love you..."

He groaned. A low, heavy sound filled with remorse, with thankfulness. He gathered her against him, cushioning her head on the unsoiled shoulder as his hands gripped her buttocks, his cock moving inside her.

Long, slow strokes caressed the inner heat of her cunt as he kissed her throat, her neck. His thighs bunched, his back tensed, but still the deliberately careful movements never slowed.

"Mine," he whispered again. "My woman. My love."

His thrusts increased then, his breath coming hard and heavy, his hips driving the fierce erection as deep, as hard as he could as she clenched his shoulders, her legs wrapping around his hips, holding on for dear life as she felt her climax begin breaking over her.

Seconds later, she felt him locking inside her, heard his groan, his hungry little growl, then the hard, heated blasts of his semen spurting in the tight depths of her pussy.

"I'm sorry," he whispered against her neck, his face damp—though with tears or his own sweat, she wasn't certain. "I am so sorry you had to see what I am."

"No, Taber." Her hands smoothed over his hair, his shoulders. "Never be sorry. I love everything you are. All of you."

Such acceptance should not have been possible. Taber stood under the hot spray of water, his eyes closed, his mind slowly clearing of the blood rage he had felt when he had seen that bastard ready to fire off a submachine gun in the women's direction. Helping to wash it away was Roni, her hands tender as she cleaned him thoroughly. She had washed the blood from his hair, his face, and had then proceeded to clean every inch of his body with the silken comfort of soap and cloth.

Hot steam and the scent of soap filled the large shower cubicle. The sounds of water rushing over him and Roni's soft hum whispered over his mind. With each rinse and careful soaping of his body, he felt more of the rage rinsing from his soul as well. With it came an incredible dragging weariness. He wanted nothing more than to curl up beside her and sleep. But there was so much left to do.

"All done," she whispered gently as she kissed his shoulder, her hands smoothing over his wet flesh, stroking him as the involuntary purr began to sound in his chest.

He flinched at the sound.

"Shh." She cuddled against his chest, kissing it, her soft licks immeasurably tender. "Do you know how much I love that sound? How much I love knowing I pleasure you? Comfort you?"

His eyes were closed against the melting pleasure seeping through him. He had never been taken care of. Ever. And here she was, so small and gentle, her voice whispering over him, her hands soothing him, taking away almost three decades of pain as she whispered her love for him.

"They can't take you," he suddenly groaned as emotion tore from him, his arms contracting around her, holding her close to his chest. "I couldn't live without your touch, without your heat and passion, Roni." His throat felt tight from the feelings sweeping over him. "I would rather die than face such a thing."

"We won't let them take me, Taber. Together, we'll be okay." She pushed his hair back from his face as he opened his eyes, staring down at her, aching with the beauty he saw in her.

"I won't let them." He shook his head. "I will have to kill again…"

"And I will be right beside you when you do." She laid her fingers over his lips. "I will always be here, Taber. And we'll face the aftermath together. Just as we are now."

Did he deserve her? Hell, no, he knew he didn't, but he knew there wasn't a chance he was going to let her get away from him, either.

He cleared his throat as he leaned back from her, groaning at the erection suddenly straining between them.

"I have to talk to Callan," he sighed. "Then we'll take care of other things." He glanced down at his stubborn organ once again.

Roni moved to turn off the shower then grabbed the large towels she had laid out before leading him beneath the spray of water. He watched her in bemusement as she dried him like a babe.

"You would make an excellent mother," he whispered, imagining her bathing their child, caring for it as tenderly as she was caring for him, or more so.

A soft flush stained her cheeks. "I love children." She moved behind him, stroking the towel over his flesh as it soaked up the last of the water.

"Will you be upset when you conceive?" he finally asked her as he cleared his throat uncomfortably. "I should have thought before forcing my first kiss on you. Before binding you so effectively. I should have explained..."

"Wouldn't have changed anything." She came back around, grabbed another towel and dried herself. "I would have wanted you anyway."

He stilled, almost uncomprehendingly. "Are you certain, Roni?"

She paused, then breathed in deeply as wry amusement crossed her face. "Taber, that nice big cock of yours isn't the only thing I had on my mind when I saw you, you know. It was you I missed all those years. It was you I dreamed of before you ever touched me sexually. It was your babies I've always dreamed of having. Otherwise, you would have found my knee driving your balls up to your throat when you did kiss me. Now are you satisfied?"

He winced. She wasn't above it. She had done just such a thing before.

"Understood." He nodded quickly.

"Good. Now I know Callan's waiting downstairs for you. I'm going to curl up on the couch until you get back. Kane and some others were bolting the glass doors in place earlier, so maybe I can still manage a few hours of sleep before this place gets crazy again."

She looked exhausted. The constant worry, sexual needs and physical danger were taking a toll on her.

"Sleep in the bed..."

She shook her head. "I can't sleep there without you. So hurry up. I'm getting pretty damned tired."

He dressed in clean clothes while she pulled on one of his large T-shirts, the hem nearly reaching her knees, before grabbing a spare blanket from the quilt rack in the bedroom and heading for the sofa.

"I'll be back soon." He bent and kissed her soft lips as she stared up at him drowsily.

"Hurry and come back. I'll need you soon."

He could smell the need building in her. He nodded abruptly and turned and left the room. She couldn't live like this much longer, he thought. She was becoming exhausted, worn down. If she didn't conceive soon, then he worried that her health would suffer. But what, he wondered, would happen when she did conceive?

Chapter Thirteen

Roni was starved the next morning. She had awakened late, showered and dressed, and headed immediately to the kitchen as she followed the scents of bacon, eggs and biscuits.

When she entered the sunlit room, it was to find the three women talking softly over heaping plates and steaming coffee. Her mouth watered violently.

"On the stove." Sherra grinned at her as she eyed the plates with starving desperation.

"I feel like someone cut a hole in my stomach," Roni sighed. "Taber's going to have to install a kitchen in that damned apartment he calls a bedroom if he insists on spending all his time up there."

"It won't be much longer." Dawn's soft, melodic voice had Roni stilling in surprise as she turned to look at the other woman.

"Excuse me?" she said, confused.

Dawn shrugged. "You'll conceive soon."

"And you know this how?" Roni asked as she lifted a plate from the center island and moved to the stove.

"Because I can smell it."

"Dawn," Sherra spoke up warningly.

Roni glanced over as the other woman shrugged and lowered her head to her food.

"So what does it smell like?" She frowned, poured a cup of coffee and carried it and her plate to the table.

"We aren't certain." Sherra avoided her gaze.

"Dawn sounded certain enough. Is it information that can only be given if you kill me later?"

Merinus smothered her laughter, though Sherra frowned disapprovingly. "No, but maybe something you don't want to hear yet."

Roni glanced back over at Dawn. "Give me a timeline and we'll see how good you are." She shoved a forkful of eggs in her mouth as Dawn turned to her in surprise.

"Within the next seventy-two hours," she finally said, and as soft as it was, her voice was more than confident. "I noticed it with Merinus, right before she and Callan were forced to run from the Council. I saw her perhaps three days later, and she had already conceived. Your scent is similar."

"So how does this scent thing work?" Roni swallowed the eggs and stared back at the other women.

It was intriguing how easily the Breeds could pick up such senses. They were completely human, no matter the propaganda Roni was certain was being spread. But the gifts their animal DNA gave them were amazing.

"It's just a change in the pheromones." Dawn shrugged. "As though a special, delicate fruit is slowly ripening. It seems whatever change is being made to the ovaries and the eggs, it produces this scent as it progresses."

Roni looked to Merinus. Ovary change? Her stomach dropped with a sudden, overriding fear.

"The baby is completely normal." Merinus laughed. "We've had several sonograms done and all the prenatal tests show everything is fine. You'll conceive a normal baby boy or girl. I promise, no kittens, as Kane is wont to tease us with."

Fury flashed in Sherra's eyes.

"Excuse me. I have work to do."

Roni watched her in surprise, almost missing the regret that flickered across Merinus' face as Sherra rose to her feet and deposited her plate in the sink.

"Tell Callan I'll be on patrol if he needs me," she told Merinus as she walked from the room. "Tell Kane to get fucked."

Roni winced.

"That's his problem," Merinus sighed as she glanced at Dawn. "She won't let him touch her."

"I don't blame her. And it's time for me to go as well. I have detail on Mr. Andrews in just a few minutes. We don't need him getting any more transmissions out."

Roni stilled, her coffee cup poised at her lips as her eyes widened. She set the cup down carefully as the ramifications of those few words hit her like a fist to the stomach.

"He's the reason they knew which room we were in," she realized painfully, swallowing tightly as the food she had eaten threatened to come back up. "He told them where we were."

Merinus sighed heavily. "We can't be certain, Roni. They're still tracking the transmission."

"He sent a transmission out yesterday and last night we were attacked. The men found every weakness in security the estate possessed by sheer luck, I guess?" she snapped bitterly as she rose to her feet. "He nearly got us all killed and he's still here, given the chance to try again."

Rage roiled through her chest. Dear God, what would it take to neutralize the threat her father had always been within her life? He was only growing more determined now to destroy her than he had been in the years before.

"Roni. Callan and Taber are taking care of it," Merinus said gently. "Let them do what they have to do."

Roni speared her with a hard, vengeful look. "I don't think so, Merinus. Not this time. Not again."

* * * * *

Roni was none too pleased with Taber. His refusal throughout the day to get rid of Reginald, or to allow her to find out what the hell he wanted only stroked her fear higher. He was dangerous—to her and to Taber. He had already proven that. The battle she had fought with Taber earlier only drove home the fact that Reginald was growing more conniving, more evil, than ever before. They couldn't prove he had made the transmission. They only suspected it. To effectively put a stop to any threat he represented, they had to be certain. Just as they needed to know for certain who he was working with.

The men who had attacked last night were no more than hired guns. Sometimes they worked for the Council, sometimes they worked for other sources. There was more than one source popping up in the world that had decided the Breeds didn't deserve life. Reginald, if involved, was only one of many.

He was her father. He was the man her mother had loved. Her sweet, gentle mother. Roni laid her head against the cool glass of the balcony door and fought the pain ripping through her chest.

Margaret Andrews had been one of the kindest, gentlest souls. Roni barely remembered her, but she remembered how her mother sounded, the soft lullabies she sang to her, the whispered promises of a better life. And she remembered her mother crying.

It was one of her strongest memories from childhood. Her mother's cries, muffled, pleading, as she begged Reginald for mercy. *Please, Reggie. Please don't hurt me...*

Roni flinched as the words echoed through her mind. It was her last memory of her mother. The last words she had heard Margaret speak. The next morning her mother left for work, an hour later she was dead.

"Weak bitch," Reginald had muttered at the funeral. "She didn't fight enough."

Roni had never been certain what he meant by those words, but as she grew older, they had stayed with her. Had he been behind her mother's accident? Or had it been another of his muttered ramblings in regards to her mother's frail health?

She had been alone then and she felt alone now. She stared into the darkness fighting the old fears, the old wounds. She could feel the brink she stood on and it terrified her, the knowledge slowly building inside her.

Her mother had loved Reggie with a single, driving obsessive emotion that had terrified the young Roni. It hadn't made sense to her, how easily her mother would bow to his demands. She'd push aside her own wants and needs in deference to him. Even more than that, she pushed aside her daughter's. How many nights had dinner been a meal of cornbread and the meager amount of potatoes her mother had grown in the backyard because Reggie had taken all the money for himself? Or the times she had watched him slap her, scream at her, because they had eaten the last of the groceries in the cupboard, leaving him to fend for himself?

Had she loved him? Or was there something more there that her mother had been determined to hide from her?

She shook her head fiercely. Whatever it could have been, her mother had kept the secret of it well.

Her fists clenched. She had sworn she would never need a man so desperately. Had sworn she would never let herself be used, broken, because she loved. And here she was, unable to break away from the man who had that very power.

It didn't matter then that Taber had always held her with tenderness, had always given her heat and security rather than his fists. Her fears raged inside her as hot and bleak as the heat that throbbed in her pussy.

For some reason nature had taken the choice away from her and Taber both. He was a man, fully mature, who had faced unspeakable horrors and beside him she felt like the child she feared she was. Frightened. Confused.

She squared her shoulders and breathed in roughly. Okay, so she knew her problem. That was the first step to fixing it. Right? Her emotions had terrified her months before, once she realized how deeply Taber could hurt her. That letter she thought he had sent had destroyed her, broken a part of her. A part of her fighting, trying to heal only now that she was with him again.

When your heart loves, Roni, there's no fighting it. She remembered the saddened words her mother had whispered to her one night after another of Reginald's attacks. *Sometimes, protecting those you love, no matter what it takes, is more important than your own heart.*

And Roni knew now that she had to find a way to protect Taber. He didn't know how vicious, how cruel, Reginald could be. He couldn't, or else he would have never allowed him to stay. Taber knew loyalty, a need for freedom. He could never believe her father would do anything it took to achieve his own aims, even destroy his daughter. And Roni knew her destruction would bring Reginald a wealth of satisfaction. Finally. He had a weapon against her, and soon, she knew, he would use it.

"Roni." Taber's voice, as dark as midnight, wrapped around her senses as he stepped into the room.

Immediately the pulsing arousal that flowed through her body intensified. She turned from the window, pulling the gun from her waistband and laying it on a nearby table as she approached him. She reached for the hem of her shirt and stripped it quickly over her head.

He was hers. Damn him. Damn Reginald and her fears.

She tossed the shirt to the floor and toed off her sneakers.

"Son of a bitch." His hands went to his jeans.

"Take me," she challenged him as she pushed her own jeans from her hips and stepped out of them quickly. "I dare you."

There was a fever rising in her body. She didn't want the bed. She didn't want gentle mindless sex. She wanted to still the volcanic sparks of heat flaring inside her as she tore aside his control. She wanted to soothe him, enrage him, stroke and flail at him.

His eyes narrowed on her. She loved it when he did that. The jade-green color sparkled dangerously, giving him a primal, predatory appearance.

He growled, a feline rumble of warning as she smiled back at him in sensual challenge.

"I could," he told her softly, watching as she moved around him, keeping her within sight at all times. "I could take you down and mount you in a second, Roni."

She trembled at the dark warning. Her pussy spilled more of its slick juices along her swollen lips as her womb rippled in anticipation. She watched him breathe in deeply and knew he could smell the incredible heat filling her body. He tensed as he did, the muscles of his abdomen rippling as his cock jerked in anticipation.

"Do you know what you're tempting, Roni?" he asked her, his voice silky as she moved behind him, stepped closer, then smoothed her hands down the bunched contours of his back.

Like rough silk. The soft pelt that covered his body tickled her palms as she stroked him. He shuddered beneath her hands.

"I thought cats liked to be stroked." She leaned forward, catching her breath as the hard pinpoints of her nipples brushed against his back.

The rumbling growl that vibrated in his chest caused her to shiver in delight. It erotically stroked her senses, her arousal.

Her hands moved around his waist, sliding across the clenched muscles of his stomach.

"I used to dream of touching you," she whispered as her lips smoothed over the striking tattoo on his left shoulder. The snarling Jaguar, its eyes narrowed in fury, ears laid back warningly. "I dreamed of making you moan, of hearing you whisper how desperately you wanted me."

"I want you until I feel broken inside from it, Roni." He stayed still, tense, as her hands moved over him.

"Can I heal you?" She laid her cheek against his shoulder, hearing the loneliness in his voice. The same dark emotion she had felt herself for so long.

He shuddered under her hands as they caressed over his own straining nipples.

"You heal me with every touch." His arms were bunched, his body vibrating with the tight leash he had on his lust.

Roni smiled slowly. Could she break the control? Could she remake them both in the fires that would explode from it? If they survived it.

Her hands moved lower, tickling over the washboard stomach, heading unerringly for the strong stalk of his cock rising from his body.

"Roni." The word held immeasurable warning.

"Yes, Taber?" She swallowed tightly as her hands caressed the crease of his thighs.

He was close. So very close. She felt him prepare to move and jumped back. She laughed low and deep at the primitive growl coming from his throat as he reached for her and missed. She had a feeling the missing part was deliberate when she turned back and realized he was slowly stalking her.

She moved along the room, watching him carefully, more than aware of the tension filling the room with a sexual awareness so thick it wrapped around her like gossamer threads of need.

"I'm going to take you down," he whispered as she skirted the couch, placing its width between them. "I'm going to mount you, Roni. Then I'm going to ride you until you're screaming beneath me."

Her cunt beat out a demand that she drop to her knees then and there. She didn't think so.

"Been there, done that," she drawled. "Be original, baby."

He snarled. Her pulse raced. Oh, that was the sexiest sound. Deep, vibrating in intensity.

He moved then, a smooth, graceful leap that had her eyes widening in shock as he came over the couch. Her second's hesitation was her downfall. Even as she was turning to run, his arm hooked around her waist and he lifted her from the floor.

Roni fought frantically. Her body was burning, her cunt throbbing in desperation as adrenaline surged through her. She bucked in his arms as he laughed, her low scream of frustration and furious lust echoing around the room as he took her to the floor.

There were no preliminaries. There was no need for them. The slick cream of her need dampened her thighs, flowing thick and hot from her pussy. His cock surged into the syrupy thickness filling her vagina as she arched back, screaming out at the pleasure.

"Been here, baby?" He pounded inside her ruthlessly, his hands holding her hips relentlessly as his cock thrust hard and deep in the tight depths. "Done this?"

The depths he reached had her shrieking in part pain, part pleasure, her cunt gripping him, the muscles clenching spasmodically as he fucked her with a hard driving rhythm.

It wasn't like the first time and only now did she realize the control he had exerted even then. A control he had lost this time.

She pushed back into each driving thrust, crying out for him, her pussy clenching on the thick intruder driving her insane with the need for orgasm.

"Talk to me, baby." His hand lifted from her hip a second before he delivered a firm, sharp slap to the rounded curve of her buttock. "Tell me if we've been here, Roni."

Shock singed her then. Oh hell. That felt too good. She whimpered with it, bucking against him, jerking against his hold. She fought him, gasping at the pleasure of his tight grip as he restrained her, the sharp sting of his hand on her ass as he punished her.

"Done this..." She dared him, then threw her head back in an agony of pleasure as his hand landed on her ass again.

"Done this?" His hand moved again, sliding along the curves, his fingers caressing, driving her insane as they dipped between her thighs, sliding through the juices collecting on the lips of her sex.

"Keep talking, baby," he growled as he circled her clit. "Let's see if this old cat can't teach you a few new tricks." His fingers rubbed, caressed, delicately milked her clit to the powerful thrusts driving into her pussy.

She couldn't breathe. Roni fought for oxygen as the almost violent intensity of sensations ripped through her. Too many, too fast. She could feel her pussy tightening, her womb convulsing.

When the explosion came she felt every emotion contained in her soul tearing free. Her orgasm slammed through her as she rose from the floor convulsively, her arms reaching back for him, her scream a strangled plea for mercy.

"More." There was no mercy.

His arm locked around her waist, lifting her, his erection sinking deeper inside her, stroking her from an angle that kept the fiery intensity of her release echoing through her body. She was being driven mad. Even her flesh became a traitor to her desperate need to fight the overwhelming orgasm.

The minute the first eased, he threw her into another. His cock was stroking inside her, fucking her with a relentless demand she couldn't deny. She arched against him, her hands falling to the tight muscles of the arm holding her, clenching, fighting for some hold on reality as she was thrown once again into an abyss of ever deepening sensation.

She was screaming. She didn't know what she was screaming, only knew the words were fighting to be free, to be heard. She loved. She needed… And then she felt him. From the position they were in she felt the first change. His cock tightened, jerked, then it seemed as though the flared head thickened. Another, smaller erection bloomed beneath it, locking his cock deep inside her as it caressed an ultra-sensitive bundle of nerves hidden there. Press. Stroke. In that second she was hurled into a kaleidoscope world of clashing colors, heartbeats, surging blood and an animal's roar. And a knowledge she knew would change them both forever.

Chapter Fourteen

Roni would have preferred to clear her mind, to drift within the safety of the world Taber was trying to build around her. At least, she had thought that was what she preferred, until hours later, after the demands of their bodies had been met and sanity began to return. It was then she knew it was time to face her own life.

She was only twenty-two to Taber's thirty. But even more than the eight years difference in their ages, there was a whole world of experience as well. He had lived with fear, unspeakable cruelty and death, even before he had become a man. He had known the evil that filled the minds of the Council, the men who created him, who trained him. He had been decades older than she had, even when he was a teenager.

Roni knew her own experiences in growing up didn't even come close to the pain he had known. She was a baby in comparison. But she was also his mate. She wanted to be more. She wanted to be strong enough to stand by his side, strong enough to fight with him. She couldn't do that if she allowed either of them to hide from the truth.

She would let him protect her to an extent, but after that, she needed to stand beside him, to ease the man who fought for supremacy over his DNA. The man who needed to love, to find at least a safe haven for his soul.

He hadn't told her he loved her, but she would deal with that later. One step at a time, she thought. One growth at a time. She would get there eventually, but first things first.

"Cats have barbs," Roni said lazily, her fingers playing gently through the long, silken strands of his hair.

He had been purring. It amazed her. He had tried to stop, had even laughed at himself earlier because he couldn't, though she had seen the worry in his eyes that it would disgust her. Quite the opposite. She now knew how to tell if her lover was pleased, happy, content. Destroying that contentment for even a moment was something she hated to do. But it was something they needed to clear up.

He tensed in her arms. His head still lay against her chest, but rather than the sated relaxation that had filled him, a watchful tension now moved over his body. The soft vibration in his chest had stopped, though her fingers had never ceased the slow caress through his hair.

"Yeah, they do." His hold tightened only marginally.

"People think because I'm young, I'm completely dumb." She laughed softly at this. "Even before you marked me, you always handled me with kid gloves, never doing or saying anything that you thought would upset me. Letting me face life isn't going to break me."

"It was never because I thought you were dumb, Roni." He sighed as he moved from her arms, sitting up so he could stare down at her thoughtfully. "I wanted to protect you. That's all I've ever wanted."

And she realized how true that was. She had known it when she had been only a child, and she saw it now. A part of him had to protect her, otherwise, he would never be content, never be secure.

"I don't want to be protected from everything, Taber." She turned on her side, moving into the embrace he created by opening his arms and pulling her close.

Her head lay against his chest now as he breathed out roughly. She could feel the protest building in him and knew he would always try to protect not just her body, but her emotions as well. She didn't want to be protected from growth.

"I don't want you hurt," he whispered against her hair. "Not in any way, Roni. It makes me crazy, thinking of it. It always has. The world can be dark, baby. Scary as hell. I never wanted you to see how bad it could be."

The dark magic of his voice couldn't hide the bitter memories running through it.

"That won't work, Taber. How can I be anything to you if I can't understand the life you've lived? Do you think I don't know some of the evil out there? For God's sake, how many times did you have to come rescue me from Reginald's enemies, from men who called and told a teenager how many different ways they were going to fuck her in exchange for her father's betrayal?" She had never told him the full extent of the terror that had her running to him through the years. The true measure of the fears she had faced. She had known he would confront Reginald, and she had been terrified of the consequences. How could she have lived if he was harmed because of her?

His arms flexed, bunched in anger.

"I would have killed him if I had known, Roni. I may kill him yet," he swore.

"You're better than he is," she sighed. "And he's not worth the complications. He's not worth the stain on your soul." She rose up, staring him in the eye. "I know what you are, Taber. I know what happens when you come inside me. You don't have to hide the truth from me. All I need is to know you'll be beside me."

"I always have been." He shook his head in confusion. "Why would I leave now, Roni? You're mine. I told you that."

She rolled her eyes impatiently. "Taber, I don't belong to you…"

"The hell you don't." Stubborn male arrogance lit every word. "I warned you before, baby, and I'm telling you now. Once I had you, it was too late to re-think the issue. I won't play games with you. I won't lie to you. And I'll sure as hell never let you leave me."

"Good thing I'm content to stay. For now," she muttered as she plopped back down on the bed, staring up at the ceiling with a frown. "Must be the animal coming out in you. Though I never knew cats to be possessive. You're going against type, Taber."

He grunted mockingly as he stared down at her, a brow lifting with an expression of superiority. "Really?" he drawled, his voice deepening. "Says who?"

"Wild Kingdom," she snapped without heat.

"Wild Kingdom needs to research a bit more." He laughed as he settled down in the bed beside her, drawing her close to the warmth of his body as he pulled the sheet over them.

"I don't know." She yawned. "They seemed pretty sure of it. You sure you can't mate anyone else?" That one worried her, more than she wanted to admit. She would hate to have to kill him after getting used to this crazy situation he had thrown her in.

"Don't know. And I sure as hell don't intend to find out," he grumped. "Mating you is about to kill me. I doubt I'll be able to walk straight when I get up in the morning. Which isn't far off. Go to sleep." He reached over, extinguishing the light on the small table by the bed.

Silence filled the room. Weariness dragged at her body.

"You should make him leave, Taber." She voiced the fear about Reginald that she couldn't seem to rid herself of. "He's dangerous."

Once again silence stretched between them for long moments.

"We'll watch him, Roni," he promised her. "Remember. Keep your friends close. Keep your enemies closer. Reginald will show his hand eventually. When he does, one of us will be there to stop him."

She sighed wearily. She couldn't push the suspicion of her mother's death from her mind. Someone had killed her. She had known the mountainous roads in all conditions. She would have never gone over that cliff on a perfect summer day.

"I'll protect you, Roni." His confidence washed over her like a comforting wave of warmth.

"I don't doubt that, Taber," she sighed. "It's not my safety I worry about. It's yours."

"Go to sleep, baby." He tucked her closer, his arms, strong and warm, sheltering her. "Tomorrow is soon enough to deal with it."

She closed her eyes, her hand moving from the bed to her abdomen. She could feel the change in her body. The desperate heat was cooling, leaving only a more natural desire now. A comforting warmth. Would it happen so soon, she wondered?

"Sleep." His hand covered hers. "Tomorrow is soon enough."

* * * * *

"Okay, listen up, kitties." Kane strode into the large kitchen like a hard wind bent on shaking up whatever previous safe zone had been established. "Get your noses out of the cream, we have problems here."

The morning ritual of after-breakfast coffee had run smoothly the few days Roni had been there. But it wasn't a ritual Kane had partaken of until now. She had seen Merinus' older, taciturn brother only once in the past days since her arrival. He watched everything and everyone suspiciously.

He was handsome, with his dark hair and striking blue eyes. He was tall, not as broad as the Feline Breed males, but exuding a powerful grace that drew the eye. This morning he was dressed in jeans that conformed to every muscle in his long legs and emphasized his tight, hard stomach. A black T-shirt was tucked into the waistband that was cinched with a plain, leather belt. On that belt he wore a holstered gun with such casual confidence that it seemed to be an extension of his body.

"He's going to call me a kitten one time too many," Sherra muttered with low violence from beside Roni as she stared down at her coffee cup.

The interactions among the small Pride of Feline Breeds fascinated Roni. They were completely loyal to each other and the other Breeds who had slowly been making their way to the estate set up for them. Like a large, extended family. They fussed and grumbled with each other, but they fought tenaciously for each other as well.

"Kane, as always, your entrances leave much to be desired," Merinus sighed as Callan chuckled in amusement.

Merinus watched her brother and the slender Feline female, Sherra, with wary concern.

"He takes some getting used to," Taber told Roni as she glanced over at the tall, eagle-eyed man holding several reports in his hand as he poured his own coffee.

Kane was dangerous. There was no other word for it. His eyes were deep pools of blue ice, suspicious and surging with an inner energy that made Roni nervous. Evidently, it made Sherra nervous as well. She shifted in her seat, casting the man a look of simmering anger.

"Merinus, keep your ass in the house. Period. You and Ms. Andrews. I don't know how the hell those snipers got into the compound but the one left living doesn't want to play with us yet and give the information out." A cruel slash of a smile curved his lips as he leaned back against the counter, lifting the coffee cup for a tentative sip. It assured those watching that soon, the sniper left alive would be more than happy to play whatever game Kane suggested. She would have shivered at the thought if the situation weren't so dangerous.

"So what have you managed to find out?" Callan asked quietly as he leaned back in his chair at the head of the table and watched the other man intently. "Other than the fact that our new friend is temporarily anti-social."

Kane grunted, scratching his cheek absently with the hand that still held several wrinkled pages of paper.

"There's a possibility this isn't a Council job." His voice turned decidedly more dangerous. "I'm not sure who is behind it yet, but we're getting close. From what I've managed to gather, it's leaning closer to a small, select group who believes the world is better off without your particular brand of genetics mixing into the soup pot."

Roni glanced at the expressions of the Breeds gathered around the large kitchen table. Their expressions varied between contempt and anger.

"Hmm, wonder if they have nice accessible daughters." Roni's eyes widened as she looked down the table to Tanner. The sexual threat inherent in his voice had surprised her.

He was a Bengal Breed, Taber had told her, and he looked it.

His thick, long black hair was lit with several shades of gold and framed his dark, intent face. He looked like a fallen angel, oozing sex appeal and lusty excesses. His amber gaze glittered angrily beneath his long sooty lashes as his eyes narrowed dangerously.

Roni had known Tanner as long as she had Taber, and the young man, though friendly and flirtatious, had always held that cutting edge of perilous intent. As though he saw into the soul and often judged it harshly.

"Tanner." Callan grumbled a hard-edged warning.

"Come on, Cal, I could mix the soup up for them right good," the younger man snorted. "I won't hurt anyone."

"We don't have time for cat fights," Kane snapped.

He was rewarded by more than one growl and several animalistic snarls in response. The grin that crossed his lips was amused and easy, despite the threats that lay thick and unvoiced in the sound.

"Get to the point, Kane," Callan told him softly, but the very silkiness of his warning told Roni much more. The older Feline Breed was growing tired of the little digs Merinus' brother was directing their way.

The sniping didn't make sense. The easy familiarity she had seen him display with the Breeds on other occasions had suggested he both respected and cared for the members of Callan's pride. Yet his actions now hinted at a deeper tension.

"Point is," Kane set his coffee down and glanced down at the papers he held, "several radical members of previous race groups have decided to band together. They call themselves Liberators. Their main agenda is the death of any and all genetically altered humans. They don't have a lot of money backing them, but they have firepower and several ex-military members. Looks like it's hunting season, boys and girls. And guess who's the catch of the day?"

Silence reigned for long, tension-filled moments.

"We expected this." Despite his words, Callan's voice was weary, saddened. "How close are we to finishing the security measures?"

"Close." Kane shrugged. "But no system is perfect, Callan. We have a lot of ground to cover and our perimeters are being tested from every angle. They're quiet for the most part, not tipping their hands, but they're watching. And rumor has it they're attempting to put a spy in place."

Roni stiffened, her fists clenching in her lap as she fought to deny her own suspicions now.

"So catch him," Sherra snapped as she glanced over at Kane. "What are you here for anyway? You socialize in the house more than you actually get any work done."

"At least I'm willing to be sociable." His smile was tight, hard. "Unlike some of us in this house, I can actually manage to remain civil for more than five minutes at a time."

"Oh, really?" she drawled sarcastically. "Funny, I hadn't noticed amid all the little snipes and half-veiled insults. Forgive me, Kane. I'm certain you're doing your best."

His eyes narrowed. The scene playing out before Roni's fascinated gaze was better than any soap opera ever invented.

"Keep pushing me, Sherra, and you might not like the consequences." Undercurrents of emotion thickened between the two of them.

"I don't like you...period." She rose to her feet, glancing at Callan. "When you have real answers, Cal, let me know. All he has is his damned conspiracy theories and I've grown tired of them."

She swept out of the room, her head held high, a mane of long, incredibly thick blonde hair swaying past her shoulders and catching the light as she passed through the doorway.

"One of these days..." Kane muttered.

"Leave her alone, Kane." Merinus' voice was flat and hard now. "You're pushing too hard."

Her brother shot her a surprised look.

"I'll push harder before it's over with," he snapped. "And you can watch it or you can tell me what the hell the deal is. Your choice, Merri. Either way, I'll get the answers I want."

"Enough already," Callan ordered, his frustration level evidently reaching its breaking point as he stood to his feet and faced the other man. "Deal with your personal life off my time, Kane." Then he turned to the youngest of the Breed males. "Tanner, get into town tonight. See what you can find out from those sources you have in place. I want to know who and what is involved in all this."

"I'd start asking our new visitor first." The rough, grumbling voice that entered the fray came from the kitchen doorway.

Roni recognized the Breed from the night before. Merc, she thought they had called him. He stared at them with placid, deep brown eyes, but nothing could hide the aura of death surrounding him.

"Meaning?" Callan asked him softly.

"Meaning, I caught him trying to sneak around the weapons shed earlier. When I put a stop to that, one of the men assigned to watch him caught him trying to break into the communications offices. That boy has the Grim Reaper sittin' on his shoulder, Callan. And I'm of a mind to set that dark visage free."

All eyes turned to Roni, and for a moment, guilt seared her chest so painfully she was forced to catch her breath to keep from crying out in denial any father could threaten his child in such a way.

"He's going to end up killing someone." She turned to Taber, her fists clenched as fury nearly overwhelmed her.

"Or he's going to end up dead." Merc evidently didn't care one way or the other about the rough, warning growl Taber emitted as he flashed the other man a dark, silencing look. "He keeps excusing his little trips from the barracks on trying to find his 'little girl'. I say we relieve the world and his daughter of the complications he's causing."

"Enough, Merc." Callan came to his feet as he stepped over to the coffee pot. "File your report of his activities with Kane as you were directed. We'll take care of the rest."

"Maybe it would be easier if you put someone else to tailing his ass," the lion Breed snapped. "I've about run out of patience, Callan."

"You're not by yourself." Roni pushed back her chair as she flashed Callan, then Taber a furious look. "I don't understand. You were forced to kill those assassins, you're living day by day wondering when the next attack will come, knowing he's behind it, but he's still here." It made no sense to her. "What's so important about him that you're allowing it to risk everyone?"

Dear God, if he actually managed to get one of them killed, how would her conscience bear it? It was her fault he was here.

"Each transmission he sends out, we get closer to finding his source," Taber finally answered her bleakly. "We're also learning the holes in our own security system. They won't make it to the house again."

She pushed her fingers through her hair, grinding her teeth together in fury.

"Fine. Use him all you like, but do it away from me," she finally snapped. "I'll be damned if I'll sleep with someone willing to risk his life so rashly. Fuck this, Taber. I've had enough of the games and your willingness to give him a chance to kill you. If you want to die, you'll do it without my cooperation."

Fury flooded her, hot and blistering as she glimpsed the amusement that flashed in his green eyes.

"Roni, you're not in any danger…"

"Do you think my life is the only one I care about?" She wanted to smack him for being so damned dense. If he was not careful, she was going to smack him. Hard. "Dimwit, it's you I'm worried about." She did smack him. Her hand landed against the side of his head as he ducked to avoid the blow before she stalked around him, ignoring the surprised chuckles of the group behind her before facing Merc. "Kill him," she snarled. "Before the adrenaline junkies behind us get their own asses blown to hell. I'm getting tired of the damned suspense anyway. We should start taking bets on whether Callan, Taber or Kane will take the first bullet. Because God's truth, their all three in the running."

Merc crossed his arms over his chest, his reply coming to his lips as she placed her hands on his hard chest and pushed him out of her way.

"Damned men always standing in front of me, blocking me," she muttered fiercely as she stalked past him. "I ought to shoot everyone of you myself and put the rest of us out of the misery of waiting to see who gets it first. None of you have the common sense God gave a goose…"

She ran up the stairs. Her gun was in Taber's suite. Loaded. Ready. Reginald would talk to her or she would place the first bullet in his stinking black heart.

"Dammit, Roni, wait up," Taber thundered behind her as she slammed the bedroom behind her.

She would have locked it, but she had a feeling he would merely run right through. Stubbornness was not always a sexy trait in a man, she thought vengefully. Sometimes, it could be damned unattractive. Right now, it was making her sick to her stomach to think of how foolishly intractable those damned Breeds were being.

"Dammit, Roni, you don't know what the hell what is going on here." Taber burst into the room, his eyes glittering with irritation as she whirled around to face him.

"Of course I don't know what the hell is going on," she yelled back at him, tired of being nice, understanding, sweet little Roni. "How the hell am I supposed to know jack shit when all you do is placate me and make excuses. I'm sick to death of the excuses, Taber. Tell me what the hell is going on. Now."

She saw the indecision flash in his gaze. This protectiveness bullshit was really starting to get on her nerves.

"Roni..." There was that tone of voice again. The dark little purr guaranteed to make her pussy wet and make her forget all about her fury.

"Forget it." Her hand sliced through the air in front of her. "It's not happening. Give me one good reason why I shouldn't go out there and shoot his sorry ass for trying to get every one of us killed. One reason, Taber. That's all I want. Just one fucking decent reason."

"Because, if he's dead, then there's no way in hell I can find out who his employers are and what they're after. If he's dead, Roni, then we're fighting blind. We know who is behind the leak in our defenses now, and we will contain him. But we have to know who our enemies are."

"No." She shook her head furiously, turning away from him as the frustration began to eat at her. This wasn't what she wanted to hear.

"Roni." His voice lowered as he moved behind her, his hands settling heavily on her shoulders as he pulled her back against his chest. "Just give us a little more time, baby. Just a little more."

"Time," she whispered, staring despairingly at the closed balcony doors across her. "How much more time will we have?"

Chapter Fifteen

She gave him until the next afternoon. A good hour after the alarms had gone off again, signaling an attempted break against one of the perimeter fences. More than three hours after she accepted the fact that it was quite possible she had conceived.

The furious, burning heat was abating. Not that she wanted Taber any less, or that the fires he started in her body were cooler. They weren't. But the desperation, the unnatural burning compulsion was dissipating, leaving the arousal at a poker-hot level that she was more familiar with. The one she had lived with before Taber had ever marked her.

But it also meant that the there was another life to consider. One she wasn't willing to risk to her father's insanity.

"I want you to make Reginald leave now." Roni turned to face Taber as they entered the sheltered garden area outside the kitchen.

It was the only outside area Taber and the others would allow the women to go to when the house became too stifling. It was a large courtyard, but stretching overhead, from wall to wall, were thick wooden beams holding a multitude of sheltering vines. Even in the full heat of the day it was a cool escape from the tension slowly filling the house.

She moved deeper into the small grotto, brushing against the thick, sheltering shrubs and low growing trees that had been placed around a central fountain.

A variety of flowering bushes filled the air with the heady scent of their blooms. The fountain splashed playfully, infusing the area with moisture, lending to it an air of sensuality and relaxation. An atmosphere she fought desperately as she tried to convince Taber to have her father escorted from the estate.

She laid her palm against her abdomen, trying to still the nerves that roiled within her stomach. The severe heat that had afflicted her over the past days was steadily easing. She was pregnant and she was terrified. More frightened than she had ever been in her life.

"Roni, let us do our job," Taber told her softly as she turned back to him, watching her with a warmth, a caring she couldn't face yet. "Upsetting yourself like this every time an attempt is made isn't going to help."

Roni rolled her eyes in frustration. "I am not upsetting myself. His presence here is upsetting me." Her hand sliced through the air between them as she went nose to nose with him.

She could feel the fear building in her, feel the sick, awful sensation in the pit of her stomach that warned her that Reginald was scheming at his worse. It had been in his gaze, in the calculating demand as he was pulled from the house the night before. He was neck-deep in trouble and determined to pull her into it as well.

"You forget, I know him just as well as you do, Roni," he reminded her carefully. "I know what he's capable of."

She hated that restrained sound to his voice. As though he was choosing each word, each move with her. As though he only gave her the parts of himself that he wanted her to see.

"Why give him the chance, Taber?" She wanted to scream at him, but she kept her voice to a careful hiss as she paced farther along the courtyard. "Why? The risk is too great."

"What can he do now?" Taber asked her logically. She hated logic. She hated *his* logic. So cool and confident. "We need to know who hired him and what he wants. If we run him off, we may not know until it's too late to contain the threat. We can't risk that, Roni."

"You're risking your life instead." She shook her head, pushing her trembling hands into the pockets of her jeans as she sat down on one of the wide stone benches at the farthest edge of the courtyard.

"My life is at risk every day, baby." He sighed roughly as he sat down beside her, pulling her into his arms. "You think I don't know what you're fighting so hard? That I don't know you're carrying my child, Roni? That I couldn't sense the change in your body as it happened?"

She stiffened in his arms. "You can't be certain of that."

But she was certain. She should have known that he would guess.

"Merinus went out of heat when she conceived. The desperate need isn't driving you insane now, Roni. It's easing." He nuzzled her neck, his warm breath blowing across her skin with such pleasure she shivered.

"That doesn't mean anything." She tried to shrug him away, to keep her mind from becoming clouded with need as another, more intense heat began to fill her. "Just because Merinus is pregnant doesn't mean I am."

The natural desire was something she thought she would never feel again. Something she could have done without. She could have denied the hold Taber had on her so much easier if he didn't make her crazy to fuck him with just the feel of his breath on her neck. It was disconcerting to realize how deeply she loved him, needed him. What would she ever do if anything happened to him?

She arched involuntarily to the caress, her breath catching on a sigh of longing. The shaded grotto-like atmosphere suddenly turned heated, too moist, sensitizing her, sucking her into the earthy lust that always shook her at the mere sight of him.

He chuckled. The sound was low, heated, as he lifted her against him, turning her until she sat draped across his lap.

"Let me up." She struggled against him, but knew her heart wasn't in being released.

His arms held her easily as he looked at her, his eyes narrowing, becoming darker, more intense. Roni shivered under the look. "I still want to fuck you crazy. Right here, Roni," he whispered wickedly as his hand slid up her thigh, beneath her soft cotton shirt then curled around the curve of her breast.

Roni felt her nipples peak in throbbing expectation. They throbbed, ached for his touch, his mouth, anticipating the feel of his tongue rasping over them erotically. Her womb clenched in need, her pussy weeping, preparing for the invasion that every cell of her body screamed out for.

"Someone will see us." She fought not to pant. "Besides, we were arguing..."

"You were arguing. I was disagreeing," he pointed out, his voice less than patient as he pushed her shirt over the full mounds of her breasts. "And I have finished disagreeing and will now begin feasting."

Her cunt throbbed at the sound of his voice, her nipples aching as his head lowered. Roni watched, seeing the sudden sensual fullness of his lips as they opened, his tongue as it curled around the stiff peak first, searing it with a blistering pleasure.

"Oh God, Taber." She couldn't stop her desperate moan as his mouth then covered the engorged tip.

His tongue swirled with wet heat around the sensitized bud, his mouth drawing on her, cheeks flexing. Roni couldn't help but watch. It was the most sinfully sensual sight she had ever seen. His dark face flushed with arousal...for her. It was for her. His attention solely on the pleasure he took from suckling her nipple, the pleasure he gave was nearly orgasmic.

His hand held the sensitive flesh, pushing the mound higher, intensifying her sensations as his tongue stroked over the elongated tip. She could feel her juices gathering from within her suddenly clenching vagina then spilling past the narrow channel, coating the rapidly sensitizing lips of her cunt. Her clit ached, pulsed in time to the rhythmic suckling of his mouth.

He moaned against her, the sound vibrating along nerve endings that screamed out for relief.

"Delicious." He lifted his head, her nipple falling from his mouth with a smooth, moist popping sound. "Come here, baby, let me undress you. I'll show you…"

"Taber, I need you back in here if you have time." Callan's voice called through the courtyard. "We'll be waiting for you in the office."

The intrusion was like a bucket of ice water, sweeping over Roni as she stiffened in Taber's arms, her eyes widening in alarm. She couldn't believe she had forgotten about the inhabitants of the house. How easily they could step outside and be witness to the erotic loveplay behind the shelter of the thickened foliage surrounding them.

"Dammit, he left me the hell alone while you were in heat," he muttered. "Now he'll be interrupting me every damned chance he gets."

"What?" She shook her head as she moved quickly from his lap, jerking her shirt back over her breasts. "Why?"

Taber winced as he stood, the ridge of his erection pressing thick and hard against the front of his jeans.

"I did it to him." He shrugged with an unapologetic grin. "We all did. Hell, still do if we get the chance. He gets irritated." There was a shrug to his powerful shoulders, an almost lighthearted grin that tugged at her heart.

How often had she seen such a smile on his face? His eyes were almost glowing with humor, his lips tipped into a comfortable smile. Boyish. Amazement washed over Roni as she realized what was so different about this smile, this look. She had never seen it on his face before, had never known him to relax enough to allow any playfulness out.

"I wish he had just kicked you, instead of waiting to punish me as well," she sighed roughly. "Go on, do whatever you were going to do. I want to sit here for a while." She sat back down on the bench, her knees weak, her heart beating roughly as she stared up at him.

God help her, he was too handsome for words and she was terrified of losing him again. Maybe this time, permanently.

"I'll be back soon." He knelt in front of her then, his gaze meeting hers as he placed his palm against her lower stomach. "Stay in the house, Roni, until I can get back. Take care of our baby."

Static pleasure washed over her body at the sound of his voice. It was husky, deep, caressing her nerve endings like a physical touch. But even more than the husky throb of his words was the unvoiced emotion behind them.

"You can't be sure." She shook her head, confused by the shifting awareness that she felt.

It wasn't just the lessening of the unnatural arousal, it was the acceptance within herself. She was learning it wasn't so much her body that couldn't stand life without Taber, it was her heart, her soul.

How bleak and empty her life had been before he made her live again. Made her fight, made her learn to be who she was. In a few short days, he had given her the very things she had longed for the most—his heart to nurture, his soul to protect, his body to enjoy and love to her heart's content, and a family. With Taber and the child they had created she had all she had ever dreamed of.

"I can smell the changes in your body," he whispered. "Just as I could smell your heat, I can smell our child. Do you have any idea the pleasure that brings me, Roni? I, who had nothing, no one to call my own in all the years of my life, now have not only you, but the child we've created together."

She could see the hopes and the fears that filled him at that moment. He stared at her, everything he was, everything he dreamed, reflected in the brilliance of his eyes. His brows lowered, his expression becoming intent, fierce. Then he lowered his head, his body bending further until he could place his lips where his hands had been.

Roni gasped as her fingers gripped his shoulders, his arms going around her, holding her close as he pressed his face into her lower stomach. He was so strong and sure in her arms, bending to her, his attention on the child he knew was forming within her.

"I love you, Roni." The words could only barely be heard but they nearly stopped her heart with emotion. "Know that. For years I have longed for you. Loved you. You complete me..."

He didn't give her time to answer him. No time to accept the emotion he whispered against her flesh. He rose quickly to his feet and stalked away from her. No kiss. No touch. No chance for her to reject what he had given her. As though she could ever reject him.

Roni lowered her head as she fought her tears, fought her own steadily rising emotions. No matter how much she feared the consequences, she loved him. Had always loved him. But damn if he wasn't too stubborn for words.

Chapter Sixteen

"Did you think you could hide from me forever, girlie?" Reginald's voice was a serrated intrusion into the peaceful atmosphere of the mansion's living room.

Roni knew she should have expected Reginald to do something stupid. He had never been the smartest man she had ever known but she hadn't expected him to be one of the dumbest either. Actually, she hadn't thought he would be inventive enough to slip past the Feline Breeds on guard while Taber was out of the house, but he did.

One minute she was alone in the living room watching the arrival of several wounded Breed males outside, the next second she was jerked around roughly to face the father she had always loathed.

"What are you doing here?" She jerked away from him, her eyes going to the open door of the room. "Do you think someone won't know you're here, Reginald?"

The look in his eyes made her stomach pitch in nervous awareness of the danger he could represent.

"Doesn't matter if they do find out," he sneered angrily. "I'm just here visiting my little girl. Or did you forget you had a father?"

"Every chance I get," she snapped back. "What the hell are you up to here? Don't you have any more sense than to piss these men off, Reggie?"

His smile was terrifying. Confident, assured, stretching lewdly across his face as his blue eyes glittered with malice.

"What have you done, Reggie?" Roni could feel the last thread of hope she ever possessed where her father was concerned, snap.

"Listen to me, Roni, they aren't natural. They aren't human," he hissed with a fanatical fervor that terrified her. "I know he put that mark on you. All I need is for you to leave with me. Just for a little while, girl, and let my friends have some blood work. Just some little tests, that's all."

"You can't be serious." She shook her head slowly, edging away from him, suddenly more terrified of him than anything else she had ever faced in her life. "I'm not going anywhere with you. If this is why you came here, then you may as well give it up now."

He frowned, a dark, sinister lowering of his brow that had her heart rate picking up nervously. He had never looked at her like that. She had never seen such hatred, such utter contempt in another human's eyes before. And she had never imagined it would be directed at her.

"You will come with me, Roni," he snapped, watching her with a feral intensity that bordered on the insane. "There's no telling what he's planted in your belly while you've been in his bed. Do you think I'm going to allow the world to know a kid of mine is a dirty animal fucker?"

She flinched at the disgust, the terrible fury in his voice.

"You're insane," she whispered. "They have as much right to live as anyone else, Reginald. More so."

"Oh, spare me your pretty little speeches," he spat contemptuously. "Tell me, girl, how long have you been fucking the bastard anyway? Was that why he threatened to kill me if I let any of my friends around you? Wanted his pussy all to himself, did he?"

Roni backed up as he edged closer to her. She could feel the hatred, black and vile, pouring from him.

"I won't answer that," she snapped, refusing to allow her fear of him to show.

"How old were you when he first found you, anyway, hiding like a snot-nosed brat in those hills? Ten? Eleven? Was he fucking you then, Roni? Is that why you followed after him every chance you got?"

She shook her head desperately, wondering where the hell the men who were supposed to be in the house were.

"I won't dignify that with an answer." She fought to put as much space between them as possible. "Not everyone has the perversions your friends do, Reggie."

"If I had known that was your fascination for him, I'd have given it to you myself," he sneered. "I could have used a little excitement in my bed after that stupid bitch mother of yours died…"

"Stop." Roni shook her head desperately. "Leave Mom out of this, Reggie."

Her frail, weary mother. Roni trembled at the memory of her. She rarely allowed herself to remember her mother. The memories were bleak, painful. Margaret Andrews had been too delicate, too gentle, for the life Reginald had dragged her into.

"*Leave Mom out of this*," he mocked her cruelly. "Fine, we'll leave dear old Mom out of it. Get your ass out the door and in my car so we can take our little trip."

"Why?" The couch was between them, but her way to the open doorway was still blocked. "Do you really think I'm stupid enough to go with you? To let you or anyone you know touch me, Reggie? It's not going to happen."

"How 'bout a trade then?" He paused, watching her intently, his expression triumphant.

"What?" He was insane. Roni could only blink at him in astonishment that he could even consider she would trade her own soul for anything he had.

"A trade," he repeated softly. "You come with me, Roni, and let the boys do their tests, and I'll tell you why your momma fought so hard to stay hidden on that mountain. I'll tell you why she let me use her however I wanted to and however my buddies wanted to. I'll tell you, girl, who your father really is."

Time seemed to stand still for Roni. She watched Reginald with a sense of fascinated horror, and yet a grain of thankfulness. A thankfulness that went so deep it nearly made her knees weak.

"You're not my father." It all made sense now. The years of abuse, the pain her mother endured. All of it was falling into place. But if her mother was hiding with Reginald from her father, then how much more horrifying could he have been?

"I can see that just breaks your heart," he snapped dangerously. "What, you think you're too good to be my girl?"

"I think a snake would be too good to be a child of yours, but that's just my opinion." She needed to distract him, to get him to shift position just enough for her to sprint over the couch and run for the door. As long as he faced her from the other side, though, she was trapped. "So tell me, Reggie, why would I care who my father is? He can't be too important or you would have sold the information already."

"Would I?" He cackled. God, he actually cackled like some old crone. Weren't crones women?

"Course you would, Reggie." She kept her voice soothing, hoping to keep him from becoming too insistent on grabbing her. She could see the intent creeping into his expression, his body bunching in preparation.

"Naw, I wouldn't tell you this, Roni. Not for all the land in Texas, little girl. Not without a reason. 'Cause it would have meant my own life. But I'll tell you now, if you come with me nice and peaceful like." Calculating and feral, his gaze reminded her of a rabid dog she had once seen.

She couldn't let him get her out of the house. If she did, his advantage would be that much greater.

"I'm not leaving with you," she told him carefully, moving farther back, watching him, knowing he had to be insane. "And Taber won't let you take me, Reginald. You won't be able to leave the estate with me. You should leave, while you can."

His eyes narrowed. "Your stinking little cat is too busy to worry about you, little girl. And I won't take no for an answer."

He jumped for her then. Roni knew she would have only a second to evade him, only the slimmest chance to dart past him and run for the door. When his hand swiped for her hair she moved. Any time Reginald became furious with her he would grab her hair first. Hold her in place for whatever punishment he deemed necessary.

She felt his fingers brush by her head as she sprinted over the couch, screaming Taber's name. Where the hell was everyone, anyway?

"Bitch." She almost made it. She was clearing the couch when he caught her ankle, jerking her back with enough force to take her breath as she fought to turn her body, to shield her abdomen and the fragile life growing there.

She bounced against the cushions, kicking out with her other foot as he fought to retain his grip on her. There was no breath left to scream for help. She needed her strength, her wits about her, to try to escape. If no one had heard her screams, then no one was close enough to help her.

She kicked for his groin and missed, but the force she landed on his thigh had him stumbling back. She jumped and rolled over the couch, her ankle an agonizing ache from the harsh twist he had given it. Stumbling, she bolted for the door, screaming out Taber's name again as she heard Reginald curse viciously behind her.

"I said you're going with me." He caught her hair again, this time delivering a sharp blow to the side of her head that left her dazed and crumpling to the floor from the pain.

"Taber," she tried to cry out his name again, to warn him, to warn someone. But darkness was closer around her, sweeping through her mind, and she knew she only imagined the bloodthirsty animal's roar that echoed in her head.

* * * * *

Rage washed over Taber in violent, nearly suffocating waves as he heard Roni's frantic screams echoing through the house. Merinus had come running for him and Callan when she had first seen Reginald sneaking into the mansion, terrified of his intent.

He had been coming through the backyard when he first heard her screams. He entered the living room in time to see the bastard, fist closed, strike her temple in a blow that sent her to the floor.

There was no question of mercy. No question of reining in the rage tearing through him. His roar echoed through the room as he threw himself at the other man, desperate to alleviate the threat to his woman.

Reginald was faster and in better condition than Taber had anticipated. They rolled across the floor, the older man grunting as he slugged Taber in the ribs with enough force to nearly take his breath and knock him back for a second.

But the animal he had kept carefully leashed all the years of his adult life was free now. There would be no escape, no mercy for the man who had dared to threaten all Taber held dear.

He was aware, only absently, of the men now moving into the room. Roni was pulled to safety as Callan barked out an order to one of the others to find the doctor.

"She's alive, Taber," Callan called out as Taber faced off with Reginald. "Let it go. Let the men take him."

Taber's throttled roar had Reginald paling as he stumbled backward.

He rushed the older man. His fist connected with the side of Reginald's head, blood spraying as flesh tore. He jerked him from the floor as he fell, shaking him remorselessly as the older man's eyes bulged from his head.

"You kill me and you know what happens," Reginald wheezed as he managed to tear himself from Taber's grip. "It will be all over the news, boy. Everyone will know."

"Ask me if I care," Taber growled, pacing after him as he backed away.

Reginald's mouth worked desperately. "I didn't hurt her."

"You die."

"Come on, man," Reginald was pleading now. He edged back along the room, trying to evade Taber as he stalked him relentlessly. "You know I didn't hurt her."

Taber stilled. He would have eased the thirst, the fury for vengeance, in that second if the other man hadn't made the deciding move. Reginald pulled a small, deadly pistol from behind his back, aiming it at Taber's chest as a smile of satisfaction washed over his face. His finger tightened on the trigger. "Die, cat."

Taber threw himself to the side as the weapon discharged. Simultaneously, several others went off as well. Rolling to his feet he watched Reginald's body jerk convulsively from the bullets slamming into his body. One in his heart. One dead center between his eyes. He fell almost in slow motion, the hollow thump of his body echoing around the room.

"Dammit, cat-boy, how many times do I have to tell you how to kill a rabid animal?" Kane snapped as he walked into the room, nudging the body carefully with his foot. "Yep, that's how you do it. One bullet at a time."

Taber turned to Merinus' brother, adrenaline still coursing through him, rage beating like a spike-edged hammer at his brain.

"You call me cat-boy again and I'm going to shove that gun up your ass and shoot you with your own fucking bullets," he snarled furiously as he went nose to nose with Merinus' brother. "You don't like what you work with, then get the fuck out, Kane."

Kane blinked down at him. Blue eyes, nearly the color of Roni's, usually hard and cold, seemed to thaw marginally. Kane lifted his hands in a gesture of surrender.

"Truce?" Kane suggested.

Taber breathed in harshly, shaking his head, fighting the rage that wouldn't seem to abate.

"How did that bastard get in the house?" He turned to Callan then. "I thought we had Merc on him. What the hell happened?"

"Somehow he caught Merc unaware. Laid him out pretty good." Callan shook his head as he motioned to two of his men to drag Reginald's body from the room. "We caught him, Taber. It's over." Callan slapped him on the shoulder as he sighed wearily. "Go to your woman now. She'll need you when she wakes up."

Roni was already awake when Taber stepped into the bedroom. Merinus sat beside her on the bed, talking to her softly as Roni held a damp cloth to the side of her face.

Her shirt was torn, her shoulder scratched, the side of her face already bruising darkly. She was the most beautiful sight he had ever seen.

"Is he dead?" He had expected tears, maybe regret. But her eyes shone with a bitter hope that he was.

"I'm sorry," he whispered to her as Merinus rose to her feet and went to leave the room.

"Taber, you did what you had to do." The other woman stopped beside him, her hand lifting to rub his shoulder consolingly. "Don't beat yourself up over it. I'm sure there was no other choice."

There was no other acceptable conclusion, Taber thought. No man who raised a child and abused it should be allowed to live.

He watched Roni as the door closed quietly behind Merinus, seeing the pain that she tried to hide, the fear. Had he finally crossed a line she couldn't accept?

"He wasn't my father." Her voice cracked then. "Why didn't Momma tell me he wasn't my father, Taber? Why did she hide it from me?"

It was as though something had finally broken loose inside her. Taber moved quickly to the bed, pulling her into his embrace, his heart breaking for her.

"I don't know, baby," he whispered painfully.

"She loved my father." Her fists clenched in the material of his shirt. "I know she did. She told me she did. Why was she with that bastard? Why did she let him hurt her?"

He could feel the rage pulsing inside her, the pain of years of neglect and emotional abuse. He hadn't been able to protect her from everything, no matter how hard he had tried. And even now, he couldn't protect her from the full knowledge of the life she faced. The life their child would face. He could only hold her and pray.

"I would give everything I am to take this hurt from you." He moved back, staring down at her, his heart hurting for her even as his soul relished the knowledge that he held her heart. She didn't hate him. She didn't fear the animal that sometimes broke free. She accepted all of him. And if he could, he would give all he had to save her from this pain.

Her eyes were dark pools of confusion, of hurt, but he could see her trust in him. Her need for him.

"I wouldn't," she finally sighed. "I wouldn't change anything, Taber. None of it, if it meant I couldn't have all of you. The rest of it doesn't matter, other than a footnote to the brutality Reginald was. I can live with it. I can't live without you."

How could she do this thing to him? Make his chest fill with pride with such simple words? Make him feel as though he could conquer the world with only her smile to back him?

"You will always have me," he swore, his voice husky, the emotion filling it surprising even him. She filled every part of him. "Always, Roni. Always, you have me."

She touched his cheek. Almost convulsively his hand rose to hers, gripping it, bringing it to his mouth as he placed a heated, soul-giving kiss into her palm.

"Then I'm happy," she sighed, a tired, weary little sigh. "Hold me, Taber. Lie beside me and just hold me. Rest with me."

He lowered her to the bed, pulling her into his arms, holding her tightly to his chest as her head tucked beneath his chin. She settled against his body as naturally as breathing. Comforting. Warming.

"Our child will be loved," she whispered drowsily.

"Always, Roni. Our child will be adored." He knew, to the depths of his soul, that it would be no other way.

She sighed heavily, relaxing against him as the events of the past days finally sapped her remaining strength. He heard her breathing deepen, felt her body go lax and he allowed the single tear to fall slowly from his eye. She was his gift. His soul. In her, salvation had come to the man who struggled daily with the animal that lurked inside him. With her, he had finally found his peace.

Chapter Seventeen

Aaron Lawrence sat still, frozen, his eyes glued to the television screen, the past rushing over him with the force of a tidal wave. The words filtering through his numb mind held little meaning. All he saw was her face. A face he had thought he would never glimpse.

Veronica Andrews. Daughter of Reginald and Margaret Andrews. His soul screamed out in protest. She was nothing to the bastard who had betrayed him. She was his. His child. The last connection he had to the woman who had completed his soul. The woman who had run in horror from the crimes she believed he had committed.

His daughter. He fought back his tears, his grief. She looked so much like her mother. The same gentle curve of her brow, the dark blue eyes, the curve of her cheek. The fear that whitened her face...

The reporters were like a pack of animals as they molested her. Tearing at her clothes. Yelling at her. He watched the taped report, fury churning in his chest.

"Get their names." He didn't look at his son. Seth would take care of everything. He would know what to do now.

Aaron's jaw clenched as he fought the rage building inside him. The mark on her neck was an abomination. Unnatural. For months, despite Seth's neutral stand on the Breeds, Aaron had been funneling money into the attempted destruction of the animals. As he watched the news reports closer, saw the brief interview that came later—after the small wedding ceremony between his daughter and her pet—he wearily acknowledged such support would have to end. If she was happy.

He frowned. What if she wasn't? What if somehow she had been forced into this? If she had, he could bring her home. He could care for her. Give her all the things he had been unable to give her throughout her life. He could be her father.

That was it, he thought, hope rising within him. Seth could do this. Of course, Aaron knew he would have to convince his son to do this his way. Seth was too direct, too damned honest. There were days he would have suspected that boy was sired by another, if it weren't for the fact he looked so damned much like Aaron.

The same dark brown hair and steel gray eyes. The same patrician features. It was like looking into the mirror of the past when he looked at his son. But he was a good boy, Aaron reminded himself. Strong. Tough. He was big enough and smart enough to get what he wanted, when he wanted it. He didn't have to cheat. Not like his dad had.

"You can't tell her." Aaron turned to Seth now, seeing the hard purpose that lined his son's face. "Promise me, Seth. I swear, if you don't tell her the truth, I'll never deceive you again."

A cynical smile crossed Seth's face, though he didn't look over at his father. He was staring at the television. Another of the rare interviews with the full Pride.

"You'll always lie to me, Aaron." Seth shrugged his broad shoulders in resignation.

Aaron winced. He hadn't called him "dad" in so long, Aaron had forgotten the sound of it.

"You can't tell her, Seth." Grief whipped at his heart. If Seth told her the truth, she would never forgive him. Never call him dad.

Seth sighed deeply. "I won't tell her."

"We'll have to be careful," Aaron warned him. "We'll have to watch things first. Let your boys check it out good. Real good. Make sure she's happy."

Seth did glance at him then, his eyes narrowing thoughtfully.

"We can stay in that town." Aaron gestured to the television report. "Let your boys check it out..."

"I can get the answers..."

"Please, Seth." Aaron put everything he had into the plea. "I swear, I won't do anything. Just let me be sure. Just this one time. Let me be sure, my way."

Seth watched him closely. Aaron was more than aware of what his son saw. The old man, broken, wheelchair bound, slowly dying. And he *was* dying. He was paying for his sins in the worst possible way. A slow, painful death. Aaron knew it, and he wasn't above using it. He wondered where Seth had found that wide streak of honor Aaron had cursed him for.

Seth wiped his hand over his face tiredly. "We'll see, Aaron. We'll see."

He would weaken. Aaron sat back in his wheelchair, turning back to the report, his heart clenching. Pretty Veronica. His daughter. His sweet, perfect little girl. She would be home soon, he promised himself. Very, very soon.

Epilogue

Sherra watched Kane broodingly, unable to keep her eyes from him, unable to continue to deny what her body had been telling her for months. She was going into heat. She could feel the tiny fingers of need clawing at her flesh, demanding that she give in to the instinct to breed. Demanding that she go to the man who had made her his woman, his mate, over a decade before.

God, had it really been that long? Over eleven years. Eleven long, torturous years she had suffered for that one night, for the fanatical plans of a brother who had been born as twisted and demented as his creators. Suffered for a man who had never loved her. Had never truly needed her. If he had done either, then perhaps, just perhaps, so many other things would not have happened.

Sherra. Baby. Yes. Ah hell, yes baby, let me in... The remembered words were like a knife sinking into her soul. And yet the more she fought the memories, the more vivid they became.

Kane Tyler. Tall, strong, his very presence had been enough to take her breath then, to fill her with a desire so strong it had nearly overwhelmed her. His touch had seared her senses, his kiss... She whimpered. She wouldn't remember the kiss. Wouldn't remember how her heart had clenched at the stroke of his tongue.

A shiver worked over her body as she jerked to her feet, forcing herself away from the window, away from the sight of Kane moving with confident, arrogant power across the yard.

How much longer would Merinus hold her secret, she wondered as she pushed her fingers through the long fall of hair that fell forward over her face. How much longer before the sister informed the brother of the child he had lost all those years ago? The child that had been murdered while still in her womb?

Her hand moved to her abdomen, running over it with a ghost's touch as her womb rippled in need. How often had she dreamed of what that child could have been? Dreamed of a precocious son with his father's deep blue eyes, or a daughter with his long black hair. A child that would have been the best of both of them.

Sherra fought back her tears, fought back all the useless dreams, the hopes that had once filled her. Life had taught her that there was no chance to redeem the past. No sense in regretting what could not be undone.

I love you, Sherra... His remembered words whispered through her mind. *I'll be back, baby, I swear it. I'll be back, and I'll bring help...* But he had never returned. He had never come back for her.

The scientists had been ecstatic to learn she was breeding. Every precaution had been taken to insure the life of the child. Every precaution except that of a mind bent on death. Her baby's death.

The whimper that echoed around her couldn't be hers, she assured herself. She had cried for that lost child years before. Cried until her soul bled out with the salty moisture of her pain. Cried until there had been nothing left inside her heart but an empty shell. Until Kane had returned. And with him, so had the memories she had fought so desperately.

Ahh, Sherra. Yes, baby. So tight. So hot and tight. Her pussy tightened convulsively at the remembered feel of his cock pushing inside it. He had watched. She remembered that. Watched as every inch of his powerful erection sank into the burning depths of her hairless cunt. He had been fascinated by that lack of hair. Had loved licking the plump lips, feeling her juices slide against his tongue.

"Stop," she whispered, her fingers pushing into her hair, gripping it, hoping the pain would tear through the veil of heartache.

They had only had one night. Only eight stolen hours during a time when he was supposed to be training her. He had trained her, but not in the lessons he had been ordered to deliver. He had trained her to his cock instead. Trained her to his kiss, to the touch of his hands. Trained her to love, and then later, to hate. She couldn't seem to rid herself of the hatred, no matter the fact that he had been as powerless as she.

Dayan. He had been her brother. Her confidante. He had been one of the few people she had trusted. His betrayal had been the worst. He had tried to kill Kane, Merinus had told her. It had been he who had slipped the drug into her food. The drug that forced the unwanted abortion on her already weak body. It had been her brother who had destroyed all that Sherra was. And now here she was, eleven years later, her body tormented with a lust she couldn't seem to control, her heart breaking with memories she could no longer fight.

God, yes. Suck my cock, baby. Yes, Sherra, oh hell, oh hell… He had tried to pull back, to keep from spilling his seed into her mouth but she had been desperate for the taste of his essence. Desperate to know every facet of the act they were engaged in.

She licked her lips at the remembered taste.

"When are you going to tell him?" Merc stood at the doorway of the office, staring back at her with bitter, hollow eyes. He knew, she thought, knew well the pain of losing all that mattered in his life.

"Who said I was going to?" There was no hiding from the fact that he knew she was in heat. Hell, they all knew. Her scent was only undetectable by Kane. Only he was unaware of what her body was going through.

"You can't hide it from him forever. He's not a fool." He shook his head as he crossed his arms over his powerful chest. "It's time to let go of the past, Sherra."

She snarled. "Fine advice for you to be giving," she snapped. "When you're strong enough to accept your own past, Mercury, then you can bitch at me for not accepting mine."

It was a low blow. Sherra shook her head as she groaned in misery.

"Merc, I'm sorry."

He signed wearily. "No more than the truth. But you have a chance now, Sherra. Your mate still lives. And he's more than ready to ease the pain beginning to build within you. Why fight it? Don't you deserve more than this?"

"Do any of us?" she whispered. "I can't, Merc. I can't." She couldn't face losing another child. She couldn't face losing Kane all over again. "Too many years, too much anger."

"He's your man," he said simply. "Soon, he won't take no for an answer. What will you do then? What will you do when he learns the truth you've hidden from him since he found you?"

A tired, bitter smile crossed her lips. "I don't know," she sighed bleakly. "I just don't know. And maybe that's the part that truly, truly terrifies me, Merc. I don't know if I can face his punishment."

Merc shook his head slowly. "Start counting the days, Sherra. Because soon, very soon, there won't be any more hiding. He'll know and when he does, he'll show you why he's your man. Maybe then you'll realize the futility in fighting."

He turned and left the room, and in that moment she realized how right he was. Soon, she wouldn't be able to hide her needs. They would invade every cell of her body, rendering her helpless and in such heat she'd be screaming for relief. She knew. She knew because it was a cycle. Every year. Every long wasted year she had been apart from him she had suffered. Suffered until death had seemed the only viable alternative. Suffered until she had cursed him, hated him and finally in a last desperate move had assured herself and nature that no child would ever come of her body. She had tricked Doc into sterilizing her and destroying forever a chance at the child and the man stolen from her. She had done the unthinkable. And now, she would suffer more. As always. Alone.

About the author:

Lora Leigh is a 36-year-old wife and mother living in Kentucky. She dreams in bright, vivid images of the characters intent on taking over her writing life, and fights a constant battle to put them on the hard drive of her computer before they can disappear as fast as they appeared.

Lora's family, and her writing life co-exist, if not in harmony, in relative peace with each other. An understanding husband is the key to late nights with difficult scenes, and stubborn characters. His insights into human nature, and the workings of the male psyche provide her hours of laughter, and innumerable romantic ideas that she works tirelessly to put into effect.

Lora welcomes mail from readers. You can write to her c/o Ellora's Cave Publishing at P.O. Box 787, Hudson, Ohio 44236-0787.

Why an electronic book?

We live in the Information Age — an exciting time in the history of human civilization in which technology rules supreme and continues to progress in leaps and bounds every minute of every hour of every day. For a multitude of reasons, more and more avid literary fans are opting to purchase e-books instead of paperbacks. The question to those not yet initiated to the world of electronic reading is simply: *why?*

1. *Price.* An electronic title at Ellora's Cave Publishing runs anywhere from 40-75% less than the cover price of the <u>exact same title</u> in paperback format. Why? Cold mathematics. It is less expensive to publish an e-book than it is to publish a paperback, so the savings are passed along to the consumer.

2. *Space.* Running out of room to house your paperback books? That is one worry you will never have with electronic novels. For a low one-time cost, you can purchase a handheld computer designed specifically for e-reading purposes. Many e-readers are larger than the average handheld, giving you plenty of screen room. Better yet, hundreds of titles can be stored within your new library — a single microchip. (Please note that Ellora's Cave does not endorse any specific

brands. You can check our website at www.ellorascave.com for customer recommendations we make available to new consumers.)

3. *Mobility.* Because your new library now consists of only a microchip, your entire cache of books can be taken with you wherever you go.

4. *Personal preferences are accounted for.* Are the words you are currently reading too small? Too large? Too...**ANNOYING**? Paperback books cannot be modified according to personal preferences, but e-books can.

5. *Innovation.* The way you read a book is not the only advancement the Information Age has gifted the literary community with. There is also the factor of what you can read. Ellora's Cave Publishing will be introducing a new line of interactive titles that are available in e-book format only.

6. *Instant gratification.* Is it the middle of the night and all the bookstores are closed? Are you tired of waiting days—sometimes weeks—for online and offline bookstores to ship the novels you bought? Ellora's Cave Publishing sells instantaneous downloads 24 hours a day, 7 days a week, 365 days a year. Our e-book delivery system is 100% automated, meaning your order is filled as soon as you pay for it.

Those are a few of the top reasons why electronic novels are displacing paperbacks for many an avid reader. As always, Ellora's Cave Publishing welcomes your questions and comments. We invite you to email us at service@ellorascave.com or write to us directly at: 1337 Commerce Drive, Suite 13, Stow OH 44224.

Discover for yourself why readers can't get enough of the multiple award-winning publisher Ellora's Cave. Whether you prefer e-books or paperbacks, be sure to visit EC on the web at www.ellorascave.com for an erotic reading experience that will leave you breathless.

WWW.ELLORASCAVE.COM

Printed in the United States
50931LVS00001B/75